THE
SAVAGE
SPIRIT

ONE HUNDRED YEARS OF BRISTOL SAVAGES

THE
SAVAGE
SPIRIT

John Hudson

redcliffe

First published for Bristol Savages in 2004 by Redcliffe Press Ltd.,
81g Pembroke Road, Bristol BS8 3EA

© John Hudson and Bristol Savages

Hardback ISBN 1 904537 16 2
Softback   ISBN 1 904537 17 0

British Library Cataloguing-in-Publication Data
A catalogue record for this book is available from The British Library

Designed by Tracey Feltham

Printed by HSW Print, Tonypandy

CONTENTS

ACKNOWLEDGEMENTS

The author's thanks are due to all members of the Bristol Savages who contributed in any way to the compiling of this book, every one of whom responded in a constructive, positive and friendly way that said everything about the ethos of the Tribe. Special mention must be made of Centenary Session President Michael Long, Honorary Secretary John Cleverdon, and most of all to Assistant Secretary Geoff Cutter for his meticulous preparatory work, continued instant and informed response to queries and unfailing good fellowship. Thanks are due to Anthony Beeson for advice on the artist profiles which form an invaluable part of this book.

Outside the Tribe, acknowledgement is due to numerous observers of the arts and social scene in the Bristol area, none more so than the art historian and critic Francis Greenacre and Gerry Brooke of the *Bristol Evening Post.* Sheena Stoddard, Fine Art Curator of Bristol City Museum and Art Gallery, is thanked for help with illustrations, as are photographers Stephen Morris, Ian Blantern, Chris Bromhead and others.

PREFACE

Artists have always been associated in the public mind with solitude, working in isolation from the hurly-burly of everyday life, concentrating or reflecting their innermost thoughts on to the canvas or paper. And yet we all need companionship, and for artists seeing fellow artists at work, working alongside them and visiting exhibitions all feed this process. These were the motivations that led Ernest Ehlers and friends to form the Bristol Savages in February 1904.

In celebrating our centenary, this book is an opportunity to show how art, music and poetry, together with friendship and conversation, have been enjoyed by the members, and how 'the Savage Spirit' has evolved over the past one hundred years.

We are fortunate to enjoy meeting in a renowned building in the very heart of Bristol, and with the Savages having given the Red Lodge to the City in 1920, we enjoy a lease which will enable us, one hopes, to see the Savage Spirit continue unchanged into the next one hundred years.

I am well aware of the honour the Tribe accorded me when they invited me to be their President for the Centenary Year. As I write this, it has already been an unforgettable experience, and I know that all our members – whether artists, entertainers or 'lay' – feel it has been a great privilege to be Savages at this time.

We wish our successors the same Savage Spirit in the years to come.

Michael Long, President
April 2004

Bookshop, Clement's Inn, London: *This etching by Stanley Anderson was made during his first year in London and was shown in the 1909 Savages exhibition.*

1

WEDNESDAY NIGHT AT THE WIGWAM

In Trenchard Street car park an irate man hammers on the ticket machine for his money. He's put ten pounds in, he groans, and it's only given him change for a fiver. I leave him to his kicking and cursing and step out into Park Row, where the rush-hour traffic is parting to let a wailing ambulance through to the Royal Infirmary. After it has passed, a woman in a blue Polo stays stationary a split second longer than she might have done and instantly a horn blares from the car behind her and another from the white van behind that. It is clearly time to leave the twenty-first century behind, a task I go about by taking a sharp right turn and doubling back down Stoney Hill, a cobbled byway I had scarcely known existed a few months ago. A smart red door, a ring on the bell and... well, nothing, actually. Another ring and there's something, but it turns out simply to be the beeping of the pedestrian crossing above the high wall back in hellish Park Row. A third ring, longer this time, and tinged with the last impatient, fractious vestiges of the world I'm about to escape. There are footsteps on the stair and at last the door opens to reveal the quizzical, friendly and resolutely Dickensian face of Steward Bob Matthews. 'They're down in the Wigwam,' he says. They're down in the Wigwam, are they? It's yesterday once more.

The date is November 26 2003, Scottish Night for the Bristol Savages, but it could be almost any winter Wednesday evening over the past half-century or longer. In the brightly-lit Studio up the steps on the right of the corridor some twenty artists are at work on their sketches, the topic set, as always, by the Brother Savage in the chair for the evening. At 5.45 p.m. prompt Marcus Ashman, the night's Chairman and a Green Feather for ten years, had walked in and written on the board the words *None So Pretty,* the title of a famous Scottish dance tune. Marcus's Scottish antecedents are previously unknown to many of the Tribe, but he wears the kilt with a swagger and when, later in the evening, he admits to dancing regularly with the guest Highland dancer Andrew Smith, there is genuine surprise mingled with statutory gasps of mock revulsion and indignation. It just goes to show, in the words of the posh Scottish doctor in the old Tony Hancock sketch, that they're 'not all Rob Roys, you know'. They're not all mean, either, and the Chairman does not neglect to send mugs of beer up to the artists to wash down their bread and cheese.

Wednesday evening in the Studio: In his Preface, Centenary President Michael Long writes of the value of artists seeing fellow artists at work and working alongside them.

When Marcus stepped away from the blackboard there were the usual gripes and grumbles, but within minutes the ideas are flowing and by the time Paul Weaver bursts in late, paint is already washing over several artists' pads. Paul opts for a Scottish landscape of a loch with mountains, as do President Michael Long and some others. Dennis Lewis is producing a woodland scene of intense colour and density, and pretty women are another thread, none more striking than Patrick Collins's whirling Highland dancer. Terry Culpan settles for a fairy in a tree. Terry's great forté is marine painting, but since he took to teaching art to 'ladies of a certain age' on courses in and around South Gloucestershire he has begun to approach landscapes with fresh zest. Where the fairies come from nobody quite knows, but they surfaced at the last Annual Exhibition, and here's another tonight. Some of his colleagues think privately that this is a pretty rum way for a man to be going, and a Yorkshireman at that; but at the end of the painting, when the Chairman is given the choice of all the works on offer, it is Terry's little fantasy that Marcus Ashman plumps for.

I descend the steep flight of stairs up which the cricketing ace Walter Hammond was allegedly carried at the end of some particularly jolly Wednesday evenings and Bob is right, 'they' are indeed in the Wigwam. Secretary John Cleverdon and his ever-present assistant Geoff Cutter are on the stage at the far end, putting the final touches to the room's Caledonian finery while Richard Long, President Michael's younger brother, an Honoured Green Feather and not at all to be confused with the famous 'stones in landscapes' Bristol artist of the same name, vacuums the carpet around their feet. The bar is already serving the first of the Men's and the Boys' brews of the evening, white two-handled mugs stacked high and each one urging us once more to *Drink Down All Unkindness*. It's a command that secretly worries some Savages, who argue that by drinking unkindness down you are surely somehow making it a part of you, but everyone knows what it's trying to say, so they let it go unchallenged. Honoured Blue Feather Louis Garcia is one of the early birds relaxing close to the bar, reflecting on his sixty years as a Savage; he says he was not around so much in his first years of membership, when many of the Tribe were away on war duty, but he has caught up a little since then. Louis was elected in 1943, the year in which the Savages' founder Ernest Ehlers died; on the wall across from where he sits he points out a caricature of himself playing the violin, a study, full of verve and passion, of a young man with a mane of dark hair bouncing to the rhythm of the music. The artist was Harold Packer, who studied under Reginald Bush, an early Savage who had been head of Bristol's art college from the mid-1890s. A living link from the early twenty-first century back to late Victorian times in just a couple of steps; in most walks of life it's a rare sensation, but not at the Wigwam.

'Drink Down All Unkindness': A mug with a message.

Violinist with verve: A youthful Louis Garcia, as seen by Harold Packer.

The clock ticks round towards eight and the volume increases as the Green Feathers pack the floor around the bar. Prompt at 7.45 p.m. the Red Feather artists lay down their brushes and in a distant corner of the Red Lodge piper Geoff Pegler and the dancing Andrew Smith practise their performance. From the hubbub of the lobby, through panelling-clad Elizabethan walls, Geoff's pipes sound plaintive, mysterious and remote. The Englishman's response to the bagpipes and Savages humour being what they are, there will soon be muttered lamentations that they did not stay that way. The last of the members are straggling through the reception hall which leads from the Red Lodge, and John Gill, the first-year Junior Lay Member whose job it is to greet them all, looks as if he feels he has earned his drink. He also has the distinguished air of a man who has not been a junior anything for a good many years, but it has been a tremendous getting-to-know-you exercise, he says, and he is pleased to have done it. The crowd waiting to sign the attendance book is now dwindling to the final few – members' attendance has always been noted, and that of visitors since 1906 – but a healthy new crop of names has sprung up on the request sheet for volunteers to sing *The Holy City* at Punch Night on the last Wednesday meeting before Christmas. They are part of a long tradition.

The Holy City, the ultimate drawing-room ballad with its rousing 'Jerusalem, Jerusalem, lift up your gates and sing...' has a special place in the Tribe's lore, its words

Versatile Charlie Thomas: Harold Packer's view of one of the great Savages.

having been written by Savage Fred Weatherly, the stern King's Counsel who spent his evenings writing some of the most sweet, sentimental and commercially successful song lyrics of the early twentieth century. That mix of sound practical worth to society and the dreaming of romantic dreams is a concept to which many a Savage can relate. There has doubtless always been singing 'at the meeting before Christmas, in vulgar parlance "Punch Night"' (minutes of 1915). In fact it was in 1910 that there was first noted 'the appearance of the Wine Warden carrying on high the time-honoured silver bowl, being greeted by the singing of *Good King Wenceslas* ably led by lusty-lunged Bro. Sav. Charlie Thomas'. The first apparent rendition of Weatherly's song came in 1938 with 'the appearance of a new choral party whose rendering of *The Holy City* clearly indicated that their presence in the Wigwam would always be welcome. Bro. Sav. George Cooksley was responsible for this novelty'. The tradition thrived in the middle years of the last century, as the Punch Night minutes from 1949 to 1953 make plain: 'The now well established tradition of *The Holy City...*' 'Punch Night sees the only appearance of the Savage Choir to sing *The Holy City*, with Bro. Sav. Reg Forward playing the organ and Bro. Sav. Harold Thomas the piano...' 'Tradition was again observed when the Chairman and the Hon. Sec. assumed the Ceremonial Feather Head-dresses of Sioux origin. Bro. Sav. G. Cooksley and his Tribal canaries embarked upon *The Holy City*. Many of them seemed to know the melody, and some the words...' 'There followed another traditional rendering of *The Holy City*, and worthy to note that Bro. Savages the Lord Mayor and Sheriff, each wearing civic insignia as official guests, took their places in the choir and sang lustily...' All was not so lusty come the 1960s, when the custom lapsed, and in 1970 the only singing noted was when, 'by tradition, punch was brought in to the Tribe singing *Good King Wenceslas*', the old Charlie Thomas favourite. *The Holy City* has made several reappearances since then, often with Blue Feathers as soloists, but it was as recently as the Millennium year of 2000 that it was firmly re-established on the Punch Night agenda by the then Entertainment Warden Ken Matthews, with soloist Jeremy Watkins fronting a Savage choir of all feathers. Tonight's response from would-be singers suggests that the tradition will not lightly be set aside again.

Fred Weatherly: Savage writer of the lyrics to The Holy City *and much more besides.*

Five to eight, and the ship's bell clangs; the five-minute call. The gleaming bell dates from the First World War and was the gift of Savage the Revd W. K. Knight-Adkin, who had been Chaplain of the Fleet. There is a general making for seats and at eight o' clock John Cleverdon rings the Burmese gongs for silence, which falls after a due period of ostentatious shushing. Marcus Ashman declares that it has been a great week of sporting achievement, with England winning the rugby World Cup on Saturday and the Hon. Sec. sinking a hole in one at Henbury on Monday, and before he begins giving out the notices and the minutes of the last meeting John Cleverdon makes it clear that the bad news is that the bar tab is closed, and had we wanted to share in his triumph we should have been at Henbury Golf Club on Monday evening. This goes down far from well, but as Moss Garcia is absent, John is allowed to read his elegantly written minutes with fewer oohs and aahs than usual. What's more, as

Punch Night tradition: The Tribe's special choir sings The Holy City.

Treasurer John Oakhill is not called upon to report tonight, he is spared all the usual stuff about the splendour of his suiting or solicitous inquiries regarding his next cruise to the Bahamas.

Marcus Ashman has taken the chair before, but he needs time to settle and in his first few words to his fellow Brother Savages he commits the grave solecism of addressing them as 'Gentlemen'.

'Gentlemen?' a querying voice pipes up.

'Gentlemen??' the more indignant cry goes up.

'There <u>are</u> no gentlemen in the Savages,' comes the last definitive word on the subject from somewhere in the middle of the hall and, good for Marcus, it doesn't happen again.

Geoff Pegler appears from the rear of the room, pipes in full skirl. 'Worst five minutes of my year,' is the usual cry, but this time Geoff makes a lie of that by playing

Piper Geoff Pegler: Despite the joking, his music is an integral part of Scottish Night.

for all of ten. Or at least it seems like ten. He drains a dram in a single draught with the Chairman before he is joined by his guest Andrew Smith, who looks old enough to be a Savage but is quite remarkably light and fleet of foot as he dances what the non-Caledonian among us would call a Highland fling. Their performance ends in the heartiest of applause, and Marcus pays warm tribute to Geoff, who finally joined the Tribe in 1999, for bringing a fresh dimension to Wednesday night's music with his Scots and Irish reels. As well as the pipes, he explains, he also plays the accordion and violin, and a voice from the back deems it necessary to explain that while yes, he did, it was never at the same time; a useful point of clarification.

Geoff Pegler is one of three supporters who join the Chairman on his raised dais to the right of the platform, its desk cluttered with relics and regalia of which the silver skull and crossbones snuff box designed by the long-ago Ernest Fabian most readily catches the eye. Marcus's other supporters are Cedric Nash, a retired bank manager – resounding boos for this – and the former Port of Bristol head Stanley Turner, of whom the Chairman opines he does not need to say much more. There is general assent to this judgement, and a shout of 'No, not likely.' The next performer is the internationally known concert pianist and avid Savage Allan Schiller, of whom more later in this book. He plays contrasting pieces with varyingly compelling Scottish credentials. The first is by the Victorian composer Rockstro, who lived some way south of the border at East Cheam but produced a jolly medley of Scottish (and in the case of *The Keel Row,* North-Eastern English) tunes which he called *Heather Bells.* Allan follows this with *Wedding Day* at *Troldhaugen* by Grieg, who, as he explains, had a Scottish grand-father and would have qualified to play rugby for Scotland had he stood somewhat taller than four-feet-ten. At least, it sounds like four-feet-ten from where I am sitting, but as Allan himself would have trouble winning a place on the Harlem Globetrotters basketball team his words might not quite have carried to me.

The pleasure of meeting regularly with friends old and new is just as much a part of Wednesday night at the Wigwam as the music, recitations and songs.

Allan Schiller is the consummate professional. Mike Alford, the conjuror who fol-lows him, is not. As a conjuror, Mike Alford makes Tommy Cooper look like the David Copperfield who appears not in Dickens but on stage at Las Vegas, perform-ing illusions of the utmost slickness and sophistication. The hand that lumbers in and out of Mike Alford's pocket producing not-so-hidden cards could not be more obvi-ous if it were flagged up by a flashing neon arrow. His rope tricks will not leave the chaps who shin high into the air over Indian market places fearing for their jobs. We

howl with laughter. We love Mike Alford. Best of all, we *think* he means it all to be as chaotic as it is, but he leaves us with just that element of doubt. It's this that gives his show its edge, and making you walk the *is-he-for-real-or-isn't-he?* tightrope is his cleverest trick of all.

The Centennial Year President, Michael Long, takes centre stage. It's a tough year to be President, and you can see why he was chosen. He's as serious as can be about his art, a full-time professional with a constant output of work; but he's serious, too, about the Savages, and about making everyone feel at home and a part of it. There's not a great deal in common between, say, a fortysomething art teacher with a burning ambition to paint exclusively for a living and an octogenarian retired grocer who sees the warmth and welcome of a Wigwam Wednesday night as the hands-down highspot of his week. By putting two and two together you know where Michael Long's empathy must more naturally lie, but by listening to him on the platform, and indeed off it, you never would. He loves the painting, he loves the history, but most of all in this corner of his busy life he loves the spirit of the Wigwam and wants Braves of all feathers to feel included and enjoy their time here. The first reference in his address is not to England's rugby triumph but to the final return to Bristol earlier in the day of Concorde, which has brought out tens of thousands of admirers all over the city; he reminds us that the revolutionary aircraft's principal designer was the late Sir Archibald Russell, who became a Savage in 1971. Michael also congratulates the Highland dancer Andrew Smith, who has apparently been practising his skills for fifty years. 'No wonder you're so good,' he muses quietly. 'You've been doing it for so long.' Just occasionally Michael Long gives the impression of a man who could read the telephone directory and make it sound funny, and through some quirk of chemistry this is just such a moment. On paper, his words of praise to the dancer look mildly quirky at most. In life, they have his Brother Savages roaring with laughter and cheering.

In a break for drinks, Dennis Lewis tells me his Archibald Russell story. 'It was one of the three sessions I was President,' he says. 'I asked him if he was able to get along to some evening or another and he said "No, Rockefeller's sending a plane for me that day". Apparently he met fairly regularly with one of the dynasty at his home high up on a mountain in the deserts of Utah or Nevada or wherever, and it really was private jet service all the way. Sir Archibald told me that one day he was there he looked down and saw a fleet of trucks labouring up the hill below. "They're bringing me water," Rockefeller said. "Water? Why don't you just drill for it?" "I tried that,"

Top, drinking down all unkindness; above left, an example of the two-hour sketches at the heart of Wednesday evenings, Dennis Lewis's So Well Remembered; *and above right, Entertainment Warden Chris Torpy in full flow.*

A song from Scot Jim Mearns, a Savage for nearly forty years.

Rockefeller replied, "but all I got was this darned oil.'"

It's time to return to our seats, and on come the Tribe's main pair of impromptu poets of this time, upholding yet another tradition that goes back to the earliest days. Hylton Dawson's theme is *None So Pretty*, followed by Alan Shellard's deftly rousing epic poem on England's World Cup triumph.

There never was such drama
or excitement in a game,

he concludes, and he still has his audience with him all the way as he follows it up with one of his compositions for piano, *The Tilt of the Kilt*. Shortly afterwards Chris Torpy is giving a rather more scurrilous account of a Scotsman's kilt and all that's under it, as well as reciting Robert Burns's short and flirty rhyme *Supper Isnae Ready* and the old forces favourite *Bloody Orkney*, the kind of graphic social document that reminds you why Orcadians used to swear that their cockerels sang cock-a-bleedin'-doodle-doo for years after the troops had gone home. In between Alan and Chris, David Reed singles out four of his artist brothers' *None So Pretty* evening sketches for praise: Michael Rummings's super-topical Concorde over Clevedon Pier; Patrick Collins's swirling dancer – 'he seems to muck around and doodle and then suddenly something like this just appears'; Terry Culpan's fairy, the praise all the more hard to administer since 'dammit, he's a Yorkshireman as well'; and finally, Paul Weaver's timeless Scottish scene, with its looming wet-into-wet sky and a fetching sparkle on the loch.

Another Blue Feather entertainer whose work is always appreciated is trumpeter Norman Golding.

Time's drawing on, and Jim Mearns, a Savage since 1966, is delighted to be listed to help ring down the curtain on a memorable night. There were evenings in the past when any number of Blue Feathers had prepared pieces but there had been time for only some of them to perform. Soft-spoken Scot Jim did not enjoy that state of affairs, but everyone knows where they are these days, and it is with verve and abiding strength of voice that he sings out *The Star o' Rabbie Burns*, accompanied by Geoff Pegler on accordion, and *Green Grow the Rashes O*, this time with Allan Schiller at his side. From where I sit, Jim is framed on stage by an illuminated display cabinet aglow with the Dixon collection of silver and glassware, classical busts, glimmering stained glass, primitive spears, the mounted horns of antelopes and wildebeests and the ornate seventeenth-century Guild of Bakers fireplace bearing the archaic inscription *Prais God For All,* a phrase which now serves as the Savage grace; and as his friends in the audience hum along with him to the last chorus of *The Star o' Rabbie Burns,* you ask yourself for the hundredth time tonight, 'Where else in Bristol? Where else in England?' To which the only answer there can possibly be is 'Where else but the Wigwam?'

Nearly ten o' clock. It's getting late. In a few weeks' time Allan Schiller, working the American cruise liners in the Caribbean, will be coming to terms with plush little theatres full of upright citizens of Dallas and Detroit standing ramrod-straight, hands on hearts, in homage to Irving Berlin's now strangely sanctified show tune *God Bless America.* Tonight he plays one last time for a very different roomful of couldn't-be-more-British men, who might almost be confused with gentlemen had they not been Savages, as they sing three rousing verses of the National Anthem, frustrating Her Majesty's enemies' knavish tricks and all. It's years since I last toasted the Queen, but they do here. 'The Queen – Duke of Lancaster' I was brought up to say, but I soon discovered that that one doesn't wash much beyond Bury, Bolton, Blackburn and other points North West; a pity, since I still feel the loyal toast sounds truncated and flat without it.

'It's been a lovely evening. Have a safe journey home,' Marcus Ashman concludes. 'A lovely evening...' I wonder how often men going back to their wives after an all-male evening out express their appreciation of one another's company in this way. Not often at all, I suspect, yet the warmth, camaraderie and most of all the sheer innocence of the past few hours make the words not toe-curlingly embarrassing, not mawkish but purely and simply true. Minutes later I hear the selfsame phrase out in the street, as elderly members of the Tribe are going their separate ways in Lodge Street: ''Night William. 'Night Charles. It's been a lovely evening.'

A little way up Park Row the pace is quickening at the two students' clubs, Dojo and Level. The night is young for them at the moment, but they'll be buzzing come midnight. A couple step out of Mamma Mia, the pizza and pasta house, and wonder where the evening will take them next. It looks as if it will be anywhere but home to the eleven o' clock news and a cup of cocoa. By now the last of the Tribe's cars are streaming out of the multi-storey and only Michael Long is still on foot, dashing about and laughing and grumbling that he's forgotten where he's parked. The ticket machine is still playing up, but somehow it doesn't seem to matter much any more.

2

WHERE IT ALL BEGAN

There has never been anything quite like the Bristol Savages, and there is certainly nothing remotely like them in Britain today. In nineteenth-century England, however, there were groups of people who gave a foretaste of what was to come, painters who enjoyed the occasional company of their peers for fun as well as inspiration and stimulation. The London Sketching Society was founded in 1799, and within a couple of decades Bristol was heading in the same direction. Artists whom we now see as the Bristol School – though the grouping was far from as precise or chronologically compact as that phrase suggests – had been out on sketching parties with others to the Avon Gorge and Leigh Woods, Nightingale Valley in Brislington and the Frome Valley from Regency times onwards. In 1824 they staged their first exhibition at the Literary and Philosophical Institution at the bottom of Park Street, and by the 1830s they had formalised themselves briefly into the Bristol Society of Artists. Of the painters we now see as being at the heart of the Bristol School, Francis Danby was there from the start and Samuel Jackson and an extremely young William Müller soon followed. Danby's early companions included the Royal Academician Edward Bird and the Revd John Eagles, who although not on a par with most of the others technically has left us with the most intriguing glimpse of those first sketching outings. Some years later, after he had moved to Devon, he wrote that 'I think of a drawing party in the woods', and enclosed a song lyric which included the lines:

For we joke and we pun
And bask in the sun,
All breathren (sic) of the brush.

There was much going on in Bristol to attract painters. In the 1820s the retired businessman George Weare Braikenridge embarked on an impassioned drive to record the local topography in watercolour drawings, a venture which had the dual virtue of keeping a number of artists happily employed while giving the city a more complete record of its life before the photographic age than any other in the country. Jackson was happy to get involved as were T. L. Rowbotham, Edward Cashin, George Delamotte, Hugh O'Neill and James Johnson, the key members of Braikenridge's band.

From pre-Savages times: William Müller was at the hub of much social activity among artists in the nineteenth century. Here, from the Bristol City Art Gallery collection, is his Swallow Falls, Betwys-y-coed *of 1837.*

In 1833 William Müller, along with Samuel Jackson, Skinner Prout, William West, Rowbotham and others, continued the tradition of the sketching society with a short-lived fraternity known informally as the Monks. At the age of fifty, Rowbotham was the oldest of the eight founder members by some years. Müller was the youngest, at 21, but all the others were still only in their twenties or thirties, and they were a jolly band for a few years. All the steam went out of their enterprise when Müller left for Bloomsbury in 1839. It continued for a few years, with his younger brother Edmund Gustavus Müller among those who tried to keep the flame alive, but it had lost its will to live by 1845, when William died tragically young in his early thirties.

It had been good while it lasted. N. Neal Solley's 1875 memoir of Müller recorded that: 'At the end of (1832) or early in 1833, several young artists living in Bristol formed a Sketching Club or Society for drawing once a week at each others' houses... The draw-

The first Savage: Ernest Ehlers, who founded the club in 1904.

C. J. Kelsey: Dentist and Savage from 1906, as seen by Charlie Thomas.

ings were all from imagination, a word (for a subject) being given generally, and they were left with the member at whose house the meeting was held... The programme was "tea and chat" at six; at seven, all set to work, ready-strained drawing boards being provided beforehand at each house... At nine, a simple supper was served – cold meat, cheese and beer, with pipes afterwards till eleven, at which the party broke up.'

A more formalised society, and one with far greater longevity, came late in 1844 when a group of painters and businessmen formed the Bristol Academy for the Promotion of the Fine Arts. Locally based artists on its founding committee were Charles Branwhite, Henry Hewitt, the marine painter Joseph Walter and Edmund Müller. Nobody was talking about a 'breathren of the brush' frolicking in Leigh Woods any more, but it was one of a number of signs of recognition, as the industrialised world took flight, that artists relied as much as they ever had done on patrons, and those patrons were no longer the Church or grand families but self-made men who had amassed their fortunes through tobacco, textile or heavy engineering. The Pre-Raphaelites tried to escape into dreamy medievalism, only to discover that that was exactly what the hard-nosed tycoons of Birmingham and Manchester wanted on their walls. Less prominent painters also saw where their future markets lay, but the more traditionally-minded among them believed, as did the Pre-Raphaelites, that there were benefits still in meeting together and exchanging views in relaxed company.

Towards the end of the century, the Bristol Sketching Club took up the challenge of delivering such a service. One member was Ernest Ehlers, born in Newfoundland of German stock in 1858 but brought up from his teenage years in Bristol, at Cotham Grove. His father Gustav had emigrated to Newfoundland from Hamburg and married Elizabeth Bennett, a daughter of the Governor, who had strong family ties with Bristol and the West Country. Ernest was the oldest of six children, four of whom were born in Newfoundland and two in Hamburg, to where the family returned. Disaster struck when Gustav Ehlers died, leaving Elizabeth and her children destitute, and it was the presence of a Bennett sister in Redland that brought the family to Bristol. As they had been in Newfoundland, where they had risen to prominence in the salt cod business, the Bennetts were very useful people to know, and in time the second Ehlers son, Bob (a Green Feather Savage from 1908), went on to manage their wine merchants' business in Queen Square. That course of action was not for Ernest Ehlers, however. He had to contend with the considerable handicap of severe deafness, but from the start it was clear that he meant business only as an artist. He found a ready market for his detailed, flower-strewn woodland scenes and was a member of the Bristol Academy of Fine Arts some years before his 40th birthday. He was happy enough with some of his companions at the sketching club – Henry Stacy, C. F. W. Dening, H. C. Guyatt, Lowry Lewis, Charles Kelsey, H. G. Pearson and W. A. Sheldon all went on to be Savages with him – but he had no regard for the talents of several of the others. Worst of all, there were women members. He was by no means immune to the charms of women, as his somewhat late marriage to Kate Collins in 1907 and the birth of their son Geoffrey would seem to testify, but he read Solley's book on Müller and quickly realised that as it stood, there was not much in the spirit of cold meat, beer and pipes afterwards about the sedate Bristol Sketching Club. He had spent some years studying art at Karlsrühe, at a time when the Germans were world leaders in training and facilities for deaf people, and had happy memories of nights of raising his Stein and drinking Bier in true Student Prince style; this played a part in his thinking, as well, and served as a further reminder that there was more to communal art than meeting in a draughty hall and going home at 9.30 p.m. He shared his dream of more exciting times with only two of his club colleagues. Lowry Lewis was a dedicated and serious professional, while Stacy had run an art school of his own at Weston-super-Mare. Both of them had seen something of life. Other sketching club members who went on to become distinguished Savages, notably Kelsey and Dening, were still extremely young at the time.

He really was Curly: A. E. Toope as portrayed in a rare caricature by George Swaish.

Back to roots: A tantalising glimpse of Ernest Ehlers' studio in the early days.

Ernest Ehlers is still remembered with affection by his daughter-in-law Mary, born in March 1910 and now living near Bath. 'My husband Geoffrey was a Savage, as was my father Dr Morgan Thomas who joined in the year before I was born, so I heard a lot about the club from as far back as I can

Above, one of W. H. Y. Titcomb's most evocative street scenes of Bristol, his St Mary le Port Street with rain-soaked pavements and laden handcart, a painting now owned by the City Art Gallery; right, two paintings that hang proudly in the Wigwam, one of Frank Stonelake's powerful horse studies and Arthur Wilde Parsons' HMS Formidable; and above far right, Stanley Anderson's humorous caricature of F. A. S. 'Padlock' Locke, Honorary Treasurer for the Tribe's first seventeen years.

remember,' she says. 'I know I was nineteen when I went to my first Ladies' Night. I remember my father-in-law as a charming gentleman with old-fashioned courtesy and manners – not very tall, quite spare, very artistic and extremely deaf. He was kindness itself, with a lovely, quiet sense of humour.' These and other qualities are highlighted in a sonnet produced by the long-serving Honorary Secretary H. E. Roslyn for a beautiful folio of original paintings and verse presented to Ehlers at the time of his marriage, a treasure now in the hands of his Savage grandson George. Just two other such folios, now back in the hands of the Tribe, were created – for Wilfred Peake, a popular early member who moved to Burton upon Trent, and James Fuller Eberle, of whom a good deal more anon. As a painter, Ehlers followed the French Impressionists in painting from nature, and as the twentieth century wore on he would become a familiar figure around the city, cycling in a Norfolk jacket and knickerbockers and often with an unbelievable amount of paraphernalia.

The breakthrough that paved the way for the Bristol Savages a decade later came in the autumn of 1894, when Ehlers invited a few gentlemen friends to join him for an evening's sketching at his studio, an upstairs room on the Portland Street corner of Alfred Place in Kingsdown. Just four of them joined him on the first night, Stacy and Lewis not among them, but then again, none had known anything about the meeting when they woke up that day; Ehlers took a morning stroll to tell his friend Arthur Wilde Parsons about his idea, and word went out to others in the next few hours. Joseph Skelton, Arthur Garrington and Thomas Kingston were the three who joined Ehlers and Wilde Parsons that first evening but others quickly followed – Stacy and Lewis, of course, but also J Miller Marshall and W. H. Quick; Francis A. S. Locke became a member in 1899 and Ehlers' brother-in-law George Lingford in 1903. All went on to become founder members of the Savages apart from Garrington, who died in 1899, and Skelton, who moved away for a few years but joined the new club as soon as he returned in 1904.

The studio was a Victorian conservatory, but it was no Crystal Palace; more a zinc-roofed lean-to greenhouse facing north, which was all very well for clear light, but dauntingly bracing when the north-easterlies were sweeping down into town and Ehlers' temperamental stove was playing up or his bulldog Angelina was hogging all the heat. The Salvation Army met down below for an hour on the same evening, which led to an intriguing conflict of interests. The irreverent among us might like to imagine the strait-laced Salvationists fretting over the rabelaisian din pounding down from the room above, but the truth was rather different. At that time of evening all the painters wanted to do was paint, and their task was made no more pleasurable by the accompaniment of voices heartily proving that while the Devil may not have had all the best tunes, God did not by any means have all the best singers.

It was all a good deal more easy-going after the congregation had left and the paints had been put away, and the artists were able to relax with talk and a good deal of joking and banter, all helped along by the bottle of whisky provided by the host to counterpoint the bread and cheese. Wilde Parsons always recalled that Ehlers had asked him along on that first evening 'to start the fun'. Fun it doubtless was, which makes it all the more a pity that an 1896 photograph of the group that hangs in the Wigwam today is a very serious affair indeed. It is wonderful to have such a memento, of course, but it has to be admitted that it is stronger at conveying period atmosphere and the constraints of late-Victorian photography than any joyous sense of bonhomie. Ehlers, Wilde Parsons and their friends perch on a variety of makeshift and otherwise chairs to paint by the light of paraffin lamps, long pipes and cigars adding further to the subfusc surroundings. No doubt it was a different story later in the evening – a good deal later, according to a tradition that makes these pioneers out to be inveterate night owls.

The subject for sketching on that first night was *Old Friends,* and Ehlers set a time limit of ninety minutes. Nothing survives of the five men's efforts, but what did live on was their enthusiasm, and their instant decision to meet again the following week and so on into the future. It was agreed that they would take it in turn to be the host who set the topic and bought the whisky, but as they did not all have a suitable room to serve as a meeting place, it turned out that the bulk of the sessions were at Ehlers' studio in Kingsdown or the workspace Joseph Skelton rented in Regent Street, Clifton.

Even before the Savages were formed, the sketching club recruited a member whose forté was not in painting or drawing but more sociable skills. Francis Locke came along for the ride – and rather a long ride it proved to be – largely for being a good mixer and a facility for writing impromptu verse, the verbal equivalent of the instant cartoons and caricatures that have always enlivened Savages evenings. He was a short, Pickwickian figure, round in both body and bald head and with a high-pitched voice that was a wonderful vehicle for his rhymes and other light verses until the laughter drowned it out. His shape and name spawned the first of the Savages'

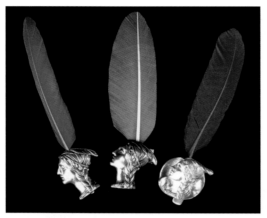

To be worn with pride: Siver-mounted feather insignia for the President, Honorary Secretary and Vice-President.

rich roll-call of nicknames – Little Padlock; but there was more to him than mere frivolity and fun. As a solicitor, he was full of sound advice as Ehlers' group of friends grew in number and moved inexorably towards a more formalised society as the Savages; his feet-on-the-ground approach was good for the artists, as when he punctured all enthusiasm for Henry Whatley's scene of cold people bearing a yule log into the baronial hall through the snow by wondering why they had not brought it in a month earlier and kept it dry; groups of people need one or two of their number to be like that, and when the Tribe eventually came into being, he was the one who first took on the ticklish role of Treasurer.

Locke's verses prompted a few others to stand up after their painting to tell a joke or tall tale. Joseph Skelton was quite an actor and particularly good at parodying the events of the evening in prose, rather as Padlock did in verse. Word was getting around Bristol that Ernest Ehlers' sketching club was about far more than an hour and a half of artistic endeavour, and more and more men were asking to join. By this time the club's ranks had been swelled by some well-organised and ambitious people. George Lingford, Ehlers' brother-in-law – the Savages' past and indeed present is rich in brothers-in-law – was one, in spite of the fact that he could be fallible in his timekeeping. He was a member of a band of men called the Diskos Club, who met in Zed Alley. They were described as sportsmen, though quite what sports they got up to in Zed Alley is lost in the mists of time; a fun-loving bunch, however, and several of them were keen to see what these Savages were all about. Lorin A. Lathrop, the United States consul in Bristol from 1892 to 1907, was another go-getter, and between them they helped push matters along. As we have noted, Ehlers was born of German stock in the New World, but he had lived in Bristol for most of his life and it would be wrong to read any meaningful transatlantic influence into the foundation of the Savages. On the other hand, perhaps there is a small case to be made for the family background of both the earlier Müller and Ehlers to be seen as something more than coincidence; in Germany there was a strong sense of *Brüderschaft,* of brotherhood, among groups of men of similar and often conservative interests, and one that manifested itself in breaking bread and drinking together to supplement the core pursuit of hunting, fishing, painting or whatever. Since both Müller and Ehlers were both very comfortable indeed in their role as Englishmen and Bristolians, however, it is not a point to be laboured.

Full glory: The President's chain and head-dress, the latter of which is worn sparingly, but always to considerable effect. Left, the Honorary Secretary's head-dress in action for the swearing-in of new Blue Feathers Ray Anstice, Stuart Edwards and Philip Gittings.

George Lingford's influence was brief but decisive. He returned to Bristol in 1903 after some successful years as an artist in Liverpool, and before long he had moved on again, this time to London; in the meantime, he had work to do. Lingford is generally credited with being among the first to recognise that the club needed a permanent home and a positive identity. He even knew where its first H.Q. should be – his attic studio above a gunsmith's shop at 39 Corn Street, in that part of the old commercial part of the city where today banks and solid commercial chambers have given way to trendy wine bars. The meeting at which this was decided, and during which the name the Bristol Savages was formally adopted, was at W. Evans Linton's house at 27 Oakfield Road, Clifton on February 18 1904. This was Day One in the history of the Tribe, and the reason the centenary is being celebrated in 2004. In years past it has been readily accepted that in all but name, the Savages first came together at Ernest Ehlers' Kingsdown studio in 1894, and the Tribe's scrapbooks are littered with press stories that trace its foundation back to that date. It is easy to see where these reports were coming from, but as a sheer matter of fact, the Bristol Savages were one hundred years old on February 18 2004. We also now know that Ehlers had written to the Savage Club in London some time before the meeting at Evans Linton's house to seek permission to use the name, which totally undermines the theory that heated deliberations over what to call themselves – the Palette Club and Lay Figure Club were apparently other ideas that had been tossed around – were brought to an abrupt end when Chairman Linton complained that they were all behaving 'like a lot of savages'. In real life, the most likely impetus to use the name came from the American consul Lathrop, who had joined the London Savage Club in 1891 and dreamed that the Bristol group might one day amalgamate with it. In fact Bristol's congenial Wednesday painting nights at the Wigwam have little in common with the well-oiled daily routine of an exclusive London gentlemen's club, with its roots deep in theatre, literature and the carriage trade end of journalism.

The concept of a Savage as a North American Indian – Native American is the politically correct term today, but the tribes themselves are perfectly happy with North American Indian – was certainly a borrowing from the London Savage Club. A society with its roots in the middle years of the nineteenth century, it has long decorated its menu cards with images of Indians, while a long-ago article in the *Illustrated London News* reported that its Wigwam – familiar word – was no less adorned with tomahawks, spearheads and tribal paraphernalia than the Park Row building is today. Happily, there has never been any serious challenge to Bristol Savages' continued use of the American Indian as its symbol. 'Of course they are not savages, but our forefathers thought of them and admired them as Noble Savages, and paid them the ultimate compliment of adopting aspects of their culture, if only on a superficial level,' says the club's Centenary Season President, Michael Long. 'In 1928 they welcomed the Chief of the Sioux as their honoured guest, and it was a happy occasion where recriminations were the last thing on anyone's mind.'

With the cinema in its infancy, the concept of the Western movie, with the Indians a cunning and ruthless enemy to the cowboys, was almost unknown in 1904. What was familiar to literate Bristolians was the series of novels on the Native American way of life created by James Fenimore Cooper, most notably *The Last of the Mohicans,* in constant publication since it first appeared in 1826. The poetry of Henry Wadsworth Longfellow, famously *The Song of Hiawatha,* was also then known to every schoolboy some fifty years after it had been written, and both Cooper and Longfellow stressed the sacred and mysterious bond between the Indians and their land, their instinctive rapport with nature. It was an appealing and inspiring message in the cramped industrial cities of a hundred years ago.

Then there had been Buffalo Bill Cody's Wild West Show. It had been seen frequently in Britain in the late 1880s and early 1890s, including a riotous week in Bristol when more than a hundred thousand people flocked up the Gloucester Road to visit it on Horfield Common in September 1891. It was pure Barnum and Bailey, of course, but what was very apparent was the off-stage bearing of the impassive Indians, who seemed to exude simple dignity and inner calm in far from dignified circumstances. These perceived personality traits, set against an often precarious and brutal existence in the wild, made American Indians very charismatic people in late Victorian and Edwardian eyes. William Gladstone had been one of the first visitors to the London show in 1887, and had spent equal time with Bill and Chief Red Shirt. There were some ninety-seven Indians in the troupe, and they were a source of great fascination. Shortly afterwards the Prince of Wales went along and enjoyed the spectacle so much that he urged his mother the Queen to demand a special performance, to which she invited most of the crowned heads of Europe. As captivated as her son had been, Victoria arranged for a further show at Windsor Great Park, a highlight of which was an Indian attack on a stagecoach. Buffalo Bill was the coachman, the Prince of Wales rode shotgun beside him and the passengers were the Kings of Denmark, Saxony, Greece and Austria. Of course none of them suffered anything

worse than a good shaking-up, and while Cody was briefly the toast of socialite London, his cowboys and Indians became legendary in Britain from that moment on, equal partners in helping bring nations and cultures together. The days of American Indians being cannon fodder in John Wayne movies or comic characters of the likes of Little Plum Your Redskin Chum and Um Heap Big Chiefie were still in the future.

Preoccupation with American Indian terms seems to come and go within the Savages. There was a time when wives really were referred to as squaws, and for a period in the 1960s the minutes are scattered with references to papooses, meaning sons of members of the Tribe. The word wigwam is interesting in itself. Technically, it means a Native American's hut, a corruption of an Algonquian term, so is technically well suited to the admittedly large permanent structure in the Red Lodge garden. A century ago, however, most people in Britain thought of a wigwam as an Indian's tent, the kind we now know correctly as a tepee, and from this distance in time it is not easy to say whether the Savages were consciously correct in their terminology or simply hit haphazardly upon the right word for the wrong reason; it seems reasonable to suspect the latter. What cannot be denied is that they put a great deal of thought into their feathers and insignia over the years. In 1912 the 'feathers and badge to be worn' were red for artists, blue for literary and white for musical, though come 1914 and the headlong rush to arms there were few musicians to be found wearing their white feathers with pride. Social members, it will be noted, wore no feather at all. It was in 1921 that today's formula was introduced: red for the artists, blue for the entertainers, and green for lay, the green following hard on the heels of a brief flirtation with yellow. In those days all the feathers were naturally coloured and came from Bristol Zoo, where a number of the senior staff were Savages. Presumably the canaries took a dim view of this arrangement, since it was quickly reported back that yellow feathers were difficult to get, and green would be a far more sensible option. Today, Terry Cleeve is the Tribe's main man for making the lapel badges and dyeing the feathers, which have been collected from the swannery at Abbotsbury in Dorset by David Langford. When he called in for fresh supplies in the summer of 2003 he found a number of them already collected in a box that looked to be marked SAUAGES and which someone had meticulously corrected to SAUSAGES. When Terry Cleeve reported this to a Friday nosebag luncheon a few days later his listeners seemed not at all surprised or put out, and generally received the news in the spirit of 'and quite right, too'. In the early days there seemed to be various experiments in how the feathers were held on, with compressed card and even miniature totem polls tried. The restyling of 1937 brought in an

American five cent piece, the nickel, as a more durable feather holder, and it was with due reverence thirty years later that the club's minutes noted the death of Chief Johnny Big Tree, the Indian whose profile appeared on the coins.

And what are we to make of the old Sioux welcome, now rendered as Ku-Woh-Wah, that has been used as a Savages greeting almost from earliest times? Long-time Secretary Frank Mole used to say its use had been suggested by a visitor well versed in Indian lore, while when the Sioux chief with the unlikely name of Dr Eastman visited the Tribe in 1928 it is impossible to imagine that its pedigree was not discussed and verified with him. For the purposes of this book, the search for definite proof proved as frustrating as others have found it in the past. The American Embassy passed on the supposed telephone number of the North American Indian Society in Britain which turned out to belong to an elderly widow in Edinburgh who swore she had never been farther west than Oban, while an internet link to a Sioux chief on a reservation in Dakota turned out to be as effective as smoke signals in a hurricane. The Sioux word for 'welcome' is Ku-Woh-Wah. Just believe it.

Quiet, retiring but always impressive: Arthur Wilde Parsons, a legend among Savages.

While on the subject of evolving attitudes and the legislation covering them, the reason why the Savages and other male-only organisations do not attract the attention of the Equal Opportunities Commission is quite simple; they are private members' clubs, and as such do not fall within the remit of the Sex Discrimination Act of 1975. A House of Lords ruling in 1973, treating a case of racial rather than sexual discrimination, decided that a society that operates a system of proposing and seconding new members, followed by the consideration of the acceptability of applications by its committee, is deemed to be a private members' club; if it genuinely selects its members on personal grounds – rather than, for example, accepting anyone who will pay a fee – it is again a private members' club. The same does not apply to clubs that are open to the public or a section of the public, maybe nightclubs or some sports clubs, and these organisations cannot discriminate on the grounds of sex. In truth, women have not fought tooth and nail for membership of the Savages over the years, but there seems to have been a brief testing of the waters in April 1967. The minutes note that the President welcomed two university guests,

'who turned out to be girls' (sic); they were then 'interviewed in purdah and respect-fully and apologetically asked to leave'. This was a little early for Women's Liberation, but it was certainly a time of social unrest on the campuses of Europe, and the two young women doubtless saw their incursion as a tilt at the male Establishment.

All of which was a long way away from 27 Oakfield Road on the evening of February 18 1904. With Evans Linton at his home that first night were the Savages' founding fathers and first committee: Ernest Ehlers, George Lingford, Arthur Wilde Parsons, Thomas Kingston, Henry Stacy, Lowry Lewis, J. Miller Marshall, Francis A. S. Locke, W. H. Quick and Frank Stonelake. Quick was appointed Secretary and Locke Treasurer, and the meeting's chief practical decision was that a gas lamp and other improvements should be introduced to Lingford's studio before they moved in on March 9. The two Wednesdays before that, meetings were held at members' hous-es as before. On February 25 just eight of the eleven turned up to Ehlers' studio, and while Quick was excused for being out of town, Lingford and Stacy each found them-selves paying a threepenny fine for their absence, one of the rules laid down from the start. There was more paying out at Wilde Parsons' house at 75 Hampton Park on March 2, when it was acknowledged somewhat belatedly that Francis Locke was a treasurer without any funds. All put five shillings into the kitty, from which he was required to buy collapsible chairs; otherwise, home comforts were still thin on the ground, and members were expected to take their own glasses along for the following week's move to Corn Street.

And so came March 9, and the eagerly-awaited transfer to George Lingford's stu-dio, state-of-the-art gas lamp and all. Nothing much else about it turned out to be particularly impressive, though it was undeniably a decently sized room. The stairs leading up to it were narrow and awkward, and in terms of winter draughts and sum-mer sweltering it was little improvement on Ernest Ehlers' Kingsdown greenhouse. Even worse on that first night, after all the build-up and anticipation, was the fact that George Lingford somehow contrived to forget all about it. He was certainly in the studio and his fellow Savages were certainly on the doorstep at the appointed hour of 7.30 p.m. with assorted chairs, sketching paraphernalia and whisky; but one way and another they failed to make any contact with the man upstairs, much to the amusement of various evening strollers and street urchins and the increasing concern of the local bobby on the beat. He was just about to move them all on when Lingford appeared at the door explaining that he had been asleep, and the knocker had not 'sounded in his ears'. The phrase irritated the Tribe for months on end before they could see the funny side of it, and doubtless Locke wove in some reference to the fiasco when after painting that night he recited a poem he had written to mark the occasion. He was also instructed to buy a corkscrew and ashtrays, and the following week it was agreed that any new member should pay an entrance fee of five shillings.

An incident a short time after the Corn Street opening suggests that Lingford perhaps had some excuse for not hearing his visitors knocking. A minute records that Mr Stonelake be absolved from the threepence fine for non-attendance as 'unfortunately he could not get in'. On that night, clearly, his knocking failed to 'sound in the ears' of the entire Tribe, two of whom were known to be deaf, anyway. The oldest of the group, at sixty-six, was Stacy, a successful professional artist and teacher. Lowry Lewis was fifty-four, Wilde Parsons and Lingford both fifty-two, Ehlers forty-six and the other artist members rather younger; the 'baby' was Evans Linton, a future RWA, who was still in his mid-twenties.

They were not, of course, working in an artistic vacuum. At the bottom of Queen's Road, Sir William Wills's fortune was giving shape to the Bristol Municipal Gallery, which opened in February 1905; Clifton Arts Club followed in 1906, with two women artists at the helm and Impressionism its first major inspiration, under the presidency of Jacques-Emile Blanche; and in 1907 came the Bristol Guild of Handicrafts in Park Street, which led in the following year to the Bristol Guild of Applied Arts. The national Guild of Handicrafts' wholesale move from London to Chipping Campden in 1902 had made a deep impression on Arts and Crafts enthusiasts in the West Country, and though C. R. Ashbee's 'Cockneys in Arcadia' formally disbanded in 1908, many of them stayed on in the Cotswolds to set standards to which all serious craftspeople aspired. From the far south of the West Country, the artists of Newlyn and St Ives were a growing source of admiration and fascination for the art lovers of Bristol.

Apart from being the Savages' foundation year, 1904 saw the creation of the Bristol Municipal School of Art. This was a renaming of the art school attached to the Bristol Academy of Fine Arts (now the Royal West of England Academy) after it had been taken over by the city council's education committee. Reginald J. Bush, a Savage from 1906, stayed on as its principal, a post he had held for almost ten years under the old regime. He was always a man of great organisational skills and enthusiasm, and the corporation's injection of stability and capital helped him mould the school into one of the most respected in the country before his retirement in 1934.

Near Heybridge Creek, by Charles Brooke Branwhite: The son of one of the most illustrious painters in Bristol in the nineteenth century, he was among the major talents of the Savages' early years. This painting was bought by the Tribe at its 1925 Annual Exhibition for £30.

All in all, the Bristol of the first decade of the twentieth century was the scene of much serious, committed and skilful artistic endeavour. The Savages could hold their heads high in such company, but so equally could the other organisations, and in the midst of them all a word of acknowledgment must go to Sir George White, a Savage from 1909. In 1895 his Bristol Tramways launched the first conventional electric tram service in Britain, from Kingswood to St George, and in the years that followed the network spread and the prospect of flitting into and out of town in one's leisure hours, whether for a show at the Hippodrome, a service at the Cathedral or a club or society meeting, became less demanding and simply more possible than ever before.

What the Savages did have from the outset was clubbability. On May 19 1904, three months after their inaugural meeting, they held their first dinner at the Café Royal in High Street. Before the event members busied themselves designing menu covers, artwork well worthy of a repast which cost four shillings a head and included anchovies or herrings, fresh salmon, steak and onions, forequarter of lamb, calves' head, new potatoes, spinach, 'asparagus in plenty', caviare, soft roes, cheese and coffee. The twelve visitors present were so enthusiastic that they were immediately accepted as Honorary Members, a move which paved the way for the Green Feathers of today. Before leaving, all present flaunted their bohemian credentials by standing on the table to drink the health of the Bristol Savages. Two pictures were produced to mark the occasion, *First Feed of Bristol Savages,* a drawing by Arthur Wilde Parsons and *Come Pick a Bone with Me,* by Lowry Lewis; it is interesting that the menu card for the London Savage Club dinner two years later was adorned with a 'prehistoric' sketch clearly based on Wilde Parsons' work.

Reginald Bush: As a prominent teacher, he introduced several talented younger artists to the Tribe.

At the end of the first session there were twenty-seven members, a number restricted by the size of George Lingford's studio. It soon became clear that this would be a strictly temporary home, but a sub-committee entrusted with the task of finding a temporary headquarters made very little progress until George Lingford announced that he had found a second floor room at the Royal Hotel which could be rented for six months a year for £5, to include lighting and heating. By November 2 they had moved in, and revelled in the luxury of a chair for all, a cheerful coal fire and lighting which satisfied them for a little while, at least; by the A.G.M. of October 1906 the Secretary was being instructed to 'dally in soft converse' with the manageress of the Royal until he could persuade her to instal incandescent lights in the room 'instead of the present wretched glims'.

An early wobble after the high adrenalin of the launch: lay members, whose subscriptions were already proving a vital source of income, were discovering that there was little for them to do at the Royal on a Wednesday night other than drink at the bar, paying rather more per shot or pint than they would back home at their local, or presumably in Zed Alley. The artists got a conscience and decided that something had to be done. Having taken the quantum leap of admitting non-painter members, they felt shamefaced about the possibility of driving them away so soon; besides, word would get around town in no time that the Savages laid on a dull night out, so there would be no chance of pulling in any new recruits. Their

Sir George White: An art-loving giant of the Bristol industrial and social scene.

answer to the dilemma was a series of 'special nights' of entertainment to show their lay colleagues just how much they were valued. Another room in the hotel was hired, one containing a piano, and an order was put in for seating and food for thirty. As an extra incentive, guests would be given the chance to ballot for the sketches of their choice, and enticing looking invitations went out to all.

It was not a good night; 'most ghastly' was the official verdict. One lay member turned up, Andrew Fenn by name, and four others had the good grace to send in their apologies. For this, Charlie Thomas had been brushing up his Devon dialect verse; the retiring Wilde Parsons, uneasy as a singer beyond the choir stalls of All Saints' Church in Clifton, was prepared to beguile the company with his party piece *Asleep on the Deep;* the story of *An 'Ole* was the Norwich painter Miller Marshall's speciality, and he had been putting the finishing touches to that; and Frank Stonelake and Evans Linton, both still youngsters but skilled in telling a tall tale, had been polishing their routines for days. Mr Fenn took mercy on them all and was forced to admit that in the circumstances it would be best if he simply joined the artists in helping them demolish thirty helpings of food and drink before taking his pick of the paintings. 'There was an excellent show of work', the minutes assert; but that was hardly the point.

Despite all this, the lay members kept on coming, and was there ever a pair of successive vintages to compare with 1905 and 1906? In the first of those years the ranks were swelled by H. E. Roslyn, a well-known Bristol journalist who became the 'Rossy' who served as Honorary Secretary from the beginning of the First World War to the end of the Second. Then, and more considerably by far, begging the estimable Rossy's pardon, in 1906 a brief note in the minutes records the unanimous election of James Fuller Eberle as an honorary member. Apportioning praise where it is due, he was nominated by Richard Quick and seconded by Ernest Ehlers, but in strict truth, he became a Savage by default. The invitation had gone out to Alderman W. R. Barker as chairman of the city's museum and art gallery committee, but he felt he was too old to accept, and put forward his vice-chairman, Fuller Eberle, instead. Apart from his powerful connections, Eberle was already well versed in the tradition of art in the city, an interest that transcended his work for the museum committee. 'He owned a collection of the sepia landscape drawings done at the early Bristol sketching meetings, and I am sure he well understood the stimulus and inspiration these meetings were to artists of the Bristol School such as Danby and Jackson,' says Francis

Greenacre, the former curator of fine art at Bristol City Museum and Art Gallery who now deals in paintings. Whatever it was that inspired him, whenever the Savages put up a prayer of thanks for 'Bongie' in the years ahead, as it seemed they did almost constantly at one time, part of it was also dedicated to Alderman Barker for his unwitting but stupendous good favour.

Among artists who joined the Tribe in the Royal Hotel years were Charles Brooke Branwhite, related to the Müllers and a formidable Establishment figure, though not to be confused with his more famous Bristol School father Charles; Charlie Thomas, just twenty when he was elected in 1904 and a Savages stalwart well into the second half of the twentieth century; Arthur 'Curly' Toope, another of the first four elected artist members, who joined in 1906 and last exhibited at the Annual Exhibition of 1952; and Charles Kelsey, a greatly influential presence at the Wigwam in the years before the Second World War. These were clearly still early days, and the process of getting to know the rest of the Tribe did not always run smoothly, as this minute from October 10 1906 makes plain: 'A regrettable incident now occurred. Mr. Parsons said we ought to have the supper first and the dinner later on, as it was quite certain that Mr. Lewis would not be able to paint anything for the exhibition if he had his dinner first. Mr. Lewis retorted "You're another", and insisted on having the supper and dinner on the same night. His language subsequently became unfit for publication, and the members finally dispersed in great confusion, assisted by the police.'

Then there was Bartram Hiles. The Savages had been a club for only two years when they welcomed this Bristol-born phenomenon to their ranks. A few better painters have worn the Red Feather, but none more remarkable. He had lost both arms in a tramcar accident in 1880, when he was just eight years old; hitching a free ride on the back of one of the horse-drawn tramcars plying the new Hotwells route, as boys and youths often did, he fell off and had his arms so badly damaged by a tram passing on the adjacent track that each had to be severed at the shoulder. Even at that young age he had shown tremendous promise in both painting and drawing, and when his life began to come together once more after the accident, he set out to learn the skills all over again by working with his mouth. Pencil drawing came first, followed by watercolour and oil. With concerned people taking up his cause, but largely as a result of his own courage and willpower, he took art and modelling classes at the Merchant Venturers' Technical College in Bristol, was awarded a scholarship at the age of eighteen to the National Art College at South Kensington, and

Left, Lowry Lewis's Come Pick a Bone; above, Harold Packer's impression of H. E. Roslyn, Honorary Secretary from 1914-15 to 1944-45; below left, Bartram Hiles's Sunshine and Shadow, exhibited at the Royal Academy in 1909 and now in the Wigwam; and below, On the Coast, a two-hour sketch by H. C. Guyatt, who joined in 1907.

In the Wigwam at Brandon Cottage, but with several still recognisable works of art and artefacts surrounding him, the armless painter Bartram Hiles displays his remarkable technique. The Savages did much to help him in his unhappy final years.

from there went on to study the French Impressionists in Paris. His talent was such that those who granted him the London college place, which came with a superb bounty of a hundred guineas, had no idea of his disability, having considered his work purely on its merits; what is more, he was the youngest person ever to win the award. He also won frequent prizes at his Bristol and London colleges, all again founded on his talent alone.

Back in London from Paris, he exhibited regularly at the Royal Society of British Artists and had pictures hung at the Royal Academy exhibitions of 1908 and 1909. The latter, *Sunshine and Shadow,* is now owned by the Savages and proudly displayed

In the Gallery, a characterful study of life in the gods at Bristol Hippodrome in the 1920s by Alexander Heaney, one of the Savages' master etchers.

in the Wigwam, as are two powerful heads of American Indians and some smaller paintings. In all, the Tribe owns some twenty pieces of his work. He also earned a living through decorative work – friezes, wallpaper, book illustrations and the like – while another string to his bow was designing postcards for Raphael Tuck. At his height, his paintings were bought for the collections of the Queens Victoria and Alexandra, and the French government honoured him for both his talent and his bravery against heavy odds.

Hiles returned to Bristol with his wife and young daughter in 1906, the year he joined the Savages; he lived on Constitution Hill, Clifton until 1927, when he died at the age of fifty-five. Unfortunately, his later years were neither healthy nor happy, and he was not seen in the Wigwam after 1919. He ceased to be a Savage in 1923, but the artist's biography at the end of this book records the varied and imaginative ways in which the Tribe aided him until the very end. Particularly touching is the story of the dentist Savage Charles Kelsey making dentures to enable Hiles to continue painting, though by then it was 1925 and all but too late. There is even a Savages link in his name, for he was christened Frederick John and it is thought that 'Bartram' was the idea of his great friend and helper Matthew Hale, who joined the club along with him in 1906. The nickname was already in place by then, a playful reference to that long-ago tram which in one way blighted Hiles's career and in another spread his name far and wide, but it suggests that Hale was tailor-made to join the ranks of the jokey, punning Tribe of that day and this.

The Frenchman Balthazar Fringes was another colourful figure from the earliest days, a man bubbling with enthusiasm which was not always shared by his fellow Savages. In May 1905 he proposed that the Tribe should meet on alternate Saturdays in summer in a forerunner to the artists' outings that are still enjoyed today; the first was to Flax Bourton by railway, and there were ten takers for the 1.30 p.m. stopping train out of Temple Meads that afternoon. A fortnight later, half a dozen of them turned out for another afternoon, and towards the end of the season a dispirited little minute records that: 'On Saturday June 24 the visit to Pensford did not seem at all popular, for only the Honorary Secretary and Mr. Fringes were present.' Nevertheless, a precedent had been set, and the innovative M. Fringes was busy breaking new ground again the fol-

The Kelsey Chain: Presidents wear it when they are representing the Tribe in public.

lowing April, when he and his son brought specifically instrumental music to the club for the first time. Up until then there had been old Padlock with his verses and the assorted talents who never did quite get to perform on that disastrous lay members' special night, but the entertainment provided by *les Fringes père et fils* was on a different level altogether. Whether higher or lower might be gauged from various recollections of the evening. The minutes tell us merely that 'After work, Mr. Fringes and his son discoursed sweet music on the cello and flute', but H. E. Roslyn, yet to be made Secretary, was somewhat more candid in his memoirs. 'To this day, some of us have not forgotten the occasion when Miller Marshall read *Tam o' Shanter* or when Fringes, a Frenchman, and his son gave us cello and flute duets for nearly two hours,' he wrote. 'The latter was a terrible infliction. Fringes brought a fat portfolio of music and would not rest until he had gone through the lot. No sooner was one doleful piece finished than another was started. The boy, intensely nervous in strange com-

An institution: Grouse was first published in December 1921 and returned after a long absence some 70 years later.

The Frenchman's legacy: Balthazar Fringes was an eccentric bird of passage, but the artists' outings he introduced are still enjoyed today.

pany, was constantly corrected or reprimanded by his father, and the more he was rebuked the more he floundered. His breath became short, and the harder Fringes scraped the cat gut, the fainter became the halting tones of the flute. It was not until everyone was exhausted that the performance came to an end. That was one of the few nights when a second round of drinks became necessary.' M. Fringes was a bird of passage who very soon returned to France, but he had made his mark.

The minutes' polite assessment of his musical contribution was not a tone that would last. In fact robust criticism has been dispensed with some enthusiasm over the years, as this entry from January 12 1938 reminds us: 'In plaintive tones, Bro. Sav. (Jimmy) Sherwood made several inquiries as to Sylvia and her whereabouts. Some of the members looked as if they could give him a few addresses, an (sic) they would. Urged to continue, he bleated some about the wench for whom he professes eternal affection. One wonders whether he has taken medical advice on this matter. Bro. Sav. Irving Gass regaled the company with some Devon tales, after which their attention was again directed to the love stuff by Bro. Sav. Reg Tappenden, who sang himself in as an Entertaining Member of the Tribe. His view of the disease was even less encouraging than Jimmy's, for he prophesied his own demise from acute haemorrhaging of the heart. After a comic tale by Fairfax Goodall, Bro. Sav. Monty Hambling hoiked the meeting back to love. His first effort treated of "a little while", "a short time" or words to that effect. The second of "violets on a grave" and so forth. One was irresistibly reminded of the celebrated surgeon who said that an operation had been a complete success, but the patient unfortunately had died under the anaesthetic...'

It seems quite bizarre to discuss Charlie Thomas in this section on the Savages in the most distant chapter of their history but the record books tell us quite clearly that he joined the Tribe in 1904; they tell us equally that he stayed on at the Wigwam until long after the end of the Second World War and (like the Centenary Session President Michael Long) he held Presidencies in three decades – 1920-21, 1932-33 and 1941-42. His entry in the Artists' Profiles section at the end of this book tells something of his many talents and contrasting character traits – who, for instance, could imagine such a challenging and irreverent character as a pillar of the church? The Savages saw him as a youth – he was a mere twenty years old when he joined – to being an old man, and whatever his status in the seven ages, he was always a pivotal figure, the life and soul. In the early days he was the joker, the rhymster, the spinner of tall tales who for years made 'tell us another one, Charlie' a catchphrase in the Tribe. In his wartime session as President in particular he made new Savages go through an elaborate marching drill before they were admitted, which some found harmless fun and others did not. In his middle years, the early times at the Red Lodge, he was quite simply the cult figure of the Tribe, Bongie apart. The early issues of *Grouse,* the Savages' magazine that first came out in December 1921, were quite simply crammed with C.T. references, and cartoons and sketches of him with his trademark pipe.

A quirky view of W. H. Quick reading the minutes, as he did as Honorary Secretary for the first ten years of the Savages' history. A play on the word 'lyre' perhaps?

Charlie Thomas can dance, flirt or paint,
And no-one would call him a saint,
He's a joy! He's a lamb!
He's a pot of real jam!
And there aren't many things that he ain't.

That was F. A. S. Locke's view of him and the way his name punctuates the minutes book for decades on end upholds that assessment. It was Charlie who first sang *Good King Wenceslas* when the punch was borne in, and the Savages are singing it still. He was the one who played Father Christmas with the gifts, went off into a concert party to entertain First World War troops, interrupted the minutes, dashed off caricatures, polarised opinion in the Wigwam like nobody before him or since. 'Bro. Sav. C. W. Thomas was in a critical mood with the result that the reading of the minutes occupied twenty minutes, and even then he vigorously opposed their adoption,' read the minutes of December 29 1915. 'He took nearly as long to recite a poem by Bro. Sav. (Windsor) Aubrey, owing to the personal explanations he felt it necessary to make.' That was one night when cries of 'Give us another, Charlie' did *not* echo around the Wigwam. He died just before Easter in 1958, four years after the Tribe had presented him with a portrait by John Codner to mark his fifty years' membership. Whether they loved him or gave him a wide berth, everybody felt the difference when Charlie Thomas was no longer around the place.

November 1905 brought the Savages' first painting exhibition, running for a full two weeks at the salerooms of Nichols the auctioneers in Broad Street. For the hire of the premises they paid a hefty ten guineas, and the expense did not end there. As well as buying display equipment they hired a sandwich board man to spread the message and paid a non-member salesman £1 5s plus five per cent commission to staff the show. When sales totalling £123 rolled in they were more than happy that their money had been well spent and that the exercise would be repeated annually. It was certainly good business for a society whose Treasurer had reported a balance of fivepence at its A.G.M. a month before.

Perhaps that three-figure profit unlocked a door. In any event, come the 1906-07 session there was a strong whiff of change and progress in the air. At the October 1906 A.G.M. 'Mr Roslyn was asked about the printing of the Rules, but he didn't seem to know much about it'. Of course he would not. It is well known to medical science that journalists fall prey to baffling but total deafness at the first sound of a small number of key phrases. 'Can you get those pictures back to us?' is one. 'Could you get hold of your West Wilts edition of February 23?' is another, in November, of course; but most fearful of all is: 'Can you see if your lot can print us some raffle/ cloakroom/ PTA dance tickets?' or variations thereof. One can imagine poor Rossy, still a complete new boy at the Savages, sitting at his desk as the mighty presses several floors below him roared and thundered and shook the building to its roots. What was he to do? Slip down to the machine room at the end of the run, sidle up to some huge man in overalls hauling the printing plates off the rollers and say: 'Excuse me, mate. I'm in this art club, you see, and I wonder if you could just run me off seventy-five sets of our rules? There's sixpence in it for you.'? When the alternative was to risk the silent wrath of Padlock and Quicky and a sarky reference in the minutes book, the choice was not hard to make.

More progress came in other directions. It was agreed to hire a piano at 10s 6d a month, after a sub-committee had failed to buy a decent one for anything like the club had been prepared to pay, and in January 1907 a sixteen-shilling blackboard and easel was added to the Tribe's list of possessions. Of rather more moment, in May that year came two associated motions, both carried unanimously, that helped secure the Savages' financial future. First, it was proposed by H. E. Roslyn and seconded by Arthur Wilde Parsons 'that it is advisable in the interests of Bristol Savages that permanent headquarters should be secured'. Next, Frank Locke proposed and Charlie Thomas seconded that 'provided we secure permanent headquarters, we form ourselves into a "club", though our title remains "Bristol Savages".' This latter motion is not quite as mysterious as it seems; what it meant was that the group would *register* itself as a club – and a registered club had the considerable boon of being able to sell alcohol to its members.

None of which would have made much sense if there had been no headquarters building to which to move; but there was. After a quiet first year, James Fuller Eberle had begun to attend meetings regularly, and he let it be known that he had a room at Brandon Cottage on the lower side of Brandon Hill, which might well serve the purpose. On the evening of Wednesday May 15 1907 members met to view it, and they liked what they saw. Their new lay member was not giving it away, though the ten pounds per year rent he was asking, to include lighting, heating and cleaning, did not appear unfavourable against the ten guineas Mr. Nichols had wanted for the hire of his rooms for a fortnight at the 1905 exhibition. Yes, they would take it, they decided, and by October 9 it was their new home.

3

THE BRANDON COTTAGE YEARS

The Savages' first permanent Wigwam was a good-sized space with a skylight up in the high ceiling. The Tribe had it to themselves from August 21 1907 onwards, which gave members ample opportunity to prepare it for the big opening night on October 9. This they did, and they would happily have done more if the man they were beginning to know and admire as Bongie had not relieved them of the task of the main decorating and furnishing the room. From the start, pictures were on the walls in profusion, along with curiosities from Fuller Eberle's private collection, and it was not long before these were joined by further spears, shields and animal heads as the word went round that they were on the lookout for tribal memorabilia. In present times even the most avid member thinks carefully before bestowing yet another cudgel or pike on to the collection; back then the Tribe soaked them up like a sponge, the more the merrier, and by the end of its thirteen-year sojourn at Brandon Hill the walls were bristling with primitive weaponry and heavy with pictures, while every horizontal surface that was not dedicated to painting groaned under the weight of ornaments, cased curiosities and mementoes. In other words, the spirit of the Wigwam in 1920 is echoed almost uncannily by the scene at Park Row today. This sense of time standing still is not a unique phenomenon, of course. The same must apply to a good number of churches in Bristol, to various rooms associated with the legal profession and to some of the older school and university buildings. What is different in these instances is that they are moulded by hundreds of years of evolution and tradition, even if not necessarily on that site; the ambience of the Wigwam was hit upon almost haphazardly in half a dozen years leading up to the beginning of the First World War, and so perfect, so absolutely right for the Tribe did it turn out to be that it will never change as long as there are Savages in Bristol.

The platform at Brandon Hill was not as prominent as today's, merely a raised dais in the corner with enough floor space for a piano and a performer to stand alongside it. Two long tables for sketching dominated the centre of the room, with the Chairman at their head, and lay members and guests took their chances around the sides. The crucial difference between Brandon Cottage and Park Row lay in the fact that in the former, all activities were squeezed into a single room; the luxury of space

'Physical Energy' is the topic for the evening as Savages meet at Brandon Cottage, then their home for less than a year, on January 29, 1908. The Wigwam has already taken on a lived-in air, but a smart appearance among members is clearly still de rigueur.

enjoyed by Green Feathers today would have been the envy of the first lay members, who, after all, included some of the most influential Savages the Tribe has ever seen.

It was the early days at Brandon Cottage that set the pattern of Wednesday nights as they are still known today. Many of the elements were already in place, but their re-enactment week after week, in an increasingly well loved space that members could think of as their own, added greatly to their air of permanence and worth. Many traditions Britons regard as ancient or medieval are not; Victorian clergymen in particular were adept at evoking Merrie England, or a genteel version of it, in any number

The more spacious scene shortly after the Wigwam had moved to Park Row in 1920. Again, much is recognisable, although the Chairman's table can be seen in the foreground, not in today's accustomed position.

of seemingly archaic activities which were in fact of their own invention. Regularly repeated rituals can quickly be seen as spanning the generations; and when, after a few years, a son joins a father in the group and so they really do span the generations, they take on a potency that tradition-minded men find both meaningful and moving. They would bore other people rigid, but these are not the kind who would ever feel at home in the Savages.

To finance this grander lifestyle, annual subscriptions were raised from five shillings to ten. There were sixty-three members when the move to Brandon Hill was made, and although artists predominated, Fuller Eberle's presence spelled out in the clearest terms that this was not solely a club for 'breathren of the brush' and would never again be so. Members who were elected on his proposal read like a *Who's Who* of the Bristol of their day, overwhelmingly Conservative in their politics. The question as to how a club that had begun in 1904 as a coming-together of artistic free spirits had become a bastion of the city Establishment by 1910 is one well worth asking. The answer lies in the fact that no one man, whatever the label he carries through life, can easily be pigeonholed. It is just as easy for an artist to prize his standing as a respected and useful member of society, maybe as a teacher or arts administrator, as it is for an accountant or barrister to appreciate and support the arts. In the Savages, both sets of people found common ground. In addition to that, many of Bongie's recruits to the Tribe were a long way from being conservative with a small c. Sir George Wills and his brother Sir Frank both had the money and the imagination to lift them far above the merely worthy and conventional, and few cities have been blessed by more lavish or far-sighted benefactors of health (leaving aside the products through which they made their millions), education and the arts than members of their family. Bongie's friend Sir George White, on the other hand, while being happily suburban in his lifestyle and a classic Fat Cat by today's definition, was a power in the land not solely as an entrepreneur but through his sheer creative genius. The only factor that prevents his being looked back on as the greatest artist who ever graced the Savages is his choice of medium – trams, motor vehicles and aeroplanes rather than oils and watercolours. In 1901, his London United Electric Tramways stemmed directly out of his pioneering tramway network in Bristol in 1895. He began building buses at Filton in 1908, and two years later, by now a Savage, he backed his hunch that air travel had a future by launching the Bristol Aeroplane, Bristol Aviation, British and Colonial Aeroplane and British and Colonial Aviation Companies. His brothers in the Tribe always swore that he would have been as famous as A. V. Roe, Sopwith, the Short brothers and C. S. Rolls if he had put his name ahead of that of his beloved Bristol. On the day of his memorial service in the cathedral in 1916 flags flew at half mast on public buildings and at the appointed hour, trams trimmed with black crepe ribbons stopped throughout the city in respectful silence: 'The passengers and staff alighted and stood bareheaded in the streets.' If you were looking for some bone-headed industrialist, you did not look for Sir George White.

Bongie completed a clean sweep of the city corporation hierarchy by nominating the Lord Mayor Edward Robinson, Sheriff Stanley Badock and Town Clerk E. J. Taylor to the Savages ranks. Lieutenant Colonel George Gibbs, who was later to be the first Lord Wraxall at Tyntesfield, the ninth Duke of Beaufort and a future Sheriff, Ivie Dunlop, were also enlisted in 1907, 1908 and 1909. For a club in its infancy it was a remarkable achievement, and it must be said that in terms of Establishment top brass, the Savages never again embarked upon quite such a concentrated recruitment drive. That having been said, no fewer than thirty-seven men who have been Mayors or Lord Mayors have found their way into the Savages over the years, by and large after their terms of office had ended, and

A busy night at Brandon Cottage, in the years when Fuller Eberle was rapidly expanding the social membership of the club.

Mellow evenings at Brandon Cottage, the Tribe's first Wigwam. On the left is Stanley Lloyd's impression of a musical interlude, while below, the scene of the artists sketching is itself a two-hour sketch, by Reginald Bush.

Fashions change, as has the venue, but most Savages will be struck by what links these paintings with the present day, rather than the differences.

Ernest Board's The Departure of John and Sebastian Cabot on their First Voyage of Discovery, 1497, *a fanciful image but one of the most celebrated paintings by a member of the Savages, now prominently displayed in Bristol City Museum and Art Gallery.*

as some served twice they totalled forty-three terms in all. The tradition was strongest in the first fifty years of the century, though there have still been fourteen Lord Mayors since 1950, the last being Derek Tedder, who served in 1988, and Peter Abraham, in office in 1991. The domination of the Council House by Labour since then has strangled the tradition rather in recent years since, rightly or wrongly, Fuller Eberle's recruitment campaign set a Conservative agenda among members from local politics which has rarely been broken. All that can be concluded is that at that time, bringing in the city's big guns must have seemed the right thing to do for the good of the Tribe, though what the fun-loving likes of Charlie Thomas and Frank Stonelake really thought about it is no longer ours to know. What could not be questioned was the fact that the Savages no longer had merely a painting club on their hands. By the end of the 1907-08 session membership had increased to 111 of whom just thirty were working (painting) members; seventy-nine were Honorary and two Life. Change had come quickly and it had come dramatically.

Artists recruited in the Brandon Cottage years between 1907 and 1920 included Reginald Bush, George Swaish, Ernest Fabian and Arthur C. Fare, while Ernest Board was also a dominant figure throughout this time; it is to him that we owe the splendid 'Three Muses' image that dominates the cover of this book and is incorporated into the design for the poster for the Savage Spirit centenary exhibition at the City Museum and Art Gallery in the spring and early summer of 2004. Board's best known work, painted in 1906 and owned by the City Art Gallery, is his fanciful account of *The Departure of John and Sebastian Cabot on their First Voyage of Discovery, 1497;* a wonderful confection concocted in Board's head from the single known fact that Cabot did indeed make such a voyage, it presents such a rich and absorbing scene that the city council had no hesitation in making it a focal point of its celebration of the five hundredth anniversary of the voyage in 1997. A less ambitious work but one with a great deal more spontaneity is his evening sketch of Charlie Thomas off fishing with his dog, *A Good Old Sport.*

George Swaish, a well-connected man around Bristol, as seen by Frank Stonelake.

A great friend of Board and a pupil of Bush was George Swaish, a well-connected man about Bristol whose Alderman father was later knighted. His paintings are still to be found in the Council House and Bristol City Museum and Art Gallery, while among his works at the Wigwam is one of the most prized paintings to be found there, the Bongie portrait. Portraits became his speciality as the years passed by, and as well as painting several of the Bristol hierarchy, including his father, he produced the only known study of his fellow Savage Fred Weatherly, locally based K.C. and internationally known songwriter. This was bought by the Savages but later presented to the city art gallery.

Ernest Fabian, elected an honorary member in 1908, is best remembered as a sculptor and modeller and, in Savages circles at least, as the creator of the President's chain of office. His suggestion was for a chain of beaten silver with two oblong links of ivory and a central shield with the legend 'Bristol Savages' and a main centre-piece of a Native American figure holding the Cup of Inspiration. Plaques worked with turquoise and moonstone representing

Sculpture and Painting, Literature and Music and Tragedy and Comedy plus two ivory bosses engraved with Indians' heads completed the adornment of this elaborate piece of work, and the committee was excited by what it saw to such an extent that it accepted his proposal with delight. That was in the May of 1908 and Fabian, a hard-working teacher at Bush's School of Art, presented the end result some two years later, in March 1910. The only charge to the club was the cost of the materials and so impressed were its members with this valuable new treasure that they honoured Fabian with the first life membership to be awarded in recognition of services to the Savages; the three previous life awards had been honorary gestures purchased by the members concerned. Five others paid for life membership before the practice stopped in 1915. In 1912 Fabian produced the club's tomahawk golf trophy, the competition having been introduced in the spring of 1910, and two

Ramrod-straight: Charlie Thomas's view of founder member Stanley Lloyd.

years later he designed the silver skull and crossbones tobacco box, engraved with the names of founders, Secretary and Treasurer, which was to be displayed on the Chairman's table and filled by him for sketch evenings. That last proviso no longer applies but as we have discovered, it sits there still on Wednesday nights. The makers of the box were the Bristol silversmiths Kemp Brothers, but a plaster model of rugby players in action still to be found in the Wigwam is all Fabian's own work. The fortunes of Bristol Rugby Club have always been a preoccupation of a good number of Savages, as has been support for Gloucestershire County Cricket Club, and there was extra spice in the early years when the Cardiff-born Reginald Bush's brother Percy was a famous Welsh rugby international.

Two other significant pieces of regalia have been added to the collection. In 1927 Charles Kelsey presented the Tribe with the ruby-studded gold and enamel jewel worn by the President at outside functions; and a later stalwart, Frank Mole, created a delicate silver Lady's Chain to be worn by the President's wife or consort on ceremonial occasions. Decorated with a turquoise matrix in a style inspired by the Navaho Indians and their symbolisms, it is adorned with silver seeds and a blossom motif, apparently signifying usefulness and beauty, and hangs in a deep crescent shape. Maybe the rationale behind its design does not bear too close scrutiny in these days of equality of the sexes, but it surely causes no offence to describe it as a very feminine looking piece, and it can be declared without doubt that it is an attractive one.

Arthur C. Fare's name is another still well known locally today. His watercolours

Another Ernest Fabian design, the silver scull and crossbones tobacco box displayed on the Chairman's table on Wednesday evenings.

Long-serving Secretary Frank Mole was the designer of the Indian-influenced Lady's Chain.

of Bristol street scenes are among the most recognisable images of the city in the inter-war years, and while his depictions of the buildings tend to bear the hallmarks of his architectural training, the everyday human detail at street level can be both enjoyable and instructive. Needless to say, he portrayed scores of medieval and later buildings which were lost to the city during the blitzes of the Second World War. We have ample photographic record of the most important of these, of course, but there is something touching about Fare's capturing them in period colour as the life of the city ebbs and flows around them.

The early years at Brandon Cottage brought in practices that still hold good today. In October 1907 it was found that the business of the club was impinging too much on the painting and socialising, and it was decided that the foundation members (or committee) would meet on a separate night for routine discussions. In the following month it was 'agreed that the man receiving the most marks should criticise the works of the evening sketchers'. On April 27 1910 Secretary Quick took the chair for the final evening; that is yet another custom that is upheld to this day, and it was reassurance that Mr Quick was back on top form. Earlier in the winter, in the minutes for New Year's Day, it had been somewhat impatiently recorded that 'The President explained that their worthy Secretary had met with an accident to one of his eyes through some domestic Christmas frivolity, and that he would not be able to be present, his doctor enforcing complete rest of his "orbicular glands"'. George Heming was appointed the first Wine Warden in September 1908, and in February 1909 it was decided to have an At Home for working members' wives or women friends, quite obviously the first of the Savages' Ladies' Nights. September 1909 brought the ruling that 'where a sketch of conspicuous merit is done on a work evening, it be purchased at the price of one guinea to come out of the Special Fund'; the first Twelfth Night supper was held at James Fuller Eberle's house in Pembroke Road on January 5, 1909, and the 1910 meal on January 6 was the first in the Club Room for working members only. It was a feverish period of activity and invention, with so many of the innovations standing the test of time.

Corn Street was a perenially favourite subject of A. C. Fare, whose Bristol street scenes are still prized by local people today. Right, still prized by the Savages is the Punch Night tradition, in which they celebrate Christmas and another year of good fellowship.

Best of all, there was the happy notion of Punch Night. It was inevitable that the Savages would be in festive mood at the last meeting before Christmas, and it was in 1910 that they hit upon the formula that flourishes to this day. In fact punch had first been served in 1908, while in 1909 came the first collection for the 'Poor Nippers of Bristol' (£4 12s 6d) which became such a feature of Punch Night. Uncle Jack's Nipper Fund was run by the *Bristol Times and Mirror,* a newspaper owned by the local Hawkins media dynasty. In fact there were three Hawkins in the Tribe from the earliest days, including the executive who wrote as Uncle Jack in his spare time, so he was well placed to recruit the Savages to his cause. In the *Times and Mirror* of December 22 1909 he wrote: 'Uncle Jack acknowledges with thanks to the Bristol Savages for their contribution of £4 12s 6d. This would provide a very good meal, a toy, an orange and a bag of sweets for two hundred Nippers.' As the sum in fact works out at something less than sixpence per Nipper, it sounds as if Uncle Jack had his head screwed on when it came to buying in his festive fare. By the First World War he was organising Comforts for the Fighting Forces, but when peace came the Tribe began to choose its good causes as it saw fit. Back in 1909 they wondered how to collect the money and decided to put it in a fez. Just like that. The elephant's foot tradition was still years away, but the custom had been established. Come 1910 the two strands came together, and 'the Yuletide ceremony of bringing in punch bowls was accompanied by the singing of an appropriate Christmas Carol'. In 1911, 'this being Punch Night... the sum raised for the Poor Nippers of Bristol was £8 4s 6d'. The figure was £13 2s in 1912, and by December 23 1913 all was carved in stone: 'In accordance with the established custom... tradition was maintained by the serving of punch with our own special recipe.' 'Tradition'; 'our own special recipe'; how quickly the Savages settled into their way of life.

There were those who shuddered at the name the evening was being given, insisting that while of course punch was drunk, there was a great deal more to the gathering than that. The somewhat uneasy reference in 1915 reads: 'At the meeting before Christmas – in vulgar parlance, Punch Night – in order to comply with the regulations of the licensing, punch was served well before 9 p.m., with the appearance of the Wine Warden carrying on high the time-honoured silver bowl being greeted by the singing of *Good King Wenceslas* ably led by lusty-lunged Bro. Sav. Charlie Thomas. There was such brisk demand for this soul-stirring liquor that the Wine Warden (George Heming) and his assistants had wet shirts by the time the supply was exhausted. What is more, in their desire to supply everybody, they failed to collect the price of every glass, with the result that when the cash was counted, it did not equal the cost.'

In the previous year, on Punch Night 1914, 'to the regret of the Wine Warden, the profits were not as substantial as usual, due to the fact that he was so slow in filling the glasses of members that when ten o' clock arrived he had half a bowl left. His conscientious observance of the veto of the Licensing Justices caused him to cut off the supplies at that hour, with the result that much good liquor was wasted.' In 2004 the general opinion is that no such problem would arise these days, but Heming obviously felt the law breathing down his neck. In October 1915 he announced that under the order of the Central Control Board (Liquor Traffic) 'members introducing visitors would be unable to supply them with intoxicants', and from then on, liquor control regulations ensured that there would be no punch again on this festive evening until Christmas Eve 1919, when 'the chair was in accordance with custom taken by the President, Bro. Sav. James Fuller Eberle. A Punch Night without him to direct proceedings would lose all character...' (In fact Bongie was never Club President, but Chairman for the evening, and because the Chairman wore the President's chain, he was often described as such in the minutes). Whatever his title, there was no doubt about who was in charge on Punch Night, and there would later be moves to restyle it Bongie's Night; even as late as 1929 one of the earliest artist members, Wilfred Peake, was calling on the Tribe to come up with a less alcoholic name for the evening. By 1920 the focus had switched to the Red Lodge, and in 1921 three hundred members and guests raised £70 for the Poor Nippers. The elephant's foot for the collection is first recorded in 1924, and that, in all but minor detail, was the last piece of the jigsaw that falls into place on Punch Night today.

While the Wine Warden was running a tight ship, elsewhere in the Wigwam in the wartime years all seemed to be disorder and confusion. In January 1916, in a mix-up over who was going to be Chairman, 'Bro. Sav. (H. C.) Guyatt arrived with a subject, but Bro. Sav. Windsor Aubrey forestalled him, for he wired his, and so beat the man from Long Ashton on the post'; a little over a year later, in February 1917, 'Our Warden (R. H. Pezzack), having been asked to take the chair, walked down to Brandon Cottage during his morning coffee hour (!) and chalked a subject on the board. No-one observed him enter or leave, so later in the day Mogford (the caretaker) saw what had been written and thought someone had taken liberties with our sacred blackboard, so promptly rubbed it out. Consequently, when the artist members assembled, they did not know what to work on. Having wasted several minutes discussing the unusual situation, they decided the subject ought to be "Waiting", and "Waiting" it was. Bro. Sav. Pezzack, who should have been in the chair, refused, because his subject had been erased.' The following week he did agree to be Chairman: 'The subject was "Ready", and it was not rubbed off the board.' When 'In Close Proximity' was the subject of the evening sketches at around this time, 'the artists said things which need not be recorded'. Even the rented piano seemed to be playing up, and a new one was bought for £100, with tuning at twenty-five shillings a year; this at a time when prices in the Canteen, as the bar was known, were eight-pence for small bottles of Guinness or Bass, beer at eightpence a pint, port or sherry fivepence, whisky sevenpence, brandy eightpence and coffee threepence a cup. This was just before the end of the First World War, and it is interesting to reflect that forty years on, in the late 1950s, beer was only just over a shilling a pint and it was still not impossible to buy a cup of coffee for threepence.

In late 1918, however, there was more on most people's minds than the price of a cuppa. With Savages streaming back from the front, or maybe less dramatic wartime duties, life at Brandon Cottage was suddenly beginning to feel crowded. Apparently

House Dinners, held in the spring, have traditionally inspired Red Feathers to flights of artistic fancy when designing the menus.

On this page are two by Frank Stonelake, in 1911, top left, and 1910, left, while another 1911 menu, above, is the work of George Butler.

Opposite, top left, is one on the best loved covers of all, The Savage Feast, produced by Arthur Wilde Parsons in 1907, while Herbert Helps designed the 1913 card lower right.

Top right, the Elephant's Foot is a symbol of the Savages' giving; it comes out every Punch Night to gather in donations to good causes.

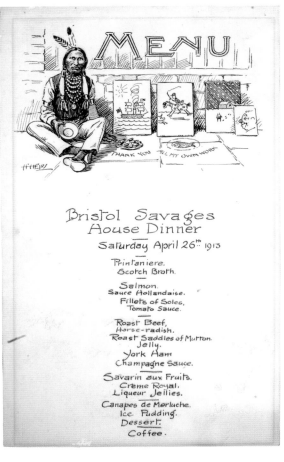

Work in contrasting styles by distinguished Savages from the early years: Above, Harry Banks's meticulous etching of Bristol Docks, and below, War, a two-hour sketch by George Butler in October 1914. Banks was best known for designing the invitation dinner cards for the coronation of Edward VII and Queen Alexandra.

most members simply believed that life would go on as before, as it is always pleasant to do after years of disruption, but Colston Waite's researches in 1971 told him that 'occasionally, Tommy Kingston would raise a croaking voice, reminding them that they should give serious consideration to obtaining fresh headquarters'. They were still pondering his words when, in 1919, James Fuller Eberle sold his coachbuilding business, and the use of Brandon Cottage along with it, and the matter was taken out of their hands. It was no longer a case of playing with the idea of whether or not to go. It was go they must. Happily, Bongie had an answer to that dilemma, a solution that still holds good to this day. The last meeting at the Cottage was on April 21 1920, with Charlie Thomas in the chair. It was not one of those Cheerful Charlie kind of evenings. His words of farewell to the Tribe's home for the past dozen years or more were sombre and sincere, and it was a tone that seemed right at the time, for the Savages were and are a sentimental crew. Little were he and the rest of the Tribe to know it, but the best was yet to come.

4

INTO THE RED LODGE

uller Eberle, his coach building business newly sold, was among the first people in Bristol to recognise the potential of the Red Lodge when it came on the market after closing as a girls' reformatory in 1917. As by this time chairman of the city council's museum and art gallery committee, he was more *au fait* than most with the building's history and could see beyond its stark and forbidding reputation as one of several reformatories founded in the city by the educationist and social reformer Mary Carpenter; she had moved in in 1854, after the house had been bought for her use by Lady Byron, the poet's elderly widow. Eberle knew that beyond the institutionalised paintwork of its corridors and partitioned rooms was a sixteenth-century house more perfect than any other in the city; he was aware that traditional plasterwork and panelling of the quality seen here was an increasingly powerful magnet to American tycoons who would think nothing of transporting entire buildings across the Atlantic; and far closer to home, and a good deal more pressingly, he knew that his sale of the business would mean an abrupt end to the Savages' days at Brandon Cottage. It was a happy chance that the Tribe was flourishing in such a way that larger premises would have been needed, anyway, but in harsh reality it was external business considerations, rather than the dynamics of the club, that precipitated the move to the Red Lodge.

Eberle put his case to the Savages on June 5 1919. He told them 'as soon as he heard that Red Lodge was likely to come on to the market he made inquiries and obtained an option to purchase; this option had been exercised. He has since received an offer of £500 for his bargain, and another £2,000 for the Great Oak Room alone. It was for the committee to say whether they were willing to move from Brandon Cottage to these new quarters. His original plan for raising the necessary funds for renovating the house, making the structural alterations and building a barn in the garden as a meeting place for the Savages was to get ten men to give £500 apiece.' The sum required, estimated at £6,000 but finally more like £7,700, was raised through £2,500 from Sir George Wills, whose daughter Margi married Fuller Eberle's son Ellison in true Bristol Establishment fashion, £2,500 from the Savages and the rest from Bongie and other of his friends. Apart from the creation of a bigger and better

Wigwam, he saw the building as a haven for the other societies in which he took a keen interest, the Veterans' Association, the Grateful Society and the Antient Society of St Stephen's Ringers. It was also to be 'in some way linked' to the museum and art gallery committee, with the donors willing to grant a long lease to the Savages before the property was handed over to the corporation. This plan met with the broad approval of the Tribe and the museum committee alike, the latter allowing fireplaces and other suitable pieces of architecture to go into the restored building.

A key figure in supervising the rescue of the Red Lodge and the design of the Wigwam was Savage C. F. W. Dening, a superb architect in the recollection of Eric Franklin, who in the late 1930s worked in another architectural practice in the same building as the great man, Gaunt's House in Orchard Street. Dening is best remem-

Splendour, a two-hour sketch by Ralph Brentnall. A distinguished architect, he did much work for Bristol University, the Cathedral and St. Mary Redcliffe.

bered in Bristol for his churches: St Alban, Westbury Park, St Barnabas, Knowle and St Christopher, Arnos Vale. He also worked on Christ Church, Broad Street and won the original design competition for the Council House before it fell by the wayside in a long-drawn-out saga. Eric Franklin remembers him as 'an elegant man who usually wore a velvet smoking jacket and smoked Burma cheroots, which he kept in an enormous silver box. His professional hours were from 10 a.m. to 4 p.m. I remember him being very cross with me for indulging in some revolver prac-

tice in the office above his when my master was away.' Eric also recalls that it was Dening and Gordon Hake, his principal at the R.W.A. School of Architecture, where he studied half the week, who first introduced him to the delights of the Wigwam. This was in the late 1930s and as Dening had predicted, this cavernous room, modelled internally at least on a medieval Gloucestershire tithe barn, was by now bristling with trophies and memorabilia. On Wednesday nights at least, its air also hung heavy with smoke from the log fires and the rich fug of Havana cigars. Dening had created just the home he knew the Savages needed and wanted, 'the large hall in the garden' of the Red Lodge which mopped up the £2,500 the Tribe had put into the pot.

Herbert Truman was one of the most prominent Savage artists in the years immediately after the Second World War, and he pleased many of the Tribe with this study of the Wigwam.

One of the considerations he had in mind was the need for space for the club's Annual Exhibition, which was already drawing large crowds, and though building work took longer than planned, the 1920 exhibition took place there in March, before the move from Brandon Cottage. Unhappily, when Dening died in the early 1950s, it was as a virtual stranger to his beautiful room. The outbreak of war seemed to undermine his health grievously, and he was never seen in either the Wigwam or the Studio from that day on.

The big move came on April 24 1920, when 180 members and guests were miraculously seated for the House Dinner. A team of Savages had been in the building strenuously decorating for days and evenings on end, and the happy atmosphere that night convinced them it was time well spent. It was doubtless also money well spent, which was just as well, since expenses rose dramatically. At Brandon Cottage the Tribe seemed able to pay its way for about twenty pounds per year, and suddenly that had soared to nearer five hundred. An effective step towards meeting this challenge was to raise membership from two hundred to three, and to raise subscriptions for newcomers. It was good news for the men on the long list of candidates for election, but for a while some older hands felt swamped by all the newness around them. Some even complained that this noble hall cramped their style when it came to heckling the Secretary, and clearly that would never do. Time soon healed that particular problem.

The Savages were granted the house on a twenty-eight-year lease before Bristol Art Gallery assumed responsibility for it in 1948. An amicable ninety-nine-year lease agreement negotiated with the city council in the 1980-81 session has given the Tribe security of occupation of the Wigwam and Studio for generations to come – 'This is a landmark in our history' – but the years leading up to the takeover, and the years after it until well into the 1960s, during much of which the site was administered by the Red Lodge joint house committee of three city councillors and three senior Savages, were unhappy times. Even before the serious wrangling over details began, there seemed cause for concern. Several years earlier the Savages had crossed swords with the council when it appeared as if it wished to make the Wigwam a museum as an annexe to the Red Lodge, quite oblivious to the spirit of the original agreement. Club members feared that this was the museum and art gallery committee's agenda once again, and sensed that some councillors were positively hostile towards them. In the original agreement there was an annual grant of £250 to the Tribe for the upkeep of its part of the premises, and this certainly seemed to be in jeopardy as handover day drew near. 'This proved to be quite a bone of contention among some of the corporation committee,' Cecil Broome recounted in 1979. 'There was a complete absence of sentiment in their attitude towards the Tribe; they were in a very strong position, and they knew it.' In fact the museum and art gallery committee's first proposal to the city council involved not a merging of the two main buildings into a single exhibition complex, as the Savages had feared, but a complete sealing off of the Wigwam and Studio from the Red Lodge, which seemed just as bad or worse. This would have caused unprecedented upheaval and expense, while Fuller Eberle's son George was scandalised at just how far such an arrangement would take the Savages from his father's original concept of their use of the Red Lodge.

By the next session the corporation had retreated from this stance, and the next proposal put forward was the one that was adopted – with one important modification, for to the Savages it still seemed fatally flawed. It involved the major refurbishment of the Red Lodge, much of which was both necessary and welcome, but there was anguish over the planned rearrangement of what was then known as the Veterans' Room. This was the space in which were exhibited relics of nineteenth-century wars stemming from Fuller Eberle's support of and collecting interest in the Crimea and Indian Mutiny Veterans' Association, fascinating scraps of the past which had been moved into the Red Lodge on the closure of the Veterans' Club. It was the council's idea to turn this corner of the Lodge into a Bongie memorial room, while the Savages, led by his son, were equally adamant that any such place of remembrance should be on their Wigwam side of the divide. Writing about the project to Town Clerk Alexander Pickard in September 1948, George Eberle pointed out that 'the main idea is in no way that of a public memorial to my father, but something which is to be very intimate to the Savages, and should therefore find a home in the Savage portion of

Complete with model house, C. F. W. Dening made yet another memorable caricature subject for Charlie Thomas.

the premises.' The contention throughout was that while Bongie had left a good deal of material to the Red Lodge, it was more of sentimental value to those who remembered him rather than a collection of obvious museum pieces. The Tribe did not by any means get all its own way in these fraught times, but Town Clerk Pickard gave heed to George Eberle's words and stepped in personally to repel the public memorial proposal. The Bongie Room today could not be more intimately involved in the life of the Savages; it is the club's office, if such a term could be truly applied to a space that looks like a cross between a cluttered Victorian study and a more eccentric corner of the props department at the B.B.C. It need hardly be said that a portrait of Fuller Eberle looks benignly down on the scene from above a memorial plaque.

The Tribe and the city council failed to see eye-to-eye on a large number of issues, not least money. Structural alterations to the Red Lodge complex were agreed in principle only after 'much discussion and argument'. They included a new staircase, kitchen, wine store, lavatory and cloakroom and the new Bongie Room on the Savages' side of the dividing door, but for a while, how it would all be paid for seemed to be anybody's guess. The Savages' portion of the work was estimated at around £1,500, it looked likely that the rent would be doubled from three hundred pounds

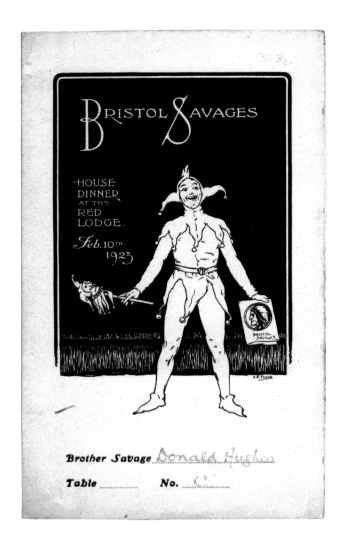

Above, characterful House Dinner menus from Curly Toope, left, from 1923 and Ralph Brentnall, above, from 1949. The Wigwam's collection of menus presents a contrasting range of artistic styles, with many of the Tribe's most memorable members represented.

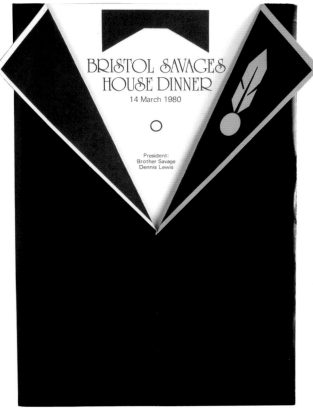

The early 1930s saw a return to the Indian theme for the House Dinner menus. The strength of the fanciful equation of the club with a Native American tribe has fluctuated over the years, but it was obviously to the fore in 1932, left, again with Curly Toope and 1935, below left, when Donald Hughes's Feb. Nine - Savages Dine card revived memories of various "Savage Feast" covers in the early years. Below, Art Deco was Dennis Lewis's inspiration for the menu of 1980.

to six hundred and there still appeared to be the threat of the corporation withdrawing that £250 annual upkeep grant. It again fell to George Eberle to save the day when, appointed the Tribe's legal adviser, he negotiated hard and to great effect to reduce the burden. Along with his brothers he also bore the cost of the conversion of the Bongie Room, which was over and above the council's demands. Such sterling service deserved reward, and even as a solicitor much in demand in the city for conveyancing he agreed that it had been granted when the Savages reclassified him as a Blue Feather.

In the following session, 1948-49, the relationship with the museum and art gallery committee was still strained when the chairmanship of the house committee was discussed. 'Their insistence that he (sic) should always be one of their members seemed unfair, but we had to concede, and the diplomacy of our President (Ralph Brentnall) must have been severely taxed,' Cecil Broome wrote in 1979. 'This contretemps may have been the reason why during this session the use of our premises was accorded to only two outside organisations, the St Stephen's Ringers and the Archaeological Society, both of which were specifically granted this privilege in our lease.'

The most colourful clash with the city council in these years, however, concerned the presence at house committee meetings of Kathleen Armistead, the curator of both the Red Lodge and the Georgian House Museum in Great George Street. A professional arts administrator, she understandably had an agenda for the building somewhat different from that of the Savages, and Frank Mole in particular found it difficult to work with her. As they each spent a considerable time in the building, that was a problem. Frank lived at the Lodge in his role as Honorary Secretary while Miss Armistead had an office there, and the concept of the two of them under the same roof has echoes of today's *Wife Swap* reality TV shows which put terminally disparate people in a house together and stand back and watch the sparks fly.

There was many a difference of opinion behind closed doors, the dispersal of the contents of the Veterans' Room remained a point of contention, and it was in the Savages' minutes that tensions were allowed to surface. By early 1953 the council had taken the decision to invite Miss Armistead along to house committee meetings. The Savages disagreed with this profoundly, and took to airing their views to the imminently retiring director of the City Art Gallery, Colonel H. W. Maxwell, who had been a member of the Tribe for well over 20 years; but it was the house committee chairman, Councillor Jones, who bore the brunt of their ire.

Intriguing, eccentric, colourful: The Wigwam is now secured for the Savages' use for generations to come, but there have been times when its future has appeared to be in jeopardy.

The committee report for February 20 1953 read: 'It was reported by the Chairman, the President and Brother Savage Milne (that Miss Armistead was at) the last meeting of the house committee and that she had had a lot to say. The Hon. Sec. read the paragraph from the lease of the composition of the house committee and the Hon. Legal Adviser gave it as his ruling that Miss Armistead was not entitled to be present at house committee meetings. The Hon. Sec was asked to see Brother Savage Maxwell and to express the committee's views on this point.'

On March 27 'the chairman reported that the general atmosphere of the last house committee meeting had been much better and more friendly than at the previous one. Miss Armistead had been present but had not entered into any of the discussions. The chairman of the house committee seemed very keen that she should be present, and it was evident that Miss Armistead had been told that she was there only to give information when asked. The chairman had assured us that we were at liberty

The Bongie Room: As administrative offices go, there can be few in the country as characterful as this. Seen here are Reg Bennett, Honorary Treasurer from 1998-99 to 2002-03 and Geoff Cutter, Assistant Honorary Secretary since 2000-01.

to bring in another member for special information and advice. Our representatives thought that it would be best to tolerate Miss Armistead's attendance, having made our protest.'

The house committee meeting held April 29 was apparently '... a very cordial one. The new director of the Art Gallery, Mr (Hans) Schubart was present, but not Miss Armistead. The chairman, Councillor Jones, had asked what our committee had decided about Miss Armistead's attendance at the meetings. He was told that while we still thought it unnecessary, as it was his very great wish that Miss Armistead should be present we would tolerate Miss Armistead's attendance, at which he seemed very pleased.'

Less well pleased was Colonel Maxwell, a Savage since 1930, who resigned on September 25 1953. Maybe he was simply intent on rearranging his entire life on retirement from work, but maybe not. What is beyond doubt is that the city council has mysteriously mislaid all house committee records between November 1951 and December 1953; and that as late as October 14 1970, Frank Mole is minuted as refer-

Savages at play: On March 2, 1932 the Chairman's Wednesday evening subject was The Objective, *which was interpreted in this way by E. Willis Paige, whose specialisation was etchings.*

ring to "that woman" when discussing the removal of exhibits from the Red Lodge to the City Museum and Art Gallery.

A social side of life that burgeoned considerably in the early Red Lodge years was the annual golf tournament, which dated from 1910. This was open to non-members, and by 1924 entries had risen to an excessive 380. A turnout of three hundred was frequent, and it was not until 1945, when "Frappy" Frapwell took over the reins from founder organiser Harry Pezzack, that it was decided to restrict the competition to Savages only. Ernest Fabian, creator of the original Tomahawk trophy, was busy again in 1925 with the creation of a scalping knife trophy and replica for the winners of the inter-club competition and also silver lapel badges showing an Indian's head for the best Savage score. These were produced between 1925 and 1930, the year before Fabian died, and the Tribe has been lucky to have had four of them returned over the years. These are now worn by the four main officers, with the President, Vice-President, Secretary and Treasurer sporting the badges first won respectively by Gordon Thompson, Percy Heming, George Heming and an

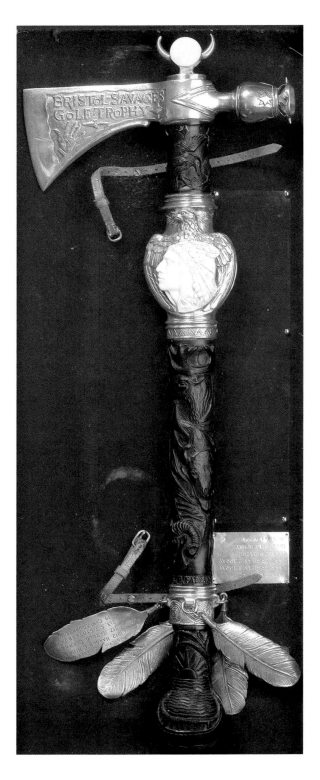

unknown Savage golfer. Ifor Davies has organised the contest since 1999, while Eric Ross and Grahame Spray have also put in sterling service over the years. The day always ends in convivial style with a supper at which Red Feathers' sketches are presented as additional prizes – and since numbers are now by no means what they were, the 2004 competition will once again welcome non-members, with Savages allowed to invite one guest each, to play for a separate prize. Late in 2001 Red Feather George Cutter, a talented wood carver, presented to the Tribe a wooden replica of the Tomahawk trophy, to be held for the year by the Savage winner of the competition. Future competitors will hope for better fortunes than in 2002, when the event was played at Bristol and Clifton, 'too many' home players won prizes, the day ran at a loss and 'dinner not the greatest; some thought the steaks were someone's old golf shoes.'

Week-in, week-out, without fail, the activities of the Tribe have been chronicled in the minutes book. Often quirky though rarely incomprehensible, the notes still have the ability, once in a while, to leave the reader asking 'what was that all about, then?' A case in point came in March 1937, when it was recorded that 'The meeting of the Savages was held in the Wigwam, Wigwaam, Wigwom, Wigwarm, Wigwomb etc.' From this distance this sounds as if it could be a parody of the upper-class English pronunciation of the day – Queen Mary, for instance, would always 'larnch' a ship – but why it was brought up at this particular point is anybody's guess. A recent visitor had been the very well connected Peter Scott, who had addressed the Tribe during the evening. Perhaps he had been the Wigwaam man, but whatever, the contorted spelling never surfaced again.

Far left, The golfers' Tomahawk Trophy was the work of the master modeller Ernest Fabian in 1912, much the same time as he produced the President's chain of office.

Left, again by Ernest Fabian, the Scalping Knife Trophy for winners of the Savages Golf Tournament's inter-club contest was first presented in 1925.

Below, a great sense of occasion surounded the first golfing tournaments. This is a detail of the splendid etching by Heaney given as a prize in 1925.

5

FATHER OF THE SAVAGES

So who was this Bongie? He was a member of a breed that scarcely exists any more, there is nothing more certain than that. The tradition of philanthropy was deeply ingrained in Bristol, and James Fuller Eberle bought into it wholeheartedly. As a major city since before the Industrial Revolution it was a place in which rich and poor had lived at close quarters for centuries; in this it was entirely unlike the towns of the North and Midlands that burgeoned throughout the nineteenth century and grew into maturity and social consciousness only in mid- or late Victorian times. A century before then Bristol had had philanthropists and social reformers whose fame spread far and wide: the Fry family, Hannah More, Edward Colston, whose involvement in the slave trade tempers our regard for him today but who locally in his lifetime was the most high-profile of them all. Into Victorian times, Mary Carpenter opened her girls' reformatory at the Red Lodge in 1854, the year in which Eberle was born in Devonport, and by the time he was attending Clifton College in the late 1860s she and Christopher Thomas the soap maker were putting the Unitarian church at the heart of philanthropy in the city as certainly as the Frys had done for the Quakers in the previous century. The Wills family was beginning to recognise that there was more to citizenship than giving a great many people work processing tobacco, and the charitable Müllers were well known for being more than simply a family of talented artists. All of this in a city studded with hospitals, almshouses and tight-knit societies of well-connected merchants and businessmen who did not neglect to spare a thought for the needy while congregating to further their members' mutual interests.

In terms of achievement and benefaction on the wider scale, the name of Fuller Eberle cannot be bracketed with any of the above in any meaningful way. In terms of Savages history and lore he is peerless, and will continue to be so as long as successive Presidents address his portrait at the beginning and end of sessions with the words: 'Bongie, we will carry/ have carried on.'

After leaving Clifton College and Manilla Hall in Bristol, Eberle joined his uncle John Fuller's coach building business and stayed in it for all his working life, building up a reputation as an enlightened employer. He was a member of the Chamber of

One of the Savages' best-loved icons, the oil portrait of James Fuller Eberle by George Swaish takes pride of place on the wall behind the Chairman's desk, along with paintings and caricatures of other officials over the years. The cleaning of Bongie's picture for the centenary celebrations revealed several details which had been lost to view for many years.

Commerce in his younger years, but resigned from it in 1886 when he was elected on to Bristol City Council as a Conservative councillor for St Augustine ward. He remained so for all but the last few months of his life, a total of some fifty-two years; his greatest interest was the museum and art gallery committee on which he served for forty years, many of them as chairman. After the First World War he received the O.B.E. for the Savages' work in providing entertainment for wounded soldiers; in 1937, some felt a little belatedly, he was granted the honorary freedom of the city; and nationally he served terms as president of the Institute of Carriage Manufacturers, and master of the London guild, the Coach Makers' Company. To most in Bristol he was Alderman Eberle, that courtesy title local authorities used to bestow on their senior councillors. In his later years he was also known as the father of the council, another courtesy title applied to the longest-serving elected representative. To the Savages, however, he was forever Bongie, after it had leaked out that that was what he was called by his granddaughter and George's daughter Mary, known as Molly, at around the age of eighteen months. The accepted wisdom is that she named him that because she could not pronounce 'grandad', but as 'Bongie' sounds utterly unlike 'grandad' even in baby talk, it is just as likely that she came up with it for no better reason than that is what little children do, give their funny old grandpas daft names. Perhaps she named him after a character in a book she had been read, or a favourite toy. 'The Savages heard of this and adopted it as a nickname, not only for its euphemism but for its aptness,' Colston Waite wrote in 1971. 'Aptness' was presumably a reference to banging the gong, but 'euphemism' seems to takes us into a realm of long-ago club slang which means nothing today. Molly died some twenty years ago, apparently embarrassed to the end at her unwitting role in Savages lore, and apt to be annoyed if anyone ever brought it up. 'She always protested that she never called him that – but she did,' says her brother John Eberle, born in 1918 and a Savage since 1946.

Fuller Eberle's benefaction took the form of selective and concentrated support for specific causes, rather than a broad sweep of interests. The *Bristol Evening Post's* obituary after his death on April 21 1939 quotes an unnamed friend as saying: 'At one time he made the Salisbury Club his hobby, much in the same way as he adopted the Red Lodge when he had secured it as a home for the Bristol Savages.' The full list, in roughly chronological order, would read something like: the Salisbury Club, the Crimea and Indian Mutiny Veterans' Association, the Grateful Society, the Antient Society of St Stephen's Ringers (he was their Treasurer for 50 years) and the Bristol

Savages. 'He was always the mainspring of some organisation,' the *Evening Post* was told. Dr White's Hospital in Temple Street and the Bristol Benevolent Institution were among his other good causes, while during the First World War, with three sons serving abroad, he was chairman of the Bristol Recruiting Committee.

'The mainspring of any organisation': reading through the Savages literature it is easy to see that he quickly acquired that status in the Tribe. His instant recruitment of large numbers of what are at least looked back upon as the city's great and good must have played an early part in that, while his solution to the club's accommodation needs from 1907 to the present and into the future is, to say the least, no small matter; but his impact is clearly owed to more than that. For a non-smoking teetotaller with a friendly and straightforward manner but 'an inborn aversion to publicity', his command of a roomful of celebrating Punch Nighters, for example, was quite remarkable. Let us recall that the minutes for Christmas Eve 1919 read: 'The chair was in accordance with custom taken by Bro. Sav. James Fuller Eberle. A Punch Night without him to direct proceedings would lose all character.' It is intriguing to speculate on quite why he held such sway, and frustrating that recorded clues to his character do not stray much beyond bland platitudes. His smile was 'encouraging, energising and infectious', one informant told the *Evening Post*. Another recalled: 'What I shall always remember about him was the wonderful way in which he anticipated the needs of others.' A maxim often used by him, and one still provided to new members, was: 'To do constantly, and carefully, and kindly, all sorts of little things, is not a little thing.' All these reflections offer tantalising glimpses without truly reaching the heart of the man. 'Of course he ought to have been Lord Mayor of Bristol years ago, and that he has not been is simply because of his modesty,' an admiring Savage wrote in 1922. The modesty cannot be denied, as cannot his lifelong habit of doing good by stealth rather than the ostentatious, but his grandson John Eberle believes he would have been prevailed upon to become Lord Mayor – he was approached several times – if his even more retiring wife Florence Mary had not been opposed to it. What is intriguing is the way in which Bongie's modesty failed to mask his merits in any other sphere of his life.

Fuller Eberle died at his home in Pembroke Road, Clifton within a year of the death of Florence, to whom he was married for some fifty-eight years. His funeral was at Emmanuel Church, Clifton, after which he was buried in Canford Cemetery. The Savages were represented by thirty-one members at the church while several others of the Tribe were to be found in the very strong city council contingent. He had become old and increasingly frail, but had looked in on a committee luncheon unexpectedly just a few weeks before he died, and members had stood up as one to applaud him in. His last night in the chair on Punch Night had been some years before, December 18 1935, at which he had put in his first meeting of the season and 'cheer after cheer was raised in gratitude for his presence'. Twelve months on, he regretted that he was not to attend 'under emphatic instructions from his doctor' and a few days earlier, on December 11 1936, the Braves had arranged for his birthday breakfast table to be adorned by a Savages mug containing 82 violets, one for every year of his age. It was at Punch Night 1937, when the committee received a note of apology signed by him but written by another hand, that the Tribe finally began to face up to the fact that his days with them were numbered. Charlie Thomas, a mighty figure in Savages history in his own right, and a great showman, took over the Punch Night chair with verve, but for years after Bongie's demise his presence was missed. The minutes for the 1937 gathering record that 'owing to the presence of an exceptionally large number of members... and perhaps too many guests, the (artists') sketches hardly received the attention they deserved. That is one of the penalties which have to be paid on such hilarious occasions. Another is that more entertaining members are present than it is feasible to call on.' In 1938 it was a case of admission by pre-booked ticket only, 'which did little to reduce the attendance but did prevent gatecrashing by most undesirable people'. Nevertheless, rowdiness on Punch Night was clearly becoming quite an issue, and there was a general feeling that 'it wouldn't have happened under Bongie'.

Five days after his death the Savages met for their last Wednesday of the 1938-39 session, with Secretary Roslyn in the chair. The minutes take up the story: 'Then the Chairman, who had been in close touch with Bongie throughout his long illness, added a further tribute. He tried to tell something of the fostering care Bongie had bestowed on the Savages for over a quarter of a century – of his generosity, encouragement and example – and how unconsciously he had created the wonderful atmosphere that always pervades the Wigwam, and has become one of our greatest assets. A few inspiring words about Bongie having been read by Bro. Sav. Donald Hughes, Bro. Sav. George Eberle gave us a message from his father: "I have enjoyed many a friendship of many still left – artist Savages and some of our political friends – but there are many among the Savages who have touched me by their pluck and perseverance in their work, and their good fellowship." Bro. Sav. George Eberle particularly stressed the last two words, because on good fellowship the strength of the Savages

Dinner at Bongie's, *a Stanley Lloyd painting from the days when Fuller Eberle was pushing the Savages up the social ladder, as well as giving the club incalculable practical support.*

had been built up, and upon the maintenance of good fellowship their future prosperity depended. In spite of the distress under which he was labouring – a distress intensified by the knowledge that his brother, Bro. Sav. Ellison Eberle, was to be operated upon – he bravely proceeded to suggest that it should become a tradition among us that on the first night of each session the President, turning to Bongie's portrait, should say "Bongie, we will carry on", and then on the last night of each session the Chairman, again turning to the portrait, should say "Bongie, we have carried on". So long as that was done honestly and sincerely, he had no fears about the future of the Savages. After the singing of the National Anthem, and remembering the words of Bro. Sav. George Eberle, the Chairman faced the portrait hanging behind his seat and said "Bongie, we have carried on". So ended the most memorable meeting in our history.'

While the Savages were wholeheartedly sincere in their admiration of and gratitude towards Fuller Eberle, his solicitor son George's role as an efficient and effective keeper of the flame should not be ignored. It was he who invented the 'carry on' tradition, he who argued most persuasively for the Bongie Room to go to the Savages' H.Q. rather than the Red Lodge, he, along with Rossy and Dean Harry Blackburne, who was at the heart of placing the annual Founders' Service on the Sunday following the anniversary of Bongie's death. 'The founders of our Tribe were few in number and diverse in character, but all were men of vision,' he said late in his life, at the Founders' Service of 1961. 'Led by my father, who was called by them Bongie, the Great White Chief, they established a tradition of comradeship and goodwill, combined with a cultural love of all that is clean and beautiful in the arts of painting, music, song and the spoken word. In the course of years there emerged that intangible something which is realised by all of us, but only occasionally referred to as the Savage Spirit or the atmosphere of the Wigwam.'

The bracketing of Fuller Eberle among 'the founders of our Tribe' was not, of course, correct in the strictest sense of the word; but let it not be supposed that the fervid respect in which he is still held today is a result of anything but his own merits and the admiration he attracted in his lifetime, rather than of anything that was said or done after his death. The second copy of *Grouse* magazine, published in 1922, carries a reproduction of the portrait of him by George Swaish which was presented to him by the Tribe in October 1921. This is the image of Bongie which hangs behind the Chairman's seat at the Wigwam and to which successive Presidents pledge allegiance, and now, newly cleansed of decades of smoke discolouration for the Centenary festivities, it can be seen in all the detail that was so much admired when it was first painted. In *Grouse,* the plate is unequivocally titled *The Father of the Bristol Savages,* and there is a note of the date on which it was presented to 'Bongey'. Both the page before and after the portrait are devoted to admiring tributes to him, including 'Fuller Eberle – 4 Es a jolly good fellow', which made readers wonder where the James in his name left him, and a reproduction of a rhyme written by Francis Locke at Christmas 1908, the year after the move to Brandon Cottage and the time when Bongie was in the midst of his feverish recruiting activity among the cream of Bristol society. The long poem – and we can only imagine what agonies a modest man would have been going through as it was recited to him in front of an excited Punch Night throng – ended:

'Hurrah', 'Hurrah', and one cheer more, again a hearty cheer,

Health, Wealth and Joy we drink to thee, our Brother Fuller Eberle.

The Bongie Room: The Savages office is named in honour of James Fuller Eberle and the great man would no doubt have appoved of its fascinating mixture of eccentricity and efficiency.

As for his grandson John, who was twenty-one at the time of the funeral in 1939, his memories are of a diffident and kindly old man whom he used to ferry around by car when his eyesight began to fail. John Eberle is still to be found in the Wigwam on Wednesday evenings, and on Friday lunchtimes too, more often than not. It means that in three generations, James, George and John, the Eberles have spanned all but the first couple of years of the Savages' history – not out. John's recollections are fascinating, but if only there were more first-hand memories to tell us what made Bongie tick.

6

IN WAR AND CELEBRATION

Britain declared war on Germany on August 4 1914, timing that convinced some at least that it would be all over by Christmas. The first question to be answered at the beginning of the 1914-15 session was quite simply whether or not to continue, and the decision to carry on was based largely on the fact that a majority of members were too old to volunteer. Many did so, however; twenty-two, according to a list drawn up by Savage Fred Bolt, who was a member throughout the war, but this estimate was later increased considerably to forty-seven. Three are known to have died, E. W. Ball, Percy Ogden and Ernest George, and there was a particular irony about the last of these. Born Ernst Hoffstein in Germany and long remembered after his death as a fine pianist, he came to Britain, changed his name by deed poll and eventually found himself in the British Army fighting against his former compatriots, a strange state of affairs that was curtailed by his death in a military hospital in Malta. Percy Ogden, a life member living in London, died as an Army lieutenant on the Somme in 1917. Towards the end of the war 'Curly' Toope was injured on active service, but one of the more bizarre absentees for part of 1916 was Charlie Thomas, who embarked for Malta and Egypt to entertain troops as part of the Lena Ashwell concert party. There was a huge get-together at the Wigwam to see him off, with the Lord Mayor heading an impressive turnout of civic dignitaries. Later in the war Thomas collaborated with fellow Savage J. G. Russell Harvey, a journalist on the *Bristol Times and Mirror,* to produce comic booklets in aid of the Red Cross Society. *Tommy's ABC* cost a shilling, and families at home were urged to buy it to cheer up the boys overseas. Produced by the Bristol master printers A. W. Ford of Denmark Street, it remains a quite superb little book, Charlie Thomas's full-page illustrations in red and beige echoing the work of the likes of Hassall and Bairnsfather and suffering nothing in comparison with either. It has its sober side. The full colour cover shows a Tommy, in the royal blue uniform with white lapels that made wounded servicemen instantly and increasingly recognisable in our towns and cities, telling his tales to a little boy and his tousled dog in the tradition of *The Boyhood of Raleigh,* and some of the rhymes are scarcely full of fun:

A is for Ambulance

motor or horse,

B is for Bandage

that binds you, of course...

The general feel of the booklet, however, and of its companion volume *Rhymes of the Times,* is one of good cheer and patriotism, with outstanding Thomas caricatures of George V and Queen Mary and a wonderfully silly little final page in which Charlie portrays Russell Harvey with panache and the writer reciprocates by drawing the artist with all the skill of a ham-fisted nine-year-old; at least he got the famous pipe in place.

By the end of the 1914-15 session the Savages had welcomed back their first serviceman member home on leave. They were to do so many times again in the years ahead, but there was something especially noteworthy about this first one. Stanley Lloyd, who had joined the Tribe in 1904 and had served as Assistant Secretary, was the first member to enlist in the Army as a private and gain a commission, so there was a ceremonial sword waiting for him when he returned briefly to the warm bosom of the Wigwam.

The Tribe kept patriotic work high on its agenda throughout the war. Many Wednesday nights became Military Evenings, at which members of the armed forces were entertained. Parties of Savages visited camps and hospitals to put on concerts and three special concerts for the public were held at Bristol halls in aid of the War Fund. In the 1915-16 session a committee was set up to bring wounded men into the Wigwam and give them afternoon tea and entertainment, and over the years this became the focal point of the entertainer members' war effort; six such concerts took place in this session, a further five in 1916-17 and two more in 1917-18. The 1915-16 session also brought a less charitable but nevertheless much-needed move. It had become the custom for every visitor to the Wigwam in uniform to have his first drink bought for him by

Top, Harold Packer's 1951 two-minute sketch Looking Up, *an unconscious reminder of the days when the Savages met in the room above a Salvation Army Hall.*

Above, Tommy's ABC, *the superb little book Savages Charlie Thomas and J. G. Russell Harvey produced for the Red Cross in the First World War.*

Image of war: Frank Shipsides' 1973 two-hour sketch Beam, *a topic he interpreted in characteristic nautical style.*

the Tribe, after which, as is the rule still today, only members were allowed to buy him further rounds. By this time strangers in uniform were becoming thick on the ground, and members' finances were eased considerably when the committee was empowered to elect the visitors as temporary honorary members to conform with Board of Control licensing regulations. One of the privileges 'enjoyed' by such members was permission to stand his round!

By season 1916-17 even older members were finding themselves drawn into war work on the home front, perhaps as special constables or locally based government officials. This had an effect on their Wednesday night attendance but they were not forgotten, since a call for a toast to absent brethren was made at 10 p.m. every meeting; besides, uniformed guests ensured that the evenings were at least as lively as they ever had been, and there was certainly no sense of the Savages having been abandoned to the old men, since Officer Training Corps cadets were out in force almost every week. Then there were cash donations. Early on in the war, two hundred pounds was taken from club funds to go into War Loan stock and the Tribe subscribed a further ten guineas to the Prince of Wales War Fund. A further hundred pound War Loan in the 1916-17 session was undoubtedly patriotic but maybe not so prudent, since the Tribe's next balance sheet showed an overdraft at the bank. And the background music to so much of this activity? *Roses of Picardy,* of course, its romantic words sung with longing by troops and their sweethearts alike. Of all the Savages who made their mark on the First World War, none did it more indelibly than the lyricist Fred Weatherly.

The Tribe's part in George V's silver jubilee celebrations of 1935 did not extend beyond having three representatives invited to join a civic procession from Queen Square to the Cathedral for a service of thanksgiving. The chosen ones were President Donald Hughes, Vice-President the etcher E. Willis Paige and Secretary H. E. Roslyn, and the Savages saw this as quite a breakthrough; it tended to be the President alone who was invited along on such occasions, but the fact that Willis Paige was a city council employee, as deputy principal of the school of art, might have helped swell the numbers. Whatever the reasoning behind it, the Savages were pleased, and they were even more so when five officers were called to the Cathedral for a memorial service to the king when he died a year later. The President alone represented the Tribe at a civic ceremony to proclaim Edward VIII king, and a few months later Savages were hard at work preparing for his coronation. They agreed to contribute towards

The war clouds lift: Hamish Milne's Pleasant Memories, *a two-hour sketch from November 1946, seems to anticipate as well as look back on happier times.*

decorations for the Red Lodge and were responding to a request for a cover design for a brochure the Bristol Development Board was producing when the abdication brought everyone back down to earth. By the time George VI was crowned in 1937 it seems that members' taste for royal pomp had waned, with the coronation of May 12 going unnoted in the club minutes.

The Second World War began for the Savages with Gordon Hake in his third year as President and Tom Burrough and Harold Thomas, a favourite piano accompanist, being called up in the early months. The Tribe had a collection and presented Harold with a leather waistcoat as a parting present, at a time when snug home-made socks and scarves were the standard clothing gifts for most men going off into the forces. This was the time of the 'phoney war', which perhaps explains why before October was out and the sad farewells had scarcely died away, Tom was back home on leave and chairing a Wednesday meeting. Despite all this, nobody was talking about it being all over by Christmas this time.

By the end of the 1939-40 session twenty-two members were in service, including seven artists, and scores more served as special constables, auxiliary firemen, air raid wardens, first-aiders or members of the Home Guard. The Royal Observer Corps was a particularly popular choice after a visit to the Wigwam by its local leader, General Sir Hugh Elles. He recruited twenty-six Savages while himself asking suc-

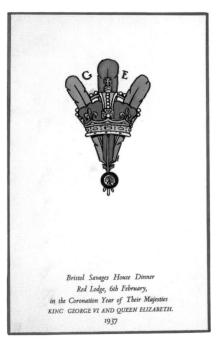

Top, Harold Thomas, one of the great Savage entertainers of the mid-twentieth century, as seen by Harold Packer.

Above, Hamish Milne's House Dinner menu for the coronation year of 1937.

cessfully to be one of the Tribe, and since the unit was newly-formed the men from the Wigwam made an immediate impact on the way it went about its serious business of keeping a twenty-four-hour vigil of the skies around the city and plotting the course of enemy aircraft.

The impact of the B.B.C.'s wartime presence in Bristol is considered in this book's Famous Faces chapter, but devolution did not begin and end with the corporation. Several ministerial departments had been evacuated to the city, and a sherry party was held at the Wigwam for some three hundred 'wartime visitors'. Civil Defence officials were called in to advise on precautions against air raids, which seemed to threaten ever more menacingly as the weeks went on, and as a result of their recommendations the cellars were declared a suitable shelter for up to sixty people and the ceilings of the studio were reinforced with steel joists to offer some refuge for those who lived in or were frequently around the building, Secretary H. E. Roslyn, the caretaker Miss Emily Sullivan and her niece. Various members were given safety duties for Wednesday evenings – or late afternoons, for a time, since meetings were rescheduled to begin at 4.30 p.m. for a brief, unloved period. Two early casualties of war were the annual dinner and the publication of *Grouse,* which never had an easy ride financially in its first incarnation from 1921 to 1940 and did not lend itself to be published on war economy paper, even if it had been available.

If session 1939-40 was a dress rehearsal for the perils to come, 1940-41 was the big show. Nobody who lived through that winter in or anywhere near central Bristol was left in any doubt about the horrors of mid-twentieth-century warfare, and like everyone else, the Savages were in the thick of it. Despite the occasional alarm from air raid sirens, there had been only one major attack on the city – a daylight strike against the Filton aerodrome – before the night of Sunday November 24 1940 rewrote Bristol's history and changed the face of its central streets forever. Everywhere was devastation and though the Wigwam was not hit directly, its roof was damaged by flying debris, some from the Princes Theatre very close by. By the following morning the roads into the city were impassable, yet thousands of shop and office workers walked in silently from home and picked their way through the shattered glass and rubble to their place of work, or the smouldering remains of it. Two days later, six members of the Tribe turned up as usual for the Wednesday meeting, which turned out to be nothing more than a sharing of experiences. They decided that having flown the flag and proved the indomitability of the Savage Spirit, there would be something approaching normal service seven days hence. They were wrong. The following weekend's air raid did not compare with November 24 for intensity, but a high-explosive bomb fell in Stoney Hill, just a few metres from the Wigwam and Red Lodge, and this time the damage was far more severe. All the windows were blown out, masonry which cascaded on to the roof devastated tiles and brought down ceilings, and the Studio, kitchen and Oak Room lay under two or three inches of dust, plaster and rubble. Tradition has it that the ceilings that fared best amid the mayhem were those in which intricate sixteenth-century plasterwork had been reinforced with horse hair.

The Tribe could scarcely have had a President better equipped for such misfortunes. Hamish Milne was the director of a building company, and the next day some of his men were around making good the damage when they could have been far more lucratively employed elsewhere. The clean-up also involved several of Gordon Hake's architectural students, who learned a great deal about the component parts of buildings and their durability or otherwise in a very short space of time, and in an extremely hands-on way. Between them they brought some order to the building, though the prospect of holding meetings in it was still out of the question. Rather than cancel Punch Night, it was held in the daytime as a nosebag luncheon; it was not quite the same, but ninety Savages showed up and seventy-four pounds was collected in the elephant's foot.

The money went to the usual good causes, of course, but by this stage the Tribe was beginning to feel something like a good cause in itself, since war was proving expensive. When the government ordered that no city centre building should be left unattended by a fire warden at night, volunteers from within the ranks soon had to be supplemented by university students who were paid 10s 6d per shift. In fact many more middle-aged to elderly Savages wished to take their turn than were able to do so, their wives being understandably reluctant to see them abandon the comparative safety of the suburbs at night to keep a possible date with the Luftwaffe down in town. The result was rather too many 10s 6d pay packets flowing out of the door, and the drama

Another affectionate Harold Packer caricature, this one of Professor Charles MacInnes.

turned into a crisis when the government introduced a compulsory war damage insurance scheme and it was discovered that the Tribe had just £19 in the bank. The long-serving Treasurer, Jimmy Sherwood, had fallen ill and found it hard to keep pace with the job, though in true Savage Spirit his predicament was treated with sympathy rather than ire and he was soon afterwards made a life member and awarded a gift of ten guineas. Nevertheless, there was work to be done, and a special sub-committee of banker and accountant members under A. K. 'Gunga' Deane set about putting the club's finances in order at a time when it had never been less able to offer members very much in the way of entertainment and enjoyment. In the hot July of 1941 it even ran out of beer, but Sidney Hobbs was able to track down some little country brewery to help out. In the circumstances, a fifty per cent rise in subscriptions was not Gunga's most popular move as the new Treasurer, but most members kept quiet and paid up. After all, there was a war on, you know.

Other risks had to be taken. For war damage insurance Savage Noel Butler, an antiques dealer from Bath, made an inventory and valuation of the Tribe's treasures. He came up with a total of £2,808, including pictures worth £700, and though the general feeling was that this was nothing like the kind of money he would have been asking for them in his shop, if it helped keep the insurance premiums down it was not an estimate to be argued with. It was decided to spread many of the items around among members for safe storage, a move that could have been disastrous in a less dedicated and honest group of people. Needless to say, with the Savages, nothing of any significance was found to have gone astray when it came to restocking the Wigwam after the lights had gone on again.

Come April 1941, with the lighter evenings and a marked fall in aerial activity, Wednesday meetings reverted to evenings, in that they at least ran from 6 to 8.30 p.m, with ninety minutes for sketching. Visitors continued to pour in: Lord Waldegrave, a Royal Artillery officer, one week, the American consul and four members of the Free French Navy another, plus frequent home front guests representing the Royal Observer Corps, the Home Guard, the anti-aircraft crew from the battery on Durdham Down. The Frenchmen were apparently 'most agreeably surprised' when Professor Charles MacInnes welcomed them in their native tongue. Those who could *parler Français* were obviously thin on the ground in Bristol in 1941, and it was not surprising to find MacInnes cast in the role of erudite welcomer. A blind Professor Emeritus of Bristol University, he was widely regarded as a national treasure among the Savages. He it was who took the art of taunting the Treasurer to a new level when, with timing that had to be experienced to be appreciated, he responded to the President's request for questions on the accounts with a solicitous: 'Did the Treasurer enjoy his holiday?' His poems about life at the Wigwam were invariably classy and subtly recited; and it is largely because of him that a spoken critique of the evening's sketches has become a feature of the Wednesday night fare. For some years, Geoffrey Ehlers, whose founder father Ernest had died in 1943 at the age of eighty-five, had described the best of the sketches to MacInnes, but on the night of January 10 1945 President Hamish Milne took the unusual step of discussing them in front of the rest of the Tribe. It might have been a one-off departure had not Charles MacInnes stressed just how much it had been appreciated; as a result, it has been a fixture ever since.

At the end of the 1940-41 session, which went on into August, a special meeting was called to discuss whether it really was worth going on until after the war was over. Hamish Milne was stepping down as President after a magnificent year's hard work and leadership, but the incoming Charlie Thomas was also a man of strength, and it was to the relief of many that it was decided that there would indeed be a 1941-42 session. The proviso was that all meetings should be finished before blackout time, which meant that there would be no evening gatherings until spring. In fact the session turned out to be as tranquil and predictable as any wartime activity could be, with the now familiar pattern of high absenteeism among Savages on Wednesdays but a packed Wigwam nonetheless. It became such a magnet for visiting military personnel and government officials that the Lord Mayor called in specifically to thank the Tribe for their hospitality; his words were appreciated, but did nothing to swell the coffers of the bar, which made another loss through its growing reputation as Bristol's answer to Liberty Hall. American troops were now in the region in some numbers, and the prospect of an evening out in a Wigwam unlike any they had ever seen back home appealed to them greatly. At the request of the Lord Mayor, one evening's entertainment was laid on just for them, while wounded troops were entertained on two afternoons a week, week after week. Perhaps not surprisingly, the Wednesday nights could get rowdy now and again. The Tribe's master of the topical verse of the time was Joe Norgrove, whose poems and songs were published far and wide, but he was given a rough ride on November 8 1944 when he stood up to recite his reflections on the artists' subject for the evening, *Solemn Stiffness*. Perhaps there was something in the title that amused the visitors. Whatever, the minutes record that while his efforts were warmly applauded by all who heard him, 'for many, the appearance of Joe on

the platform signalled the moment for noisy conversation, and they continued to misbehave until the end of the recitation. This lapse from our customary good manners has led to the posting of a notice at the canteen (to the effect) that drinks will not be served while a member or guest is performing,'

It was always a great pleasure when Savages looked in when on leave; the Wigwam was invariably one of Tom Burrough's first ports of call after he had stepped off the train at Temple Meads, and they made a great fuss of the now Major Harold Thomas when he mounted the platform to take his place at the piano again. There was even more pleasure at the reappearance of Ralph Brentnall, who had been seriously injured while defusing an unexploded bomb; Wednesday meetings were a great escape into another world of traditional bonhomie, but scratch the surface and you soon found yourself in a roomful of tired, anxious men who had seen scenes that they did not wish to share with others and were missing loved ones maybe half the world away. The pattern continued in subsequent sessions and records for 1943-44 show that apart from a preponderance of American troops there were also Norwegians, Belgians and Canadians; in a single evening in November 1945 guests included a lieutenant from Ithaca, New York, 'where there is a Savage Club', and three members of the Chinese air force. The latter said little in public, but it must be admitted that those who did wish to speak of their experiences had some stirring tales to tell. Flying Officer Tony Rooke D.F.C. had bagged one of the German bombers that had raided Filton aerodrome, while Flying Officer Brown stood on stage and recounted some of the forty bombing missions he had flown over Germany. Probably the most welcome visitor of all was the R.A.F. pilot who helped make the Punch Night of 1942 a memorable evening. The previous year's Punch Night had started at 6 and ended at 8.30pm, not least because there had been no ingredients for punch, but this year it was very different. Our hero had just flown in from Lisbon with not only unprocurable lemons for the drinks but bananas, oranges, grapefruit and that holiest of all fruity grails, a pineapple. These were all auctioned, resulting in the elephant's foot groaning under the then unprecedented sum of £181; such was the jollity that the festivities roistered on until after midnight, an astonishingly late hour for the times. From today's perspective it seems to confirm that the *Catch 22* novelist Joseph Heller's military aircraft systematically ferrying consumer goods around Europe at the height of the Second World War were not so much figments of his imagination as mere exaggerations of the truth. At least, let us hope they were exaggerations; whatever, the Savages were certainly not complaining that evening.

However iconoclastic the early Tribe might have been – and in truth, it seems that any bohemianism about it was invariably couched in the most gentlemanly of terms – the Savages made another bow towards convention when the first annual Founders' Service was held in the Lord Mayor's Chapel on College Green on April 23, 1944. There has never been any religious agenda to the Savages, and at the time some members saw such a move as a retrograde step, an apeing of the 'respectability' of the Merchant Venturers or St Stephen's Ringers. On the other hand, the city had come through much in the previous years, and the concepts of praying to God for deliverance and giving him thanks for safekeeping had not inconsiderable potency when the bombs were raining down on your street. The clincher was the Very Revd. Harry Blackburne, the Savage Dean of Bristol who had emerged as one of the city's great wartime leaders on the home front. The Founders' Service was his idea, in conjunction with George Eberle, and he put it to the Tribe at a time when tens of thousands in the city would have walked on water for him, or at least given it a try. Of course the Dean should have his service. More than eighty Savages turned up, and in truth the annual numbers are still around the sixty-plus mark on a day that ends with the anniversary of Bongie's death being marked by tea back at the Wigwam.

As 1944 progressed there was a feeling that the shackles of war were being loosened. The Civil Defence authorities eased the financial burden of nightly firewatching when they agreed that the lookout at Savage Harry Savory's premises across the road provided sufficient cover. There was a frisson when an H.M.S. *Savage* found itself in the news for helping to sink the German *Scharnhorst,* and the Tribe sent the crew half a dozen of its beer mugs in appreciation. Some members in uniform

The House Dinner menu cover of 1951 incorporated the Festival of Britain logo, which helped launch Britain's fresh postwar approach to art and design.

were finding themselves a little nearer home and paying occasional visits, and more good news that filtered through was that the now Colonel C. R. Reynolds had escaped from prison camp and was somewhere in Switzerland. Peace was by now only months away, and its impact on the Wigwam was immediate and happy. First, and most important, all the Tribe's treasures were pouring back in, every one apparently unscathed; and second, and almost as important, the departure of all the foreign

At work in the Studio in April 1951. The Savages staged a successful display at Bristol's Our Way of Life *Festival of Britain celebrations.*

Hamish Milne's totem pole, made for the 1951 Festival of Britain and still an eye-catching feature of the entrance hall at the Wigwam today.

forces and devolved civil servants meant that at last the bar stood a chance of making a profit again, which it did to the tune of thirty pounds or more in the first nine months of the year. It was far from true that there was no longer such a thing as a free drink at the bar, but suddenly and mercifully there were now far fewer of them. While counting the beer money was not the noblest way for the Tribe to draw a line under these traumatic times, at least it was a reminder of everyday reality, and there had not been too much of that since 1939.

The Festival of Britain in the summer of 1951 is looked back on with affection today, a sign that the country was at last allowing itself to dream of brighter times ahead. The legacy of the Second World War was still everywhere in the form of shortages, rationing and bombsites, but from a twenty-first-century perspective we can see why the authorities latched so enthusiastically on to the centenary of the Great Exhibition of Victorian times and encouraged the nation to enjoy it. With hindsight, now, we must suppose that had they known a coronation was coming along two years later, they might not have been so festival-minded. But they had no such foresight, so the message to the country was: 'Rejoice'.

Britain is not good at rejoicing to order, as Lady Thatcher discovered after the Falklands War and Mr Blair at the Millennium. 'It was decided that although many were not at all enthusiastic over the festival, the city authorities were committed to it and it was felt that we should give it our support,' read the minutes for the Savages meeting of March 16 1951; joy was clearly not unrestrained, but it was such that a proposal to spend fifteen pounds on a display panel for the city's festivities was amended up to twenty. The focus of Bristol Festival of Britain Fortnight in July was an *Our Way of Life* exhibition at the Memorial Ground, now Stadium, at Horfield. The Savages' main contribution was a panel some forty feet long and eight high on which members' work was exhibited, while Hamish Milne's still familiar totem pole was another favourite, especially with the children. After the show, the artists' sub-committee that organised it was congratulated on a 'magnificent job'. Ernest Andrews was the linchpin of the operation, and the Duke of Gloucester was one of the many visitors he enjoyed showing around. It was Ernest who designed the Savage tie, and asked that his should be buried with him when he died in 1976; as the artists' profiles at the back of this book affirm he was also, briefly and improbably, almost Diana Dors's father-in-law. Before the festival he was one of a minority of people who recognised the fact that it presented an opportunity to introduce the public to the concepts of art, design and architecture in ways unknown since the 1930s, and after the event several Savages were happy to acknowledge that he had been absolutely right. All in all, *Our Way of Life* was very well received, and it certainly did not deter (non-Savage) Frank Buckley, the barrister who was Bristol's Festival Fortnight mastermind. Fifty years and more later and by now a nonagenarian, he was still beating the patriotic drum and organising Battle of Britain and Golden Jubilee anniversary events for the city in the early twenty-first century. The Savages salute and admire people whose public life goes on for so long that they seem to be living in a time capsule all of their own. The Tribe itself has enjoyed the services of a score of them over the years, and it applauds Frank Buckley's contribution to the Bristol scene; doubtless even now he is laying plans for the Queen's Diamond Jubilee eight years hence...

Bristol's Festival of Britain booklet included six illustrations by Savage Herbert Truman, including one of the Wigwam in colour, while nationally, the club made a more quirky contribution to Britain's rejoicings. It had – and indeed still has, on the platform, in good working order – a bizarre 'talking head' automaton described as a comic electric telegraph, which had been made for the 1851 exhibition and was later passed on to the Savages by its inventor's member son, J Lason Smith. It had somehow been tracked down to the Wigwam by the Victoria and Albert Museum, whose contribution to the Festival of Britain was an *Exhibits of 1851* show, and the Savages were happy to let it go to

Another Studio scene from April 1951. The Wednesday evening's sketch subject was Together, *a concept that still had resonance in postwar Britain.*

London for a few months, insured for a hundred pounds. It had recently been restored, and a brass plate now records its two starring roles in the capital, a hundred years apart. Two years later, the coronation of 1953 was marked with very little ceremony, apart from the president representing the Savages at a civic service at the Cathedral and procession and the date of the tea for old people from the almshouses being brought forward to June 4.

As part of the Bristol's *Our Way of Life* theme for the Festival of Britain, the BBC West of England Home Service asked for a recording of the Savages' minutes to be made on a Wednesday evening. The plea was not well received, since 'the committee considered that the minutes were of too intimate a character, much of which depended on chance, for such a recording to represent the Savages satisfactorily'. Savage Mitchell Michaels had more luck when he asked to bring his 'tape recording machine' along to a Wednesday evening a couple of years later. The suggestion was welcomed, and though it is hard to imagine that the equipment coped very well with the hubbub of an open meeting, there was much jollity in the playing back, since few Savages had heard their voice on tape before that night. Since then the cameras and microphones have been allowed into the Wigwam on a number of occasions, notably for the B.B.C. regional television show *Jolly Good Company*, which was screened in 1969 to mark the Tribe's 65th anniversary. It did not, it must be confessed, portray a typical night at the Wigwam. Wives were present as Blue Feathers went through a number of routines with all the paraphernalia of an outside broadcast milling around them. The programme was the brainchild of Savage Bill

Captain Scott attended the House Dinner at the Royal Hotel in April 1910 as part of a fund-raising tour to help finance the ill-fated British Antarctic Expedition in which he was to lose his life two years later. The Savages own several pieces of Scott memorabilia.

Laird, then head of light music for the B.B.C. in the West of England and a self-taught painter talented enough to become a Red Feather in 1970 after ten years as a Blue. It is generally agreed that *Jolly Good Company* would make decidedly excruciating viewing if it were shown today, but at the time it was well received and seen as a force for good in spreading the name of the Savages. At much the same time there was more positive publicity for the Tribe when it donated twenty-seven paintings for auction in aid of the high-profile restoration of the Theatre Royal in King Street, and so helped swell funds by £250.

And what of the Millennium? It proved only that the Savages needed no new clothes in which to go into the new century. They were quite comfortable enough in the old ones, thank you very much. At Punch Night on December 22 1999 Chairman Malcolm Popperwell's subject for the artists was *Christmas Scenes* – 'somewhat complicated and hard thought-out', as the Honorary Secretary so loyally opined – and all was jollity with a particularly pungent punch, music ranging from *Trumpet Voluntary* to *The Dance of the Snowmen* and *Madonna and Child,* and all the old carols with a stirring cornet accompaniment to *O Come All Ye Faithful.* A week later, Quiet Night on December 29 lived fully up to its name with just fifty-nine members present for the Savage century's true swansong (with not too sincere apologies to the pedants who still swear that it ended a year later). Grahame Spray took the chair, chose as his subject *1900-2000: The Best* and might have been surprised to discover that Vincent Neave chose for his critique a portrait of an airman by David Reed, a dogfight involving two First World War aircraft by Paul Weaver and the sketch by John Palmer, who according to the minutes 'had only arrived at twenty past seven and produced a very recognisable automotive, a great improvement on his sketch on Ladies' Night, may I say'. Ernest Woolford played *Stardust* on the new Yamaha Millennium piano, Terry Cleeve told the story of Quiet Night through the years, and just before everyone went home to bed to prepare for the real late night two days later, Bob Payne sang out the Savages' twentieth century with two sentimental songs from the 1960s, *What a Wonderful World* and *Try to Remember.* He even leaned in his trademark pose with his right arm resting on the new piano, a sure sign that the Yamaha was now conclusively part of the furniture. Seven days later, and '2000' was now the outlandish new date we were writing on our cheques, usually after we had crossed out '1999'. Would the Savages ever be the same again? President Anthony Carder was in the chair, the subject was *Ave atque Vale* – 'which he translated as Hail and Farewell for the uneducated members', Bongie's grandson John Eberle was among the chair-

Anthony Carder left, was the Savages' President as the twentieth century moved into the twenty-first. Above, Chairman for the last Wednesday evening of the twentieth century, Quiet Night on December 29 1999, was Grahame Spray.

man's supporters and there was 'an unusually large number of interruptions during the reading of the minutes, mostly from Grahame Spray but adroitly handled, as was to be expected, by your Hon. Sec.; following the usual protests they were signed by the chairman as being more or less a true record of the same...' Would life carry on as normal for the Tribe in the new century? Judging from this evidence – and the fact that on Founders' Night, 2000 the chair was taken by Geoffrey Ehlers, the son of the first Savage of them all – it most certainly would...

7
FAMOUS FACES

The first major non-artistic celebrity to be a Savages guest was Captain Robert Falcon Scott, who attended a house dinner at Brandon Cottage in April 1910 to help raise funds for the Antarctic expedition on which he would perish in a tragedy which is still a part of British lore nearly a century on. He set sail from Britain later in the year, and his reward from the Savages, apart from a most enjoyable evening, was five guineas. With this his team purchased a sleigh dog that was named Brandon and which, in Savages legend at least, survived longer than most in the desperate trek back from the Pole. It is interesting to reflect that the heroic explorer against whom all who have followed are measured and judged was reduced to scouring the country in the vital months leading up to his ordeal, scrambling for five guineas here in Bristol, six guineas there in Liverpool... One of his ice axes from that final journey still hangs on the Wigwam platform wall, along with others from expeditions led by Ernest Shackleton in 1908 and the Canadians in the Antarctic in 1913. These axes were bought by Fuller Eberle as part of a collection some years later, but there are more immediate mementoes produced by two of those who had been at dinner with him that evening, for Frank Barton and Charlie Thomas both presented the Savages with portraits of him in the months following his death. Barton's was a formal framed painting but Thomas's was one of his famous lightning caricatures, dashed off on the night and signed by the great man before he hurried off into the winter night on the next stage of his fund-raising tour. This is another story that all but spans the history of the Savages. In 1937 his son Peter, the future Sir Peter Scott of Slimbridge, spent an evening sketching as a guest artist at the Wigwam – and in October 2001 the wheel turned full circle. The Red Feathers had been on a sketching trip to the Wildfowl and Wetlands Trust beside the Severn in the Berkeley Vale, and as a result, Sir Peter's widow Lady Scott paid a visit to the Wigwam. She was interested in all she saw, as newcomers invariably are, but nothing intrigued her more than sight of that long-ago Wednesday night sketch, of which she had previously known nothing. Scott's great Norwegian rival Roald Amundsen was a later guest at the Wigwam, while a call for afternoon tea came in October 1953 when Sir Edmund Hillary and some of his Everest team were touring Britain in the wake of their first ascent of the mountain in the June of that year.

A superb memento of Bruce Bairnsfather's visit to the Wigwam, a large message of greeting to the Tribe as from the cartoonist's legendary character Old Bill.

Several names that mean little to us now caused a flutter of excitement at the time. Two years before Captain Scott's visit the special guest was Laurence Irving, the novelist and playwright son of Sir Henry. He read from Thomas Macaulay's account of the Civil War Battle of Naseby, and at least popularised the cult of recitation on Wednesday evenings. Wilfred Peake even went as far as crediting him with starting it, though there is ample evidence that prose and verse resounded around the Savages' meeting rooms from the very beginning. In 1914, six years after Irving's visit to the Wigwam, it was his unhappy fate to be one of the celebrity casualties of the *Empress of Ireland* disaster in the St Lawrence River; visiting the early Savages might have been a pleasurable experiece, but both he and Scott proved that it did not guarantee a long and danger-free life. Others who fared rather more cheerily were two of the most influential popular artists of the twentieth century – Bruce Bairnsfather, whose Old Bill soldier character raised a rare smile in the First World War and John Hassall, arguably the father of modern poster design with such classics as his skipping fisherman telling the world that Skegness Is So Bracing. Cartoonists in the Tribe such as Frank Stonelake and Charlie Thomas revered the work of these brilliant men, and their visits to Bristol were highly prized occasions; a large lightning sketch of Old Bill, dedicated to the Savages, remains one of the treasures of the Wigwam to this day.

Although not an artist, Fred J. Weatherly perfectly encapsulated the Savage spirit

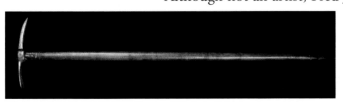

James Fuller Eberle presented a number of explorers' ice picks to the Wigwam, this being one of Captain Scott's from the tragic 1910-12 expedition.

in a double life that combined conventional worth to the community with boundless creative flair. A barrister and ultimately King's Counsel with a flourishing criminal law practice, he also found time to write some three thousand song lyrics and have fifteen hundred of them published. Not just any song lyrics, either. *Danny Boy* was one, and others were the First World War anthem *Roses of Picardy* and the Punch Night favourite *The Holy City*. These are the words that established him as a superstar around the world, but the Wurzels and TV commercials mean that his *Up from Somerset* – 'Oh, we'm come up from Somerset, where the cider apples grow' – is also still known by millions.

A good deal of folklore surrounds *Danny Boy,* which was of course set to the traditional *Londonderry Air.* Its musical score was first published in 1855 but it enjoyed an orchestral revival when the folklorist Percy Grainger reissued it in 1911. Weatherly had written the words with no tune in mind a year before that, and it was only in 1912, when his sister in America sent him sheet music of the tune, that the two were found to fit perfectly together. There is a theory that the haunting lyric – the little-heard second verse is particularly enigmatic – was based on Weatherly's premonition of his son Daniel's death in the trenches in the First World War. One thing that is definitely known is that Fred Weatherly never set foot in Ireland...

For the Portishead-born son of a country doctor, he was astonishingly well connected. As a private tutor after Oxford University, he counted the King of Siam among his pupils; Beatrix Potter's first published illustrations were to his verse *A Happy Pair;* he studied law under a son of Dickens; and through his collaboration with another giant of the drawing-room song, the Italian-born composer Francesco Paolo Tosti, he found himself entertaining Queen Victoria at her Diamond Jubilee party at Balmoral in 1897. Tosti, who taught the royal children music, was knighted in 1906. No such honour came Weatherly's way, but both Bath and Portishead remember him with house plaques and road names, while the Savages always took great pride in his achievements. He was granted life membership in 1925, four years before his death. Perhaps his ultimate Tribe moment, however, came at the Colston Hall on November 12 1914, when his jingoistic *Bravo, Bristol!,* with music by Ivor Novello, was sung at a Clara Butt concert by his fellow Savage Percy Heming, a relative of Dame Clara. It was all about the brave men of Bristol answering the call to arms, and sat well with his image as the 'People's Laureate'. 'I don't

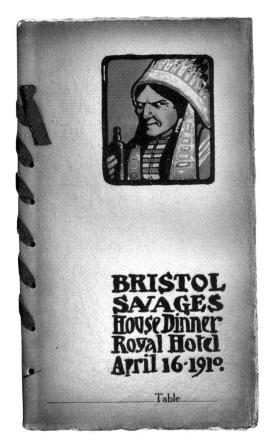

The House Dinner menu from April 1910, the event memorably attended by Captain Robert Falcon Scott.

Ohiyesha, Chief of the Sioux Tribe, who was a guest at the Wigwam in 1928.

Many members enjoyed rubbing shoulders with fellow Savage Walter Hammond.

claim to be a poet,' Weatherly once said. 'I don't pretend that my songs are literary; but they're songs of the people, and that's enough for me. People love to sing them. The heart of the people is still simple and healthy and sound.' Blue Feathers certainly loved to sing them; for years Wednesday night gatherings lapped up Brother Savage Fred Weatherly's world-famous ballads with a special sense of pride, and as we have noted, Punch Night would not be the same without *The Holy City*. A signed photograph of him still hangs to the left of the platform, while a very fine portrait by George Swaish was presented to the City Museum and Art Gallery in 1927 and is still part of its collection. Finally, let us remind ourselves that not all Fred Weatherly's verses were as sombre in tone as *Danny Boy* or *The Holy City*. This is *Salve*, hand written in a Savages scrapbook in 1925 and dusted down by Entertainment Warden Chris Torpy for *A Century of Savage Verse*, published late in 2003:

Happy the man, who, when he's young,

Keeps honest heart and kindly tongue;

And happy too in middle age —

If he has friends for heritage;

But happiest he, beneath time's ravages,

Who finds a welcome from the Savages !

On March 15 1928 those Savages welcomed the Chief of the Sioux Tribe, Ohiyesha, to the Wigwam. On the wall of the Studio is a splendid photograph of the gathering, with Ohiyesha resplendent in feathered head-dress and a dove-grey doeskin suit with all due fringes and adornments. He was apparently seventy years old, but does not look it. Also on the wall is a full-length portrait of the chief in profile, reminiscent of the sepia cards of Red Shirt and his men that Buffalo Bill would have been selling to the crowds up on Horfield Common near-ly forty years earlier. It spoils the effect only slightly to know that on less obvious view in the Wigwam is another photograph of the gathering, a happy scene, but one marred for the romantic by the fact that this time the chief is in civvies and looks like nothing other than an Identikit American businessman of his day – and one, moreover, who was better known as Dr Charles Eastman in the real world.

The Prince of Wales, the future Edward VIII, had lunch in the Great Oak Room at Red Lodge on November 6 1934 and went on to spend two hours with the Savages, 'considerably longer than the schedule of his visit provided'. He was in Bristol primarily to inspect the Unemployed Welfare Centre – it was five years since he had famously declared that 'something must be done' about the plight of Depression-hit working men and their families – but his lunch appointment was clearly a welcome relief. It was one of the years in which the Lord Mayor was a Savage – F. C. Luke in this instance – so the Prince was in good company. In the Wigwam he was 'anxious to have many things explained'.

The Bristol-born concert pianist Joseph Cooper became a member in June 1951, decades before he became a familiar face through the television show *Face the Music*. He was invited 'in view of his eminence in the world of music and his visits to the Wigwam as a guest, when he has most generously played for us', and within hours of receiving the summons, he wrote back to Frank Mole: 'Your letter touched me very deeply. There is nothing I can think of that would give me more pleasure than to become an hon. member of the Savages... I always enjoy my visits... apart from the delightful friendliness and informality, it is without doubt the finest audience in the world!' Cooper had first played at the Wigwam during the early part of the Second World War, when he visited as part of a party from the B.B.C.; a section of the corporation had been devolved to Bristol until it was realised somewhat belatedly that a large industrial city in the South of England with extensive docks, major aircraft works and important rail links was not the ideal refuge for its staff. It later moved on to Bangor in North Wales, which proved a rather more sensible option.

The B.B.C. was just one factor that brought a stream of familiar faces to the Wigwam in the wartime years, with Sir Adrian Boult's and Sir Walford Davies's among the most notable. Sir Adrian attended a Wednesday evening meeting and returned with the B.B.C. Orchestra in June to perform a public concert in aid of the Red Cross in the Red Lodge garden; Walford Davies was one of music's most gifted communicators of the twentieth century and was justly hailed as such by the time of his visit in the 1939-40 session. His zeal as a performer and lecturer and his inspired

use of broadcasting had done more than perhaps anything else to promote the glories of European instrumental, orchestral and choral music in Britain. On not quite such a rarified plane but still a classical musical giant of his day was the Russian concert pianist Benno Moiseivitch, who had settled in London and was so much at home there that he was a member of the Savage Club. He came along to the Wigwam one Wednesday night in the 1942-43 session with fellow members of the London Symphony Quartet, and it is hard to imagine that it was not the Savage-Savages link that drew him there. Fashions in musical taste come and go, but there are still music lovers around who admire Moiseivitch greatly for his interpretation of Chopin and the Russian Romantics, and he is said to have performed quite brilliantly when he was 'eventually persuaded' to play that night. After the National Anthem he stayed on to lead a sing-song around the piano – the high or low point of which, according to one's sensibilities, was Blue Feather Sidney Hobbs's famous rude song concerning an elephant's anatomy. The virtuoso, who came back for more in the following session, signed a note to confirm this unusual teaming of talents – and needless to say, it is in the Wigwam still. There are also fading memories of his later visit, in April 1944, when 'Benno Moist Savage' struck up the *Volga Boat Song* and even improvised a parody striptease in the key of A (furnished) flat. He obviously felt comfortable and at home with the Tribe.

Queen Mary looked in one afternoon when she was living at Badminton, where she spent a good deal of the war with her niece the Duchess of Beaufort and the tenth Duke, the master foxhunter who was a Savage like his father before him. During her stay in the West Country, a multitude of affectionate stories grew up around the old queen. One was that she would take workers on the estate out on war economy-minded logging parties, chopping down the Duke's beloved trees for firewood. Another was that when she visited other stately homes in the area, as quite naturally she would, she would be profuse in her praise of this piece of furniture or that oriental vase to the extent that the owners felt obliged to offer it to her, however half-heartedly. The gallant Savages do not record whether or not this was the case on her conducted tour of the Wigwam with H. E. Roslyn, but she was certainly full of knowledge and enthusiasm about what she saw. What she did get was a set of Red Lodge postcards and, in the post some time later, two copies of *Grouse* magazine, sent on to her by Donald Hughes, which contained Rossy's account of the visit and respectful portraits of her and the duchess. In reply, he received the gift of a tapestry, which is now in the City Museum, and a 'very appreciative' letter from her secretary. No doubt they were just

Death or glory? The spectacle of war is encapsulated in the cavalry charge scene by current Red Feather and immediate Past President David Reed, which now hangs in the Wigwam.

what she had always wanted. Dated Spring 1940, it was the last issue of *Grouse* before its revival in 1991 by John Anstee, and it was clear that Rossy had greatly enjoyed showing the royal party around. 'In the Veterans' Room there is a print of a picture by Sir John Gilbert R.A. showing Queen Victoria receiving wounded soldiers from the Crimea.' he wrote. 'Upon looking at it Her Majesty remarked "We have the original in Windsor Castle". Then, turning to the duchess, she said: "You have never seen it, because it hangs on a back staircase".' Such were the queen's impeccable manners, everyone accepted that any patronising undertone to this remark was entirely accidental. Rossy also found himself accompanying the Crown Prince of Ethiopia around Savages HQ, his father Emperor Haile Selassie, King of Kings, Lion of Judah, being in exile in Bath. In 1941 British troops liberated Ethiopia from Italian rule and the two returned home, but there was no fairytale ending. When the prince's chance to rule eventually came, in 1974, it was as no more than the puppet of army officers who deposed his father after the country had fallen into chaos. Reading about this, so long after the event, those with long memories at the Wigwam recalled Roslyn's story of the polite and nervous young man he had shown around that day.

There had been hopes in the 1948-49 session of welcoming Winston Churchill, licking his wounds in opposition after Labour's victory in the 1945 general election, to be guest of honour at the annual dinner. Not for the last time hope exceeded reality, and it was eventually J. E. Barton, a former headmaster of Bristol Grammar School, who found himself honoured. At the annual dinner for the following session, 1949-50, the special guest was George Baker, Secretary of the Savage Club in London and a singer best known for his nursery rhymes on *Listen with Mother;* and in 1950-51 the spotlight fell on Covent Garden opera singer and veteran Savage Percy Heming, filling the breach after Sir Thomas Beecham had declined. The dinner was in Bristol's Festival of Britain Fortnight, on July 10, and the committee warmed to the idea of inviting Sir Thomas to be their guest, as he would be conducting in the

John Gielgud visited the Wigwam in 1943 and discovered there several mementoes of his forebears in the Terry family.

Colston Hall the night before. They were quite optimistic about the prospect: 'It was considered likely that he would come, and Brother Savage Charles Lockier would use his very considerable influence,' it was recorded on March 16. Eventually, however, 'important engagements in London' put an end to that particular dream.

Nevertheless, in the middle years of the twentieth century, a host of prominent names from the world of theatre and music did perform or sing for not even their supper at the Wigwam, and the reason they were there truly was Charles Lockier, an impresario who staged major concerts at both the Hippodrome and Colston Hall and did not find it hard to lure the stars up the hill for an hour or two after their performances as an alternative to killing time in some drab hotel room. If nothing else, this arrangement made for some extremely late nights, and much fretting about last buses and anxious spouses. In 1943 John Gielgud called in after appearing at the

Hippodrome, gossipy as ever, and told many members something that even they did not know about the Tribe: that it possesses portraits and letters of his great-grandfather Ben Terry, of the legendary theatrical dynasty, and his grandmother Kate, elder sister of Helen. All had been bequeathed to the Savages by Gielgud's (non-Savage) uncle Fred Terry, and they can be seen in the Blue Room still. Other performers in the Lockier years included the New London Orchestra, Themeli, the blind Greek pianist, members of the Rome Opera Company, Donald Adams of D'Oyly Carte Opera, who was later made an honorary member, the choir of St Paul's Cathedral, Jack Train and the Hippodrome panto cast, the percussionist James Blades, who like Joseph Cooper became a television face late in his career – and Sir John Barbirolli, twice in quick succession in around 1960, first with members of the Manchester wind ensemble the Paragon Orchestra, and second with a quintet from his beloved Hallé. Sir John was another who was made an Honorary Blue Feather, and his popping into and out of the Wigwam said much about the stardust Charles Lockier was able to sprinkle for a while. There are happy memories of a young John Ogdon in around 1960, fresh from his breakthrough triumph in the world Liszt competition in Moscow and in the highest echelon of concert pianists until mental illness gnawed away at his brilliance and all too soon ended his life. He shambled on to the platform, a great, shy bear of a man with a Manchester accent, and set the Savages gasping. They instantly made him an Honorary Blue Feather and when he reappeared later in the session, to an even more rapturous reception, it was with his feather firmly in place. An earlier memory to cherish was the December Friday afternoon in 1949 when the London-born ballet dancer Alicia Markova called in with her long-time dancing partner Anton Dolin and signed a ballet shoe 'To the Savages'. On the previous Wednesday Dolin had performed at the Wigwam with some of his company's male dancers, which struck a number of members as being akin to asking Fred Astaire along on the proviso that he did not bring Ginger Rogers. There are some art forms that adapt to the Wigwam's all-male rule more happily than others, and ballet is not one of them.

The peerless Gloucestershire and England batsman Walter Hammond was elected a Green Feather in 1935 and taken off the books through non-payment of his subscription in January 1953, by which time he had emigrated to his second wife Sybil's home city of Durban, South Africa. Never a man abounding in bonhomie, he was an unlikely Savage in many ways, but Secretary H. E. Roslyn was a committee man at Gloucestershire, and some of what he told the county's star player began to make sense to him. Hammond had learned to prize his off-the-field connections, not least after he had become England captain and had felt constrained by the Establishment to turn amateur. He began to earn his bread-and-butter in the Bristol motor trade, and though his job description tended to be vague, the thrust of it was that his employers wanted to sell cars or tyres and there was no shortage of men who would take pride in buying them through 'my pal Wally'. Marsham Tyres, his last employers in Bristol, were shocked when he resigned on the same day as their sales manager, with whom he had hatched plans to set up in business in South Africa. Indeed, he left behind him a string of unhappy people far more enmeshed in his complex world than the Bristol Savages, and his emigration gave him a welcome chance to wipe the slate clean. In his defence, his wife was desperately depressed in grey, austerity Britain, and South Africa must have beckoned the couple and their young children like a land of milk and honey.

There is little in the Savages' records that tells of Walter Hammond's impact on the club, though years later a fellow member recalled: 'At the end of one evening, I had almost to carry him up the flight of stairs from the Wigwam'. Evidently he had his moments of conviviality, though celebrities known for liking a drink are always apt to fall prey to this kind of reminiscence; even today you will not find an elderly man in Swansea who is not owed a beer by Dylan Thomas, or a Second World War Guardsman who did not help an inebriated Winston Churchill up to bed in his quarters in the Admiralty.

The Queen's is always an impressive name to drop, and although she has never visited the Savages, denizens of the Wigwam have visited her. That was on an April evening in 1957 when six Blue Feathers went to entertain a formidable array of royals while they were staying with enthusiastic Savage the Duke of Beaufort during the Badminton Horse Trials. It was at fairly short notice, but all the team knew their material well. Harold Thomas was the accompanist, Maurice Grove compered, Sidney Burchall sang an elephant song which was presumably a good deal cleaner than Sidney Hobbs's with Moiseivitch, there were more cheerful songs from Dick Foweraker, Alan Nicholas was *A Wandering Minstrel* and Ellard Hughes spun some old nonsense about the Kangaroceros, which escaped from Bristol Zoo but was chased back to its cage

A Green Feather turned Blue: The tenth Duke of Beaufort was a master on the hunting horn.

By royal command: In April 1957 six Blue Feathers travelled to Badminton to present a programme of entertainment to the Queen and her party, who were staying with their fellow Savage the Duke of Beaufort. From left to right, Maurice Grove, Dick Foweraker, Alan Nicholas, Harold Thomas, Sidney Burchall and Ellard Hughes.

with full view-halloo by the Duke and his hounds. It was surreal for the Savages, grouped around the piano, to be introduced to the Queen, Prince Philip, the Queen Mother and Princess Margaret as they entered the room, but all was relaxed enough at the end when sandwiches and drinks were brought in and the party sat around talking for a good hour. It was then that the thirty-one-year-old Queen, who regarded 'Master and Mary' as surrogate parents, made her famous suggestion that the Duke should be a Blue Feather as well as a Green, since he was a dab hand at the hunting horn. Life does not always move quickly in Savages circles but on Cricket Night in March 1960, with the Duke of Beaufort in the chair for his sixtieth birthday, he duly presented a recital of calls on his horn and was awarded his Blue Feather in a special holder in which there was also room for the Green. He completed the set in 1981, very shortly before his death, when he was created Patron and was given a unique badge holding all three feathers. Princess Margaret already had a grasp of Savages lore before the Badminton concert, having been invited to lunch at the Wigwam by the Lord Mayor in March 1949. Again, her escort the Duke of Beaufort felt very much on home ground, and he called in President Ralph Brentnall to answer her questions about this extraordinary room.

A year before the Badminton concert – on April 3 1956, to be exact – the Wednesday night guests included a jazz trio that numbered Mr. Roger Bennett (clarinet). Maybe the B.B.C. Radio Bristol presenter should pencil in a fiftieth

The Rev. Louis Ward has been a Savage since 1934, and there is a strong mid-twentieth-century feel about the finest of his work. This canvas of the River Avon and Clifton Suspension Bridge is typical of his output around fifty years ago.

anniversary return visit with his regular musical partners in crime the Blue Notes in 2006, when their erstwhile double bass man Michael Long would doubtless be happy to lend them a hand. An even more eyebrow-raising interlude came when the Twelfth Night gathering of 1958 featured a skiffle sextet which included a highly unlikely Louis Ward and Harold Packer in its line-up. Louis continued to spring surprises, none more so than in the mid-1970s when he took holy orders. Word had got out that he was a little apprehensive about the reception he would get the first time he showed up at the Studio in his clerical collar, but he need not have worried. When he walked in, everyone else was wearing one, too. Another skiffler was the late Roy Mickleburgh, an avid collector of and national authority on pianos, musical boxes, automata and other forms of mechanical music. Several of his pianos, including a number of Bristol products, form an absorbing display at the City Museum, while the dispersal of his mechanical instruments at auction brought in enthusiasts from far and wide.

Of all the Blue Feathers who have entertained in recent years, the diminutive Bristol-based concert and recording pianist Allan Schiller is unique in enjoying an international reputation. He first found fame when he made a sensational debut with the Hallé Orchestra under Sir John Barbirolli at the age of ten, and while still in his teens he made his first appearances at the Promenade Concerts and the Edinburgh Festival. In his native Leeds he studied with Fanny Waterman, founder of the city's International Piano Competition, and after spending two years with Denis Matthews, one of the most stylish Mozart players of his day, he became the first British pianist to win a scholarship to the Moscow Conservatoire. Now Allan has played with every major U.K. orchestra and has toured widely in the United States, South Africa, the former Soviet Union and Europe. His fame for playing Mozart brought him invitations to Salzburg and Cape Town to take part in the commemorations of the two hundredth anniversary of the composer's death in 1991, while closer to home he famously performed all his idol's solo piano works in a single day to raise funds for the Bristol Cancer Help Centre.

Former Green and Blue Feather Roy Mickleburgh, avid collector of musical instruments, as seen by Harold Packer.

'Allan Schiller has the rare quality of playing the piano in the vocal way, which was treasured by all the great composers and, until recent years, by the vast majority of pianists,' says a critic. 'Instead of hitting the keyboard, he coaxes sound from it in such a way as to make one forget the piano is a percussive instrument whose sound is forever dying. Such skills are highly valued.' They certainly are by the Savages. Allan might play to larger audiences than the Wednesday night turnout at the Wigwam, and he will enjoy many a better pay night; for instance,

shortly after his last performance of 2003 there, in late November, he and his wife were embarking on three successive Caribbean cruises aboard luxury liners over Christmas and New Year, at which he would be playing for his supper on just two evenings a week. 'He's there to add that touch of clarse,' a friend joked. Allan knows the largely American audiences love him – but nowhere in the world does a group of people admire and appreciate him more than the Tribe that gathers off Park Row.

Masterly Blue Feather: Allan Schiller's skills as a concert pianist have taken him all over the world as well as making him a greatly welcomed performer at the Wigwam.

8

TREASURES OF THE WIGWAM

To list all that is to be found at the Wigwam would call for a book much longer than this, as well as an encyclopaedic knowledge of some of the most obscure and arcane artefacts known to man. The Tribe has been lucky to have enjoyed the services of a succession of dedicated keepers of its treasures, none more so than H. E. Roslyn, Frank Mole and Terry Cleeve, but over the years even they have had to shake their heads occasionally and admit to some bafflement over the exact nature of an artefact, especially when it comes to tribal weaponry and trophies.

Today, the Secretary John Cleverdon, a dealer in paintings for much of his working life, takes great delight in what he sees around him at Park Row. There is a strange intimacy about painters coming together as the Savages have done, combining the social with the artistic. In any group of people, a hundred years is a long time, and makes an anniversary well worth celebrating; but when it comes to creating something as abiding as art, it is really not so very long at all, and the Ehlers and Wilde Parsons, the Ernest Boards and Bartram Hiles who seem increasingly receding figures in written history still assert themselves vigorously on the walls of the Wigwam, still at the heart of and central to the thinking of the Tribe.

One of the most prominent paintings in the Bongie Room is *The Cherry Orchard, Combe Dingle,* by Matthew Hale, presented to the Savages in 1922. It harks back not only to one of the most prominent early members but to a part of Bristol which was central to the city's painting community from the eighteenth century, and continued to be so to the interconnected and fluctuating groupings of artists which eventually led to the Savages. It is some distance away in spirit from the big Wilde Parsons canvas in the corridor, showing a seventeeth-century sea battle between *The Honour of Bristol* and *The Angel Gabriel.* Another striking Wilde Parsons ship hangs in the Wigwam, a painting of Admiral Lord Rodney's flagship *The Formidable* in full sail. This vessel has particular links with the region, since she ended her days in the Bristol Channel as the forerunner of the Portishead Nautical School.

Bro. Savage Terry Cleeve

John Collins' view of Terry Cleeve with the "tabernacle" that protected the Wigwam's treasures during the early 1990s.

The two most striking images left to the Tribe by Bartram Hiles, which now hang on either side of the Studio doors. The character on the right strikes observers as a most unlikely looking Indian, but his true identity now seems to be lost in time.

There is much American Indian activity around the Studio doors, both in the corridor and in the entry to Red Lodge. Ernest Board's iconic *Three Muses* hangs here, as does his sensitive pastel study of an Indian's head, and the entrance to the Studio itself is flanked by two portraits of chiefs by Bartram Hiles, panels which originally adorned a sideboard. One looks every inch the noble savage, but the other has distinctly European features and is doubtless based on one of Hiles's friends; or even an enemy, maybe, since it is not a particularly flattering piece of work. Also in this corner is one of Frank Stonelake's favourite horse portraits, of a Shire mare with its foal. A companion piece hangs on the stairs to the Upper Studio while two more satisfying Stonelake studies of horses, *The Harrow* and another of two teams of three harrowing and planting, are rightfully well displayed in the Wigwam. Both works honour

Clifford Hanney was one of the most talented Red Feathers of the middle years of the twentieth century. This snow scene of Cumberland Basin hangs in the Wigwam and is ranked by experts among the most satisfying paintings on show.

the sheer controlled strength of the animals, which Stonelake never tired of portraying. His fellow Savages used to rib him gently about somehow turning every Wednesday night sketch back to horses, but his best work went beyond the mere knack of painting them well. To bring us up to date, hanging beside Stonelake's Shire horses and Board's pastel is a 3-D panel of Indians' heads by Geoff Molyneux, created for the Savages' centenary and bought for the Tribe.

On the stairs down to the Wigwam is an eclectic display. There is a fanciful A. C.

Eric Craddy, President on three occasions and a prolific cigarette card designer through his pre-war work with Mardon, Son and Hall, is rightly recalled in the Wigwam through this fine painting of the sailing ship Pamir *seen against the light.*

Fare account of the Bristol Great House of 1574, Frank Shipsides' memento of the oak trees planted on Brandon Hill in 1973, a Board fantasy based on a knighting by Elizabeth I and Louis Ward's cheerful portrait of the tenth Duke of Beaufort, a proud Savage like his father before him, in the regalia of Master of the Horse.

Into the Wigwam and working clockwise, one of the first images on view is Herbert Truman's impression of this very room, more on which in the next chapter. Close by, we are back among the founder members with a stream painting by Ernest

BUTLER,
THE
"Palate" TICKLER

Stanley Anderson 1908

A courtly George Butler in a detailed caricature by Stanley Anderson.

Ehlers first exhibited in 1912 and a study of Kelston Hill by Henry Stacy; moving on, we discover a snowy scene looking down from Brandon Hill by Clifford Hanney, a prolific painter who joined the Tribe in 1951. Many of his works have been at auction in Bristol and surrounds in recent years after the dispersal of the contents of his studio following his death. This is one of his very finest, and a discerning art critic in the city has been heard to say that if he were given the choice of any one painting in the Wigwam, it would be this one.

Caricatures abound in this corner – C. F. W. Dening as a domestic architect and Charles Kelsey as a dentist, both by Charlie Thomas and several by Harold Packer, including Ernest Bibbing, George Heming, Colston Waite and one of the Tribe's singing quartets. Packer has even depicted himself here, the well known sketch of him as an ancient but amiable-looking chap on two walking sticks. Back to more serious work, John Whitlock Codner has captured many of the characteristics of Donald Hughes in a good portrait, there is one of Eric Craddy's finest, the sailing ship *Pamir* seen against the light, and Hamish Milne makes his mark with a floral study. Also to be seen on this side of the room are works by Bill Laird, Sir Stanley Anderson, A. J. Heaney, 'Curly' Toope, with an atmospheric *November Mist with Sheep,* Herbert Helps with a brave with a kayak beside a lake and a clutch of modern painters in a very satisfying grouping – Brian Lancaster, David Reed, Roy Barber, Derek Joynson and Reg Batterbury.

The Fuller Eberle portrait by George Swaish dominates the walls around the President's desk, but Bongie is in good company, for all the most distinguished office holders in the Tribe's history are commemorated here; the Ehlers portrait is by John Codner. There is a further array of caricatures here, including yet another work that goes back to the roots of the club, a 1908 impression of George Butler 'the palate tickler' by Stanley Anderson. Dening, Arnold Robinson, Swaish, Stuart Richardson, Rossy,

Bristol street scene painter A. C. Fare seen in a different role by Charlie Thomas.

Brooke Branwhite, Padlock, Board, Fare, Stonelake, Wilde Parsons, Ehlers, Bush... all are depicted with wit and affection, pillars of the Tribe honoured in the most unstuffy of ways. The caricatures also set the records straight in some instances. For instance, some of today's Savages might imagine that 'Curly' Toope was so named simply as a play on 'Curly Top', or maybe even because he was bald. The documentary evidence does not lie: 'Curly' Toope was most definitely curly. A. J. Heaney also boasted a shock of hair, and while the record books tell us that Lowry Lewis was an old stager among the founder members, they do not tell the story nearly as graphically as his cartoon. Working back towards the doors, Bartram Hiles' *In Sunshine and In Shade* is kept company by a bleak seascape of 1910 by Arthur Wilde Parsons and H. C. Guyatt's lake scene. After this, caricatures again predominate, and while the work of Harold Packer is again very much in evidence, so is that of the current Mark Blackmore and John Collins. Again, those portrayed read like a who's who of Savages, this time over the past fifty years: Louis Ward, the Garcias, Norman Morgan, Alfred Moores, Rex Hopes, Frank Shipsides, Gordon Jones, Walter Skeens, Phil Woodland, Ralph Egarr, Terry Cleeve, Ken Matthews, Charles MacInnes, John F. C. Bedford *et al*.

John Bedford, Honorary Secretary in the years around 1980, viewed by Harold Packer.

Dominating the furnishings of the Wigwam are three towering fireplaces. To the left on entering is the most highly regarded of them, brought from Canynges' House in Redcliff Street by Life Green Feather Eddie Welch and with its lower part dating from around 1350. It was commissioned for his banqueting hall by William Canynges the Younger, a generous benefactor of St Mary Redcliffe, and was well established there when the family entertained Edward IV in 1461. The two figures at hearth level, showing Canynges in his roles of both merchant and Dean of Westbury-on-Trym, are of a later date, as is the spectacular upper part of the fireplace. This dates from the mid-seventeenth century and carries an elaborately carved account of the judgment of Solomon, who sits omnipotent in the centre. Somehow, Adam and Eve have also strayed into the picture, or at least Adam has, Eve's recessed panel having been vacated. She was apparently far too risqué for some previous owners' tastes, long before the fireplace found its way to the mannish Wigwam.

On the platform, as we have noted, the stone fireplace is seventeeth-century and bears the arms, in true heraldic colours, of the Guild of Bakers, along with the legend

The Guild of Bakers' fireplace on the platform of the Wigwam dates from the seventeenth century and bears the words that have become the Savages' grace, "Prais God For All".

Prais God For All. It came from the long-gone Goat in Armour Inn on Broad Quay, which is taken once to have been the residence of the master of the guild. The third fireplace, to the right on entering the room, dates from much the same period as this one and is again in carved stone with armorial bearings. It came from a house on St Michael's Hill which belonged to Richard Stubbs, a wine merchant who was Sheriff of Bristol in 1671; a vine decoration confirms its owner's profession. By tradition, the moose's head hanging above this fireplace is the finest specimen in existence in Europe, if not in the world, but then again, there was a time when superlatives flowed more freely than they do now. The snowshoes are said to have belonged to the man who shot the beast, but whose unhappy lot it is to appear as if he might well have been eaten by it, leaving behind only his oversized footwear.

The cabinets to the left of the platform and on it contain glassware and china, silver and pewter, some pieces of intrinsic worth and others of curiosity value. A tall bottle contains rum looted from the Mansion House before it was torched in the Bristol Riots of 1831; a silver shaving tray is designed to be held by a footman under his master's chin to save him from damaging his cravat with soap; punch dispensers work through a system of trapping and releasing air in thumb holes, rather in the manner of puzzle jugs. These are intriguing and amusing exhibits, but in the cabinets containing the Dixon and Strachan collections there are also choice pieces of glassware, including Bristol blue, which go back some three hundred years.

Weaponry and armour hang heavy on the walls, prompting Wyn Calvin, the comedian who has recently been elected an Honorary Life Member, to glance around in mock awe and declare the Wigwam 'your arsenal'. It comes literally from every corner of the world. There are kukris, African spears, Malaysian krees knives in wooden scabbards, European bayonets, Arab and oriental swords, a Cromwellian helmet and spurs, rifles from Imperial Russia and the American Civil War, a shield from Borneo with human hair attached. Less threatening tribal ware includes cooking utensils, drums and tom-toms and such bizarre souvenirs as European wine bottles covered in skin by African tribesmen...

Eclectic is the only word to describe much else that is on show. Mementoes range from a tomahawk owned by Chief Rain-in-the-Face, who was involved in the fighting at Custer's last stand, to a walking stick that had belonged to Haydn, with bars of music carved into its handle; from a Mexican saddle to an African harp gourd; from the Wills magnate Lord Winterstoke's ram's head snuff coaster to a Crimean war lantern identical to the one immortalised by Florence Nightingale. It is treasures such as these, crowding together to create an impression of oddity and outlandishness maybe greater than the sum of its parts, that makes a visit to the Wigwam an abidingly rich experience. And for a group of men with tradition at heart, it is endlessly absorbing to look at photographs of the earliest members of the Tribe surrounded by paintings, mementoes and even such simple nuts and bolts of life as wooden chairs, which are still instantly identifiable today.

Two glimpses of the contents of the cabinets to the left of the platform, which contain glassware, china, silver and pewter, with some pieces of intrinsic worth and others of curiosity value. Some items of glass, including Bristol blue, go back more than three hundred years.

Right, The Canynges fireplace once graced the family's great house in Redcliff Street and its lower part was in situ more than a century before Edward IV dined there in 1461. The upper part dates from the mid-seventeenth century with a scene of the judgement of Solomon as its central feature.

9

POST-WAR RECOVERY

The end of the Second World War brought about domestic changes which served as a reminder that while for most involved in the Savages the Red Lodge was a building to be walked through once a week, for others it meant a great deal more. To H. E. Roslyn, Secretary since 1914, it had been quite simply home, as it had for the housekeeper, Miss Emily Sullivan. Of all the stories of time-warp longevity that are sprinkled throughout the Savages' history, even the present-day likes of Louis Ward (1934) and John Codner and Eric Craddy (1937) can scarcely hold a light to Miss Sullivan. Mary Carpenter had been dead for less than a decade when she arrived to help at the reformatory at the Red Lodge in 1886, and she was a veteran of more than thirty years' service when the institution closed in 1917. In 1920 she was back as the Savages' caretaker, and in her later years she acted as housekeeper to H. E. Roslyn until his death. As early as March 1945 'long tradition and the rule of the Savages were broken' when she was invited on to the platform on a Wednesday evening in honour of her twenty-five years of service to the club and nearly seventy in residence at Red Lodge. Her gifts included War Savings Certificates, a cheque and best of all, a brooch made by Frank Mole in the style of the turquoise matrix in the Lady's Chain. She retired in October 1956 along with her niece, Miss Richards, who had worked alongside her for many years, and in the final years of her life the Tribe took to treating her as something of a national treasure; when in 1964 she was given an eviction order from the city council, the Savages agreed to pay her rent in lieu of the hundred-pounds-per-year pension it had previously provided for her. In the late 1960s, by this time well into her nineties, she was still attending the annual exhibition and 'carrying her years almost as a woman of seventy'. She died during the course of the 1973-74 session, a few weeks before her hundredth birthday. Her portrait still hangs above the stairs to the Upper Studio.

Rossy, who had built up an encyclopaedic knowledge of the house and the treasures of the Wigwam, stepped down midway through session 1944-45 and spent his last two years in a nursing home before dying at the beginning of January in the hideously cold winter of 1947. The war years had taken a considerable toll on him, not least in arranging firewatching duties and overseeing the extra use of the Wigwam

A memory of Doris and Ernie Trott, seen on the right of this picture with John Broadbelt and Mervyn Evans in the early stages of clearing the Wigwam for the great roof restoration of 1992.

for war work. For a time his body 'lay in state' in the Red Lodge Reception Room, and a hundred pound legacy he left the Tribe was put to commissioning the painting of the Wigwam by Herbert Truman which now serves as his memorial. It was a time when Truman was at his peak with his views of Bristol and this one proved a popular piece of work, with five hundred reproductions produced to further remind members of Rossy's forty years' service. The good news in this centenary year is that a number of these have recently been rediscovered and made available to members.

Frank Mole succeeded Rossy as Secretary in time for the tortured negotiations over the house's changeover to city council control, and in the summer of 1948 he expressed an interest in living in it as Roslyn had done. For some reason it was three years before his request was granted and he technically became a lodger of Ernest and Doris Trott, the caretakers, 'for as long as he was the Honorary Secretary of Bristol

Professional window dresser and lover of the performing arts, Rex Hopes always had an eye for the spectacular. This is his 1955 two-hour sketch on the subject The Yellow.

Savages'. The house was open to the public on Wednesdays and Saturdays and Frank took extremely seriously the, to him, very pleasant task of showing visitors around. He wrote the city council long letters detailing his public relations experiences of the previous weeks, and was particularly keen to introduce the delights of the Red Lodge to children and teenagers from Bristol's inner-city areas and rapidly expanding council estates. Both Miss Sullivan and Mrs Trott are remembered in the Centenary Mural, incidentally, the former through a reproduction of her portrait and the latter selling Remembrance Day poppies, as she did for many years. She is also remembered for her hard work in making the cooked lunches on the last Friday of the month.

As life settled down again after the war and men returned to their jobs, a strong pattern that emerged within the Savages was the considerable presence of artists, lithographic artists and other workers from Bristol's large printing companies. Mardon,

Son and Hall, with Imperial Tobacco its chief client, was the dominant force, but E. S. and A. Robinson of Redcliff Street was another steady supplier of Savage talent, and there were many other smaller companies making a contribution at a time when Bristol was a commercial printing centre second only to Watford. Among those who worked or had worked at Mardon's, with the year in which they joined the Savages, were R. B. Hooper-Jones (who also worked at Robinson's) and Louis Ward (1934), Harold Packer and A. J. Wilson (1936), Eric Craddy (1937), Frank Duffield, Alan Durman, John Keenan and Alfred Moores (1946), Ken Cooke (1947), Brian Lancaster (1968), Frank Shipsides (1969), John Palmer (1971), Peter Harrison (1972) and Roy Barber (1983). Robinson's men included Ernest Andrews (1945) and his son Peter (1952), Edwin Penny (1957) and Michael Long (1971) – not to mention, among other non-Red Feather members, the current Secretary John Cleverdon – but the real pioneers of the trend, Savages with strong links with the earliest times, were Herbert Helps, a member of the

Rex Hopes as seen in 1939 in a two-hour sketch on the topic Flamboyant *by John Codner, who for a time styled himself Whitlock to differentiate from his father.*

Tribe from 1911 and again a servant of both Robinson's and Mardon's, and Ernest Godding, Reginald Bush's son-in-law, a Mardon's artist and a Savage by 1927. Dennis Lewis, a night-school colleague of Edwin Penny, learned his trade at another company, Bennett Brothers of Kingswood, and along with many other Savages went on to flourish in smaller studios and advertising agencies. He was with Ford Advertising, which had stemmed from the distinguished printers A. W. Ford, at a time of rapid expansion for the company, and at one time Edwin Penny, Peter Harrison, Brian Lancaster, Bernard Hawkins and Ken Cooke all worked in the studio there with him, while Louis Ward was a busy freelance. No wonder the art teachers and architects who made up most of the rest of the Red Feathers of the 1960s thought they had walked in on a Ford design meeting on some Wednesday evenings. Francis Greenacre, the art historian and critic, has a firm view on the importance of those Mardon's and

Time marches on: With his eye for humour undimmed, this is how Harold Packer saw himself towards the end of his life.

Robinson's years. 'The continued vitality of the society through the 1930s, '40s and '50s, when provincial museums and art galleries were struggling, as were academies such as the Royal West of England, was undoubtedly due to the large number of Red Feathers who were working as commercial artists in Bristol's strong packaging, printing and tobacco industries,' he says. 'Today, with those industries in such sharp decline, the artist members are again largely self-employed or in education. Significantly, they have recently and wisely betrayed one the society's traditions: they now sketch not only from imagination but also from the model in life classes. Almost all good artists return to the model. Today's equivalents of such early members as the marine artist Arthur Wilde Parsons or the excellent head of the municipal art school, Reginald Bush, will soon see the light, recognise the inadequacies of their own art school education, swallow their misplaced pride and seek to join the fold.' In fact life classes were first held in Brandon Cottage in 1912 and have been held intermittently throughout the years; Francis Greenacre voiced sentiments very similar to the above when he opened the Annual Exhibition of 2001, as a result of which, as he points out, life classes did indeed begin again. The indisposition of Michael Rummings, who was the chief figure behind the revival, has meant that they are not currently being held, but it is certain that they are not gone forever.

The first Green Feather Supper was held in November 1956 and has never missed a year since then. The Tribe has among its souvenirs commemorative menus illustrated by Alfred Moores, colourful and elaborate fold-outs very much in the spirit of the pop-up children's books that were popular at the time; not that the skimpily dressed can-can girl who sprang out of the very first one was anything for the kiddies.

The menu over the years rarely strays significantly from green pea soup, boiled beef and carrots and Stilton, the latter being ushered in with all the pomp of the punch on Punch Night with perhaps a little to spare. In place of *Good King Wenceslas* there is a version singing the praises of *Cheese, Cheese* to the tune of *The Quartermaster's Store* – wafting on the breeze, humming like the beeze, full of gert big fleaze, and so on. At the gathering in November 2003, by the time all had joined in with Ray Anstice's singing of the loyal toast and enjoyed a full evening's entertainment, it was clear that the supper will sail on to its golden jubilee in 2006 and well beyond.

The 1950s saw some notable departures; 1954 brought the death of Stanley Lloyd, the last surviving foundation member, the only one who could look back fifty years to that exploratory first meeting of February 18 1904; the fact that even today, a significant number of Savages can look back on sharing a Wednesday evening with Stanley reminds us once more that time moves in a different way in the Wigwam than in the world outside. There is a lasting memento of him in the Tribe's hands in the shape of the ceremonial sword which was presented to him by his fellow Savages when he enlisted in 1914 and returned by his daughter seventy years later. In March 1958, the Tribe lost Charlie Thomas. In spite of his failing health he took the chair for his final Wednesday meeting, a sentimental gathering which included the Lord Mayor, the Sherrif and two high court judges. His connections in high places were also reflected in the very large turnout for his funeral, at which a quartet from the Savages sang a requiem. These were not, it must be admitted, happy times. A new lease for which negotiations with the city council began in 1961-62 at last brought the long-suspected suspension of the £250 maintenance grant paid to the Tribe, as well as a rent increase and an enforced undertaking to have the premises rewired at the Savages' expense. Subscription increases were inevitable – from four-and-a-half guineas to six for lay members in the 1963-64 session – and continued to be frequent in a time of rapidly rising inflation, and it seemed that every approach to the authorities was doomed to failure. When rates became applicable to the club's area of the Red Lodge complex it applied for charitable status and failed. When the new lease was finally signed with the council in the 1963-64 session, George Eberle was so dismayed with it that he resigned as Honorary Legal Adviser, to be replaced by Don Dolman. Someone who had fought the Savages' corner for so long had no reason to feel any sense of failure, as he was constantly assured by all at the Wigwam, but George Eberle, more than anyone, knew the spirit in which his father had provided the Red Lodge for the Tribe, and he also knew that he had rescued the situation almost single-hand-

Bringing in the cheese at the Green Feather Supper, a tradition that goes back to 1956. The Stilton comes in with all the pomp of the punch on Punch Night, perhaps with a little to spare.

ed when the city council took over the Red Lodge in 1948. This time there were no urbane hand-written letters to his friendly acquaintance the Town Clerk to help turn the tide; life had moved on.

In fact life was moving on on so many fronts in the early 1960s. It is fair to suppose that the launch of the Beatles and the Rolling Stones did little to shake the Wigwam to its roots, but with the emergence of the youth culture came an iconoclasm and questioning attitude against the *status quo* which ran through a considerable section of society. The Conservative government, in office since 1951, was faltering and clearly likely to fall in 1964, long before the Profumo scandal and *That Was The Week That Was* helped to clinch Harold Wilson's (in the event, surprisingly narrow) victory. Bastions of the Establishment, a term which in many people's eyes fitted the Savages, through the club's long patronage by Conservative civic leaders,

The future takes shape: Re-roofing the Wigwam in 1992 in the shadow of Trenchard Street multi-storey car park, the building of which had caused considerable structural problems to the Savages' home a few years earlier.

were the new whipping-boys, and there was no great 'feel-good factor' in being a member of the Tribe at that time. In the early 2000s, the term 'post-modern irony' is bandied about with some abandon, often with no great knowledge on the part of the user of what it exactly means. What it does seem to imply is a personal freedom to enjoy whatever it is you wish to enjoy, so long as it is legal and harms nobody, and if it is conventional, old-fashioned or corny, so be it. Forsaking muesli and going back to childhood cornflakes? Post-modern irony. An unashamed lava lamp on your mantelpiece or Blue Lady on your wall? Post-modern irony. Going along to a room full of middle-aged-to-elderly men on a Wednesday night, listening to people talking about paintings, hearing classical music and laughing at friends telling jokes or singing funny songs? Maybe not post-modern irony but nevertheless, a pursuit that no longer puts one at odds with a society that says if that's what you want, baby, just you get on with it. Some might believe that there is a degree of over-tolerance abroad today, and there is a case to be made for that; but when it comes to allowing for and understanding the innocent quirks and eccentricities of other people's tastes, modern Britain fares more admirably than at any other time in living memory. Life at the Wigwam will always be out of step with what goes on in the world outside, and all Savages will say amen to that. But the more the public hears about and understands the ethos of the Tribe, the more likely it is to applaud a group of men who are simply, happily and successfully 'doing their thing'.

10

MODERN TIMES

Modern times at the Wigwam, with all their challenges and frustrations, truly arrived in 1964, when the towering multi-storey car park looming up beside it created cracks in an outer wall. The city council declared the building unsafe, with the result that the A.G.M. was held in the Studio and Ralph Brentnall and Tom Burrough were given the task of overseeing shoring and under-pinning; more misery and expense. By the following session everyone was assured that all was totally safe, but more big spending followed instantly with redecoration, carpeting and heightened security on the advice of the police. In 1967 came the creation of the Upper Studio, where today Blue and Green Feather 'Second XI' artists paint and prepare works for an annual exhibition of their own in late autumn. Previously this space was a true 'glory hole' in which Red Feathers used to frame, glaze and etch; there were even two etching presses up there and one of them, which had belonged to the turn-of-the-century art school principal Reginald Bush, was presented to the West of England College of Art. The Upper Studio is now a spacious and well-lit room entered via a staircase teeming with paintings hung more densely than in any other part of the building; beside it is a storage space with the capacity to house new paintings for years to come, even given the Savages' prolific rate of production.

Despite these steps into the late twentieth century, there continued to be room for old-world courtesy and old-fashioned caustic wit in the minutes. The former was reflected when, after discussions about a Müller painting which had been lent to the son of a former Savage who apparently no longer had it, 'it was agreed distasteful to take punitive action', and the matter was dropped. As for caustic minutes, the record for January 6 1971 recounts that: 'A visitor was a raconteur of ability and wit... his verbosity was such that the Chairman had to intervene with the gong, but we did get to bed on the same day we had arisen.' In 1973 an even later evening was the Ladies' Night to mark the Bristol 600 charter celebrations, when most people turned up in medieval costumes and Rex Hopes, showing a combination of a scant regard for history and the flair for costume that had once made him the star window-dresser of Austin Reed's Oxford Street store, decided to be Queen Victoria. Perhaps it was an oblique reminder that he always swore that as a child he had once seen her in a procession, bobbing up and down in her carriage as if she were on a rocking horse. Chronologically, the tale was just a short step away from his proud boast that the doctor who had overseen his coming into the world had been none other than W. G. Grace. Dennis Lewis also has a Rex Hopes dressing-up story. 'It was a Twelfh Night Supper when we were all to go as Impressionists,' he recalls. 'I went as D-Lewis Lautrec, pretty well down on my knees, and my wife Maggie went as his model Yvette Gilbert. As we made our grand entry Rex came bounding up to us, ignored me completely and greeted my wife rapturously: "Yvette! Yvette!" It turned out he had once met the real Yvette, so instantly knew who Maggie was supposed to be. I thought that was impressive, but then again, Rex always impressed me. He was a wonderful artist, designer, actor, poet, raconteur... A snappy dresser, too, doubtless a legacy of those Austin Reed days.' Dennis and Maggie Lewis's snappy dressing at the Twelfth Night Suppers earns them a special place in the Savages Mural on display at the Centenary Exhibition at the City Museum and Art Gallery from April to June 2004, for they are the splendidly attired couple to the right of the final panel.

A link with Brandon Cottage was revived just before Christmas in 1973 when the Savages planted eight oak trees on Brandon Hill across Great George Street from the house, which at that time was in a poor state of repair. It was a happy occasion with the spotlight falling on Charles Baker, the only member of the Tribe present who had joined before the move to the Red Lodge. Sad to say, the trees have not fared well since then, and have been replaced. Another event that earned publicity was a musical 'first' in the Wigwam in March 1986 when Percy Grainger's *English Country Garden* was played on two pianos by four pianists with eight hands. Nigel Dodd, Michael Butterfield, Michael Wilson and Bill Laird played 'stridently, positively and stiff-wristed', as the composer had instructed, and were helped along by the audience whistling along with them.

To the man in the street, the best-known current Savage artist by quite a distance is Frank Shipsides, who is much admired for his nautical paintings and impressions of Bristol and the West Country. He is rarely seen at the Wigwam these days, but was on the top table for a Friday lunch in October 2003, shortly after his 95th birthday. Was he still working flat-out, he was asked on that occasion. "More quickly and confidently than at any time in my career," he replied. "That's what happens when you're painting well. It's when you're unsure and hesitant that things start to go wrong." His latest book, with a narrative by his fellow Savage Sir Robert Wall, was published in

The Chairman's subject for the Wednesday night sketches has always been open to broad interpretation. This is Paul Weaver's response in October 2001 to They don't make 'em like that any more.

2002, and he has produced scores more paintings since then, working every morning without fail if he is not making model ships, fiddly little sixteenth-of-an-inch-to-a-foot things that would drive most men half his age to despair.

He and his late wife Phyllis moved to Bristol just before the Second World War, and of course he is of that familiar commercial art clan, having come down from the Midlands to work for the printers Bennetts and then, in 1948, moving to that cradle of the Savages Mardon, Son and Hall as a senior artist. It was only then that he began to fly as a painter. Frank regrets that he was there too late to work on cigarette cards for Imperial Tobacco, but there was a welter of promotional material to be turned out, and

Frank Shipsides' painting of the December day in 1973 when the Savages planted eight oak trees on Brandon Hill close to their first Wigwam at Brandon Cottage, which at that time was in a poor state of repair.

in his spare time he became a keen observer and chronicler of the still busy dockland scene. His approach is traditional, but he has a ready answer if this prompts the reflection that even when he was growing up in Mansfield, the Cubist movement of Braque, Picasso and Derain must already have been pushing art into a joltingly new direction. He will be far too gentlemanly to make an issue of it, but the final word will be his. 'Humphh,' he will chortle dismissively. 'Cubism? Came and went, though, didn't it?'

English Night, perhaps surprisingly an event with no lengthy pedigree among the Savages, has provided some memorable moments over the years. In 1990 the Entertainment Warden Bob Payne arranged the programme in tribute to his predecessor Hamilton Scott, and a highlight was when the quartet sang Sullivan's *The Long Day Closes* unaccompanied. Rather more robust was the entertainment in 1994 when it was 'on with the minutes – well, nearly. There was the predictable interruption by Alfie Moores (who by now was losing his sight) and he was then guided to his seat (he thought), only to realise he had been locked in the store cupboard beside the stage.' The longest-serving member on record was Blue Feather Colston Waite, who died in 2000 having been a Savage for nearly seventy years. He first sang at the Wigwam in 1930 at the age of nineteen, and his last performace was in January 1998. This was a Brave who had been sponsored for membership by Ernest Ehlers, Fuller Eberle and long-ago Honoured Green Feather Wilmot Houselander, and not many people could claim that at the beginning of the twenty-first century.

Honorary Secretaries since Frank Mole stepped down at the end of the 1969-70 session have been Tom Cutter, John F. C. Bedford, Eric Franklin, Terry Cleeve and Norman Parker. John Cleverdon took over in 2000-01 with Geoff Cutter, Tom's son, as Assistant, and Charles Baker, Eric Franklin, Terry Cleeve, Norman Morgan and Richard Long will also be remembered as able Assistant Honorary Secretaries over the past thirty years, as well as John Cleverdon for two sessions before he took on the top job. In the same period Gordon Jones has done the lion's share of the Honorary Treasurer's duties, but the Tribe has also been well served in this role by Tom Cutter, 'Staff' Stafford, Ralph Egarr and Reg Bennett. John Oakhill took over from Reg at the beginning of the 2003-04 session.

Following plans drawn up by the House Warden, Jeffrey Yandell, major reroofing work of the Wigwam and upper Studio in the early 1990s caused considerable upheaval; happily, it also brought the fleeting delights of Terry Cleeve's Tabernacle, a room-within-a-room in which all the Tribe's treasures, including its two grand pianos, were stored in protected safety. In this work, as in many other instances, there was invaluable input by the Heavy Gang, whose history can be traced back to the creation of the post of Officer for Special Duties in 1967. That was the year in which the Royal Society of Arts asked to hire the Wigwam for a dinner, and at the same time request-ed that the table and chairs should be laid out in a particular way. Savages, for all their many virtues, are not all throbbing of thew, and some of the ones who were were hastily assembled to do the donkey work. The gang continues to do so to this day, at first under the direction of Dickie Ware but with a succession of mighty men at the helm since then.

Above, Friday lunch in the Studio is popular all through the year, with the Last Friday cooked lunch especially enjoyed by many members. This is the cheerful scene on February 22 2002.

Two noted members of recent times. Left, Reg Bennett, for several years keeper of the "Savages Budget" and a devotee of the calculator, as seen by Mark Blackmore, who with John Collins produces many of today's caricatures; and right, Frank Shipsides in his pomp in 1974, as viewed by Harold Packer.

Frank Shipsides
President.... Bristol Savages.

A highly successful and high-profile centenary venture was the Savages' contribution of Bristol area scenes for a fund-raising 2004 calendar for the city's St Peter's Hospice. Above is Richard Pope's eye-catching Bristol Bridge from Welsh Back, and below, in much the same area but in a very different style, John Collins' The Arnolfini and Prince Street Bridge.

Two more views from the St Peter's Hospice calendar, which presented the monthly illustrations in detachable postcard-sized form. Left is Brian Lancaster's impression of St Michael's Hill, another of the best loved and most pictured corners of Bristol; and below, the familiar sight of Bristol City Museum and Art Gallery and the Wills Tower take on a mysterious air at the hands of John Palmer.

11

CENTENARY SESSION

In this their centenary session the Bristol Savages are at full numerical strength at four hundred, with nineteen Life Members, ten Honoured Savages, six Honorary Savages, twenty-nine Red Feathers, thirty-six Blue Feathers and a very healthy crop of Greens. Waiting list numbers are not disclosed, but at present there is a two-year wait. Red Feathers among the Life Members are Eric Craddy, Dennis Lewis, Frank Shipsides and Louis Ward, while Ken Cooke is a Red Feather who enjoys Honoured Savage status. In their life beyond the Tribe, Reginald Batterbury, John Codner and Dennis Lewis are Senior Academicians of the Royal West of England Academy, while John Palmer, a master of urban landscapes who was happily back at work at the end of 2003 after suffering from a stroke, is an Academician. Four Savages were represented in the R.W.A.'s 151st Autumn Exhibition in 2003, John Codner, Dennis Lewis, John Palmer and Richard Pope, and all but six elderly members exhibited at the Savages' Annual Exhibition in May 2003, when 142 works were on show with prices ranging from £85 to £1,250. Art has been and always will be the lifeblood of the Tribe.

The highlight of the Centenary Session is an exhibition at Bristol City Museum and Art Gallery from April to June 2004. A Centenary Mural prepared especially for the event by Red Feathers is a focal point, but Savages' works now held by the City Art Gallery collection also feature, as do paintings, caricatures and treasures from the Wigwam. An eyecatcher among these, as it was at the 1951 Festival of Britain exhibition for which it was made, is the arresting looking totem pole made by Hamish Milne in memory of his wife, who died within the Red Lodge complex. It is hoped that a welcome spin-off from this high-profile event will be a bumper attendance at the Red Feathers' Annual Exhibition fortnight at the Wigwam in May.

In June 2004 a *Centenary Cavalcade* evening of music, song and verse is to be presented by the Blue Feathers under Entertainment Warden Chris Torpy. He also compiled *A Century of Savage Verse,* published a few months before this book. Poetry is one of the supporting arts that are the foundation of the Tribe, as testified by the Ernest Board painting which features on the cover of this book, and Chris had plenty of work upon which to draw. In the early days, Francis Locke and Charlie Thomas

The centenary was a time for looking back on past work. Back Home *was the subject for the two-hour sketches on January 19, 1977. This is how Patrick Collins saw it.*

used to write verses by the yard – 'poetry' was not and is not always the purist's definition of these outpourings – and while the magazine *Grouse* was a useful reference tool, it was by no means the only source of material for Chris. The lyrics in the book written by the most celebrated and successful of Savage writers, Fred Weatherly, are not his most famous but were all produced by him during the life of the Tribe, and many relate either to Bristol or directly to the Savages, as is reflected in our Famous Faces chapter. 'One of the many unwritten traditions of the Tribe, from its early days, is writing verse to reflect the subject chosen by the chairman for the Red Feathers to paint in the two hours before the evening entertainment on a Wednesday night,' says Chris, 'and there are many of these in the book. This challenge is met today by several of our members, particularly Hylton Dawson and Alan Shellard, who are continuing a tradition that dates back via Jack Clee, Donald Hughes, Jim Knight-Adkin, Joe Norgove and others to the foundation of Savages. Others we look back to with respect include J. G. Russell Harvey and Rex Hopes.' Joe Norgrove was by no means

A detail of University Tower and Park Street by Centenary President Michael Long, which formed the cover of the St Peter's Hospice calendar.

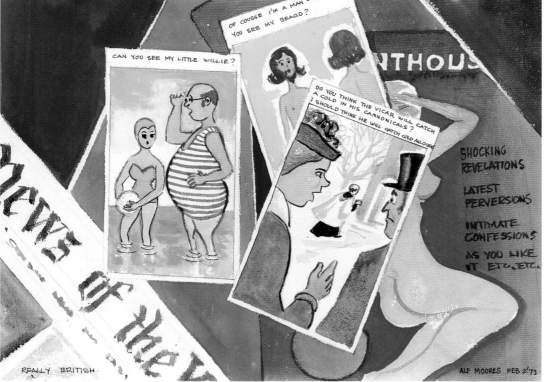

Two-hour sketch work by two versatile Savages whose art has involved them in teaching plus a great many other occupations besides. Above, Something to Remember by Dick Pope in March 2003 and below, the late Alfred Moores' satirical Really British from the same month in 1989.

John Cleverdon, Honorary Secretary since 2000-01. Before and since then his years as a gallery owner and knowledge of the art world have been a valuable asset to the Tribe.

as well known as Fred Weatherly, but he was still a lyricist and versifier with a national audience, and Chris Torpy has singled out one of his most evocative works in his First World War song lyric *Apples,* the one that begins:

Ribston, Newton, Cox's Orange Pippins,

Heap'd in baskets, gleaming row on row.

Colour'd with the sunshine, veined with vermillion

Redolent of gardens where the Apples grow.

Here, 'mid the roar of overcrowded London

How they tug my heart-strings, calling me again

Back to the orchards of Glo'stershire and Somerset,

Where the happy robins are singing in the rain...

Hub of activity on a Wednesday evening: The Chairman's table, covered with and surrounded by mementoes of the Tribe's tradition.

Still available from Bristol Savages, *A Century of Savage Verse* costs £15 plus £1.50 for postage and packing.

Another high-profile and highly successful venture in the Bristol area for the centenary session has been a 2004 calendar published by St Peter's Hospice, with twelve detachable postcard views of the city and its surrounds painted by Roger Gallannaugh, John Collins, David Reed, Brian Lancaster, Paul Weaver, Terry Culpan, Dennis Lewis, Frank Shipsides, Richard Pope, John Palmer, Anthony Pace and Patrick Collins. The calendar's cover, a superb Impressionistic view up Park Street towards the Wills Tower, is a detail of a painting by Centenary President Michael Long. Other officials in this centenary session are Anthony Pace, Vice-President; David Reed, Immediate Past President; John Cleverdon, Honorary Secretary; John Oakhill, Honorary Treasurer; Geoff Cutter, Assistant Honorary Secretary; Frank Harrison, Assistant Honorary Treasurer; Chris Torpy, Entertainment Warden; Jeremy Watkins, Assistant Entertainment Warden; Bob Matthews, Canteen Warden; Jeffrey

Surroundings that make the Wigwam special. Right, anticipation of a memorable evening begins as soon as members walk through the Red Lodge and sign in beneath the superb vintage model of The Bristolian. Below, after signing in, it just gets better and better...This is Irish Night, March 2002, in which Chairman Fergus Lyons was admirably supported by Hugh Knifton, Jack Greenland and Vincent Marmion.

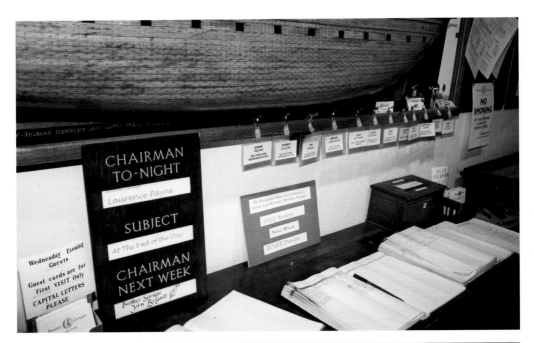

Yandell, House Warden; John D. Bedford, Honorary Legal Adviser; and Alan Stevenson, Chairman of Committee.

Michael Long, the Centenary President, has a lengthy Savages pedigree. Born in Bristol in 1940, he was taken to an Annual Exhibition by his father when he was aged about 11 and introduced to Alfred Moores, who surmised that if he kept working hard at art he, too, might become a Savage one day; indeed – who knows? – perhaps he could even find himself President. As an early intimation of greatness it is not quite in the league of Harold Wilson being photographed outside 10 Downing Street as a young tyke down from Huddersfield for the weekend, but it still says much about the intense sense of tradition that has bound together and still binds successive generations of Savages. In fact Michael Long has gone one better than Alfred Moores by becoming President on three occasions, the previous two being 1976-77 and 1987-88. It is far from inconceivable that in a dozen or so years' time he will be up for the challenge again.

After many years in the Tribe, most members look back fondly on the established artists who were the mainstays when they first joined. For Eric Franklin, recalling pre-war days, the men to look up to were C. F. W. Dening, Gordon Hake, Louis Ward, Colston Waite, Ralph Brentnall and A. C. Fare. Michael Long is happy to reflect that Alfred Moores was still a member when he joined at the age of 31 in 1971, with Ward and Tom Burrough two other venerable figures. The sense of continuity is not lost on Michael, who has never strayed far from his home city. After school he studied at the West of England College of Art, and most of his professional career was in teaching art, design and illustration before he took early retirement from being head of art at Brunel College. Now he paints full-time. One project that has spread his name far beyond the West Country is his substantial book on extinct animals, *Mammal Evolution,* which was published by the Natural History Museum and put out in translation around the world, including a version in Japanese. Work from the book formed the basis of two exhibitions, first at the Natural History Museum and later at Bristol City Museum and Art Gallery. As a painter he has had solo shows at various galleries in the South of England and has exhibited at the Royal West of England Academy. Several of his paintings are now available in limited edition prints. It is the varied and fulfilling *curriculum vitae* of an artist at home in a number of media and disciplines, and the Savages have always welcomed and nurtured such men. As is reflected in the first chapter of this book, Michael is also mindful of the world of the Savages beyond painting and strives to make all members feel valued and appreciated while stressing

that, first and foremost, this is a society of artists. The Tribe has never wavered from the principle of a Red Feather being at the helm as President, and it is to this that many informed observers attribute its longevity and success. It was a point taken up clearly and firmly by Blue Feather Colston Waite in his book *The Story of the Bristol Savages* in 1971, and one reiterated today by the art historian Francis Greenacre. 'The Bristol Savages are a remarkable and happy survival; are they the only social society of artists outside London to reach their hundredth birthday?' he asks. 'Perhaps the most important ingredient behind the society's continued success is the balance of its various categories of membership. It is this that produces such exceptional entertainment week after week, together with an audience to enjoy it, and yet keeps the artists at the centre of things. There must surely be occasional discreet battles, but from the outside looking in I have never caught the faintest whiff of gunsmoke at the Wigwam – only the enviable warmth of innumerable friendships.'

Amid all these extra celebrations, the week-by-week life of the Tribe goes on – but it seems to be with greater verve than ever in this special session, with attendances high and the atmosphere buzzing. There is a sense of history in the air, but there is also a great awareness of the here and now, and of the Tribe's strength as a vibrant and much loved institution. Members whose attendance has been sporadic are making Wednesday night a Savages night once again, while the great majority who put in regular appearances are doing so with a new spring in their step. One of the great merits of the club as a place for sociable gatherings has long been the sheer volume of the attractions it sets before its members, with three or four special events almost every month of the session. Those of 2003-04 have resounded with fun and laughter in a way of which the founding fathers would doubtless have approved. Art is still paramount, at the very core of the Tribe, and always will be; but that extra sociable element which was sought by Ernest Ehlers and his painter friends from the very start is also a key ingredient, and it is flourishing.

The Savage Spirit was certainly to the fore on the Wednesday evening of February 18 2004, the meeting that marked the exact anniversary of the inaugural meeting at Oldfield Road, Clifton. The one note of regret was that President Michael Long was laid low with bronchitis, though of course David Reed, the immediate Past President, David Reed took to the chair with aplomb. He told the Tribe that Mary Ehlers, daughter-in-law of the founder had sent along a display of roses, Ernest Ehlers' favourite flower, with a card congratulating the Savages on their Centenary and conveying all best wishes for the future. The roses were on the Chairman's table

For the Centenary House Dinner in March 2004 each Red Feather was asked to produce a hand-made menu to supplement the printed one designed by President Michael Long. Seen here, incorporating postage stamp images from the years 1904 and 2004, is the contribution of John Shipley. At the end of the dinner, all the hand-created menus were distributed through a simple competition involving the diners seated close to them.

throughout the evening. David Reed was supported by Louis Garcia and George Ehlers, the grandson of the founder, who on behalf of the family also presented a portrait of Ernest Ehlers to be hung in the Studio. The artist, A. B. Connor, was on the staff of Weston Art School and a colleague of its founder and Savages founder member H.E. Stacy, who was a great friend of Ernest Ehlers.

When it came to entertainment there was conjuring not, on this occasion, by Mike Alford but from the President of the Magic Circle, Alan Shaxon, who travelled from London to give a wonderful display of his skills. A fine programme also included Allan Schiller on piano, Norman Golding on trumpet, tales from Grahame Spray and songs by Bob Payne and Rod Young. The apt evening subject for the painters was *Gathered Together,* but when John Palmer gave the critique he broke from tradition by selecting two-hour sketches from the 100 years, by Ehlers, Helps, and David Blake, as well as the evening's work of the latest Red Feather member, Barry Herniman, which was bought by the Tribe. As so the evening passed, with all there going home in the belief that it had been an honour and privilege to help celebrate the centenary in this way. The public in Bristol and beyond has become increasingly aware of this centenary year, and the impact it will make on the region in various ways. It is only the Savages, however, who truly know how much this anniversary means to them. As they have promised Bongie, they are carrying on; but it is the spirit in which they are carrying on that has put them in such good heart for the years ahead.

Profiles of Bristol Savages artist members

(references to members becoming Savages can be taken as
meaning as artist members, unless otherwise stated)

Abbreviations CSD Chartered Society of Designers **FSAI** Fellow, Society of Architects and Industrial Designers **NEAC** New English Art Club **PS** Pastel Society **RA** Royal Academy **RBA** Royal Society of British Artists **RCA** Royal College of Arts **RBC** Royal British Colonial Society of Artists **RE** Royal Society of Painter-Etchers and Engravers **RI** Royal Institute of Painters in Water Colours **RIBA** Royal Institute of British Architects **ROI** Royal Institute of Oil Painters **RP** Royal Society of Portrait Painters **RSA** Royal Society of Arts/Royal Scottish Academy **RSMA** Royal Society of Marine Artists **RWA** Royal West of England Academy **RWS** Royal Society of Painters in Water-Colours/Royal Watercolour Society

ANDERSON, Stanley RA, RE

Born in Bristol in 1884, son of a heraldic engraver, Alfred E Anderson, to whom he was apprenticed at 15. Studied at Bristol Municipal School of Art under Reginald Bush (q.v.), and later at Royal College of Art and Goldsmiths' in London. Maintained he learned most studying art works at National Gallery and the British Museum. Elected an Artist Member of Bristol Savages in 1907 and remained a member until 1918; a caricature by Bush shows him as a clean-shaven, serious looking young man with a thick crop of dark hair. The Savages hold five framed examples of his work and two evening sketches. Won a British Institution Engraving Scholarship 1909, moving to London, and went on to become an outstanding engraver, notably in depicting country crafts such as hedging and hurdle-making. Became full member of the Royal Society of Painter Etchers and Engravers in 1923 and of the Royal Academy in 1941. For many years was in the engraving faculty at the British School in Rome. Was sole British representative of line engraving and drypoint at the Venice Biennale in 1938. Created CBE in 1951. Work widely held in British, Commonwealth and American collections. Latterly lived near Thame, and died in 1966.

ANDREWS, Ernest George Henry

Born in Bristol, 1896. Savages President in 1959 and 1970. A modest and friendly man, he worked in watercolours, painting with remarkable delicacy. In 1912 joined E S and A Robinson, and was first head of their Artists' Department. Mentioned in despatches in First World War, after his battalion was 'severely mauled' at Ypres. Lived in Stoneleigh Crescent, Knowle. Designed the Savage tie, and when he died in 1976 asked that one should be buried with him.

ANDREWS, Peter

Born 1925. Son of Ernest Andrews, when a student at Swindon College Art he courted Diana Fluck, later to become famous as the actress Diana Dors. Joined E S & A Robinson as a graphic designer, working with Edwin

Penny (qv). Later became a studio manager with Allen Davies & Son, before going freelance. Joined Savages in 1952. A fine figure artist, he worked on various accounts for London advertising agencies, and illustrated serials for *Eagle* comic. Although not a Mason, he played a leading role in James Dewar's television documentary on the Masonic movement, which led to more television appearances. Died suddenly in 1993.

ARMSTRONG, Francis Abel William Taylor RBA, RWA

Born in Malmesbury in 1849, moving to Bristol in 1905, when he lived at 42 St Michael's Hill. Elected to membership that year, by which time he was a well established artist exhibiting in London, Bern, Dusseldorf and Paris. Elected member of the Royal Society of British Artists in 1895, and of RWA in 1908, acting as committee chairman for some time. Although exhibiting regularly at Savages exhibitions, felt unable to do justice to himself at the two-hour sketch. Best known as a landscape painter, with work in Bristol Art Gallery and the RWA collections; he also illustrated periodicals, as well as an edition of *Lorna Doone*. Died in 1920.

AYTON, Robert Norton

Elected an artist member in 1980. A fine draughtsman and illustrator, including the strip feature 'Jack o' Lantern' for the *Eagle* comic. Illustrated Ladybird children's books for many years and worked freelance for the BBC in Bristol. Also a part-time teacher of illustration at the West of England College of Art, he lived and worked in a large farmhouse near Backwell.

BAKER, Richard E

Born in Bristol in 1928, was elected a Savage in 1967. An officer in the Merchant Navy, his links with the Savages were short, although he exhibited regularly at the annual exhibitions from 1969 to 1973, specialising in watercolours. No examples of his work are held at the Wigwam. Settled in New Zealand in 1975.

BANKS, Harry ARWA

Born in London in 1869, he was educated at Goldsmiths' College and Antwerp. In 1902, designed the dinner invitations for the Coronation of Edward VII and Queen Alexandra (a copy is held in the Wigwam). Once well known as a watercolourist, exhibiting three times at the Royal Academy from 1918 to 1920 and in France and the USA, he specialised in strongly coloured landscapes of Dorset (he lived at Thorncombe) and Somerset and continental views. He was a friend of Lucien Pissarro. Banks is remembered today as a fine etcher, often of Bristol scenes. Bristol Art Gallery has several examples, six being reproduced in *City Impressions: Bristol Etchers 1910-35* by Sheena Stoddard, in which is reproduced Dorothy Woollard's portrait of Banks at work. He also exhibited at the RWA. For a few years from 1917, he lived in Clifton during his daughter's term time, becoming a Savage and continuing to exhibit in the city long after he had left. He remained a Savage until 1945, and died soon after his resignation.

BARBER, Roy Stuart

Studied at the West of England College of Art before joining the studio of Mardon, Son & Hall, where he met many Savage artists. After then working for advertising agencies, he became a freelance. Continuing to paint, he developed a soft, harmonious style, to convey the tranquillity of his beloved British countryside. Has exhibited in London and the provinces, and had the indignity of one of his paintings being slashed in Chelsea. Rarely talks about his work, believing that paintings should speak for themselves. Elected to the Savages in 1983, he was President in 1997, serving also as archivist. He designed the cover of the *Savages Carol Song Book* and has illustrated *Grouse* magazine.

BATTERBURY, Reginald John RWA, ATD

Born in 1913 in West Ham, London, he was a teacher who became head of Lockleaze Comprehensive in Bristol. He was elected to the Savages in 1959, exhibiting at the annual exhibitions and also at RWA, where he later became a full academician. Was Savages President in 1980. The Wigwam holds seven examples of his two-hour sketches. Moved to Bridport in 1988.

BEAUCHAMP, C Philip ARIBA

Born in Bristol, educated at Clifton College and Cambridge. Elected an artist member in 1933, the year one of his paintings was accepted by Bristol Art Gallery. An architect by profession, his artistic interest was in wood and lino cuts, some of which were reproduced in Grouse. The Wigwam has two of his paintings. He moved to Bath and then Tunbridge Wells, where he was still in practice in the mid-1970s.

BLACKMORE, Mark Rupert

Born in Bristol in 1944, he won first prize in the Bristol Schools Poster Painting Competition when at Westbury School. At Bristol Cathedral School he was taught by painter Ian Black, and is currently a governor of that school. A chartered accountant, he became a partner in Grant Thornton, in 1990 leaving to practise with his wife, Maureen. He joined Bristol Savages in 1982 as a Green Feather, eventually being invited to paint with the artist members. Time constraints saw him switch from oils to pastels, and from landscapes to portraits. The Wigwam has two examples: a portrait of Terry Cleeve, past Honorary Secretary, and an Indian study. His commissioned portraits include one of David Shattock on his retirement as Chief Constable of Avon & Somerset Constabulary. Savages President in 1992 and 2001. An enthusiastic fencer, he has represented the South West at both foil and sabre for many years and is currently the region's vice-president.

BLAKE, David Nelson

Born in Hereford in 1944, studied at the West of England College of Art before serving an apprenticeship at the studio of Mardon, Son & Hall, where he met Frank Shipsides (q.v.). He was elected to the Savages in 1971, and later went freelance, working mainly in watercolours and specialising in studies of cats and small mammals. His work is known for the granular effects in his backgrounds and his mastery of painting fur. He later began producing backgrounds for cartoons, working in the TV and film industries in Britain and abroad, including Hollywood. His promising career was cut short by his sudden and premature death in 1992.

BOARD, Ernest RWA, ROI

Born in Worcester in 1877, he moved to Bristol at an early age. He was educated at the Merchant Venturers Technical College, and later at the Royal College of Art and the Royal Academy Schools. He later joined the studio of E A Abbey, and exhibited at the Royal Academy in 1902. A Savage from 1907, he was President in 1918. His most famous, and often reproduced, painting is The Departure of John and Sebastian Cabot from Bristol. This hangs in Bristol Art Gallery, which holds other examples of his large-scale work. Also represented in the RWA Permanent Collection. Several of his portraits hang in the Wigwam. He was commissioned to carry out mural decorations at the Houses of Parliament and in the old Council Chamber of Bristol City Council. He was also an excellent artist in stained glass. He remained with the Savages until 1932 when, short of commissions, he unsuccessfully tried his luck in London. He then moved to Farley Green in Surrey, where he designed an altarpiece. He died in 1934.

BOLT, Frederick E MIA

Elected in 1909. Apart from 1916 and 1917, when he served in the Royal Artillery, he was an active Savage until his death in 1934. As well as a competent painter, he was a fine pen-and-ink artist. A good writer of verse, he regularly contributed poems and sketches to Grouse, for which he used the signature 'Blot'. His fine illustrations of the famous story became known as the Rip van Winkle folio, purchased from him by the Savages in 1929.

BRANWHITE, Charles Brooke RWA

Born in Bristol in 1851, the son of Charles Branwhite ARWS; painting had been the main family interest for many years, his great-grandfather being a close friend of Gainsborough's. Studied at the South Kensington Schools, and at 22 was exhibiting oil and watercolour landscapes at the RA, the Paris Salon, RI etc. He became a Savage in 1905 and a member of the RWA in 1913, serving as its Hon. Secretary. Portly, silver-haired and amenable, he was an ideal choice of Savages President, serving for five successive years. He loved the open air, painting and fly fishing throughout the West Country and North Wales. A keen cricketer in his youth, he took to cycling in later life, not to save on tram fares but to reduce weight. A professional artist, he presented two paintings to the Wigwam. He is

represented in Bristol Art Gallery with Bristol Harbour and A Wet Afternoon on Dartmoor, and his St Michael's Mount, Cornish Sunset hangs in the Mansion House. He died at his home at 41 Elliston Road, Redland in 1929.

BRENTNALL, Ralph Herbert MBE, MA, ARIBA

Born in Bristol in 1901, he was one of the first students of the Royal West of England Academy School of Architecture, qualifying in 1929. He joined the architects Oatley and Lawrence, becoming a partner and in 1951 head of Oatley and Brentnall. Suffering severe injuries while defusing a bomb in London in 1942, he was awarded the MBE for gallantry. Post-war, he was involved in the design of many university and other buildings in Bristol and the restoration of the Great Hall after fire damage in the Blitz. He was architect to the fabric of Bristol Cathedral and St Mary Redcliffe. Joined the Savages in 1935, serving as President in 1948 and 1964. He specialised in pastels, of which 22 examples are in the Savages archive. He died in 1980.

BROWNE, Alan Charlson FRGS, FRES, AR(Cam)A

Born in Liverpool, he moved to New Zealand before returning to England, where he exhibited widely in the provinces. He specialised in watercolours and etchings, mountain scenery being a favoured subject; he had climbed Mount Tasman, the highest peak in New Zealand. After serving as a camouflage officer with the Air Ministry in the Second World War, he moved to Bristol in 1963, exhibiting at the Clifton Arts Club and meeting Donald Hughes, who introduced him to the Savages. Clean-shaven, good looking and quiet, he walked with a limp, the legacy of a mountaineering accident. The Wigwam has no examples of his work. After a spell in Sussex, he moved north, living near Wigan. The Carnegie Trust of Washington DC purchased a set of hand-painted slides.

BUCKLE, Claude N RI, RSMA

An architect, he was born in London in 1905. He moved to Keynsham in the late 1920s, when he was engaged in the building of J S Fry & Sons' Somerdale factory. He later lived in Kent Road, Bishopston. Around 1928 he devoted himself to painting, and quickly made a name in poster work. Elected an artist member in 1930, he almost immediately left for London to join Wallis, Gilbert & Partners, architects specialising in factories, although he retained his membership until 1934. In that year, his poster design of Buckfast Abbey was accepted by the Great Western Railway Company. He was elected a member of the Royal Institute of Painters in Water-Colours. Moved to Andover and in 1964 was elected a member of the Royal Society of Marine Artists.

BUCKNALL, Ernest Pile RWS

Born in Liverpool in 1861, he was educated at Dulwich College, later studying art at Lambeth and South Kensington, where in 1876 he won the Queen's Prize for Perspective. He specialised in landscape painting in watercolour, exhibiting at the RA, RBA and the RI. In 1919 he moved to Bristol, living in Gloucester Road, and was elected an artist member at the age of 58. In 1924, wrote an article for *Grouse* on the charms of English rural architecture. He died in 1940.

BURROUGH, Thomas H B TD, FRIBA, RWA

Born in Newport, Monmouthshire in 1910 and educated at Clifton College. Articled to architects Oatley and Lawrence, when demobilised after the Second World War, he resumed work with Hannam and Morris and became architect to the Bristol Diocese. Architect to the Royal West of England Academy, he oversaw restoration work following war damage. He was identified with the modern school of architecture and widely acclaimed for the design of churches at Lawrence Weston and Lockleaze. He was an authority on Georgian and ecclesiastical architecture and a special lecturer at Bristol University. He was President of Bristol & Gloucestershire Society of Architects. Architect to Gloucestershire Cricket Club (he was a keen cricketer and rugby player), he designed the Grace Memorial Gates. He travelled extensively in Europe, launching an appeal, 'Florins for Florence', to assist in salvaging art damaged by floods. His several books included *South German Baroque, An Approach to Planning* and *Bristol Buildings*. Elected an artist member in 1935, he served as Savages President in 1945. He worked especially in watercolour, buildings his preferred subject. His work is in the RWA Permanent Collection, which also has a striking portrait of him by John Codner (q.v.). Died in 2002.

BUSH, Reginald Edgar James RE, ARCA, RWA

Born in Cardiff in 1869, he studied at the Royal College of Art and in 1893 won the British Institute Scholarship for Engineering with a travelling scholarship, which took him to Paris and Italy. He exhibited widely, including the RA, RWA, RE, Walker Art Gallery, Liverpool and the Paris Salon. In 1898 he was elected Associate of the Royal Society of Painter-Etchers and Engravers. In 1895 he became Principal of the Bristol Municipal School of Art for 39 years, teaching many future Savages. Notable etchers taught by Bush included Stanley Anderson (q.v.) Malcolm Osborne, Nathaniel Sparks and Dorothy Woollard. Elected in 1906, he was a regular member of the Savages, a genial figure with beard and commanding appearance. He was keen on all sports, especially rugby (his brother Percy being a Welsh international) and an active fisherman. His etchings are well represented in the Bristol Art Gallery, and illustrated in Sheena Stoddard's *City Impressions: Bristol Etchers 1910-1935*. In 2002, the Gallery acquired a collection of oil portraits by Bush of W D & H O Wills employees commissioned by the company in the 1920s. The Savages hold examples of his work, along with an evening sketch of him by Charles Thomas (q.v.), with his dog and fishing rod, entitled 'A good old sport'. He left Bristol for London in 1950, dying there six years later.

BUTLER, George Edmund RWA

Born in Southampton in 1872, he was taken at 12 to New Zealand, where, in the backwoods, he practised his obvious talent for drawing. Back in England, he studied at the Lambeth School of Art, the Academie Julian in Paris and at the Antwerp Academy, where in 1900 he won a medal. He then came to Bristol as art master at Clifton College. He also ran a school and studio at 92A Whiteladies Road, with classes in figure and landscape painting. Became a Savage in 1907; he was described as tall and lithe, with a mop of dark hair and greying beard. Children were often the subject of his sketches. In 1904 he first exhibited at the Royal Academy, one of his pictures selling for £300. He was elected a member of the RWA in 1912. He was a regular at the Wigwam, which possesses 41 of his paintings, mostly landscapes in oils and watercolour, though he later became well known for his portraits. In 1917 he was appointed official artist to the New Zealand Expeditionary Force, which purchased some of his pictures. He was an active Savage until moving to Twickenham in 1920, later living in Felixstowe, where he died in 1935.

CARDER, Anthony N

Born near Manchester in 1940, spent his early childhood in Harrogate. He then spent 10 years at Clifton College, where he first learned of Bristol Savages, an Eric Craddy painting being an inspiration. After a business career, which still left time for landscape painting, he returned to Bristol in 1994 and became an artist member of the Savages, whose president he was in 1999. Long before then, he had fallen in love with Venice, and has painted many scenes of the serenissima. He describes the red feather of the artist members as 'my most treasured possession'.

CHALKER, Jack Bridger ARCA, RBA, RWA, ASIA, HonFMAA

Born in London in 1918, he studied at Goldsmiths' from 1936 to 1939. Spent much of the Second World War as a Japanese prisoner of war in Singapore and in the Thailand-Burma railway camps. He also worked alongside the renowned Australian surgeon 'Weary' Dunlop, a fellow prisoner, documenting the ravages of disease, wounds and starvation as well as the ingenious medical equipment fabricated in the camps. Many of his surreptitious diary notes, sketches and paintings are now in the Imperial War Museum. After the war he continued his studies at the Royal College of Art. He came to Bristol and became Principal of the West of England College of Art in 1959. A painter and book illustrator, he was elected a Fellow of the Society of Medical Artists of Great Britain. He became a Savage in 1959, resigning in 1991, and exhibited at their annual exhibitions in the early 1960s, as well as at the RBA, RWA and RP. In 1987 the RWA staged his 'Images of War', drawings and paintings from a POW Camp in Thailand'. He also had one-man shows at the Dixon Gallery, London. He now lives near Wells.

CHARLTON, Evan

Born in London in 1904, he studied art at the Slade, 1930-33. Began teaching at the West of England College of Art in 1935, became head of Cardiff School of Art 1938-45, and was a war artist during the Second World War. Was a transient member of Bristol Savages while living in Worcester Terrace, Clifton. He married the daughter of Hartland Thomas, the well-known Bristol architect. Elected an artist member in 1936, but there is no record of any activity at the Wigwam. In 1938 he resigned when he moved to Hampstead. A modestly surrealist painter, he had a memorial show at the

National Museum of Wales in 1985. The RWA gave him and his wife, Felicity, a show in 1986, and hold a painting of his in their Permanent Collection. Died at Porthkerry, South Glamorgan, in 1984.

CHASE, William Arthur ARWA

Born in Bristol in 1878, he later studied at the City and Guilds School in London, where he won national silver and bronze medals. Also won a silver medal at the Regent Street Polytechnic Art School. When he moved to Bristol in 1908 he was an established portrait painter and specialist in flower paintings. He was only a transient Savage, in the pre-First World War years, with three evening sketches from 1909 and 1910 in the Wigwam collection. After leaving Bristol, he spent much time painting in northern Italy and South America. He settled in Blewbury, near Didcot, where he died in 1944. Queen Mary purchased his *The Flower Jug*, while *A Coloured Group of Sweet Peas* and *A Chintz Bunch* were bought by the Queen of Norway. His principal work is considered to be the Rowley inlaid wood panels.

CHETWOOD-AITKEN, Edward Hamilton PS

Born in Bristol in 1867, he lived in Westbury-on-Trym and was elected an artist member in 1908. A bank manager, he was a self-taught artist, although he doubtless received advice and guidance from the Savage founder members. He specialised in watercolours and pastels of landscapes and flowers. A passion was his garden and the design of rockeries. He was elected a member of the Pastel Society in 1918, and exhibited at the Royal Academy, Liverpool, Birmingham and RWA. Although a regular at the Wigwam, he does not appear to have been active in the studio. He seems to have ceased membership by 1932.

CODNER, John Whitlock RWA

Born in Beaconsfield in 1913. His father, Maurice Codner, whose subjects included King George VI and Queen Elizabeth, was a successful 'Society' painter. John was educated at St Edward's School, Oxford and London Polytechnic under Harry Watson. He excels in portraits and still lifes, especially flowers. He painted the late Duke of Beaufort three times and his Savage sitters have included Tom Burrough (q.v.), Frank Mole (q.v.), John Eberle, Charles Thomas (q.v.) and Norman Parker. Oils are his preferred medium, watercolour being 'too difficult'. Now an RWA senior academician, he joined the Savages in 1937. Specialising in camouflage with the Royal Engineers, he was mentioned in despatches. He has exhibited at the Royal Academy and Royal Society of Portrait Painters, and wonders whether modern art hasn't 'reached rock bottom'.

CODNER, Maurice Frederick RP

Born in 1888, he was the father of John Codner (q.v.). A portrait painter in oils and watercolour, he exhibited at the RA, RP, ROI, RI, NEAC and the Paris Salon, where he had an honourable mention in 1938. Was Hon. Secretary of the Pastel Society. His work is in the collections of the Imperial War Museum, the Stock Exchange and the Baltic Exchange. His official portrait commissions included King George VI and Queen Elizabeth the Queen Mother. He died in 1958.

COLEMAN, James ATD

He was elected an artist member in 1964. Lived at Southwood Drive, Coombe Dingle and taught art at Filton High School. He was also a violinist of some talent, specialising in Irish jigs. In 1966 held a one-man exhibition at Weston-super-Mare, to which town he moved in 1970 after resigning his membership.

COLLINS, John F

Born in Wells in 1930, he studied at the West of England College of Art. Worked for various commercial studios before, in 1986, starting his own business as illustrator and designer. Has illustrated various children's books and as a painter exhibited widely in the West Country. His ambition is to paint full-time, his liberal view of art being 'there is a place for everything'.

COLLINS, Patrick Geoffrey ARIBA, FSAI

Born in Bristol in 1936, he was educated at Bristol Cathedral School before attending a part-time RIBA course at the Merchant Venturers College in 1953-58 and a Diploma Course at the RWA School of Architecture 1958-64. Formerly with Burrough & Hannam, E S & A Robinson and the BGP Group, he is now a freelance architect. A Fellow of the Architects and Industrial Illustrators, he has shown in open exhibitions and had a one-man exhibition at the David Cross Gallery. He specialises in a pen-and-wash technique with colour highlights.

COOKE, Kenneth

Born in Bristol in 1924. At East Bristol Central School he was taught by Savage Frank Mole, later taking an apprenticeship at the studio of Mardon, Son & Hall, where he met other Savages such as Frank Duffield (q.v.) and John Keenan (q.v.). After war service, he returned to Mardon's and was elected to artist membership of the Savages in 1947. In the early 1960s he became assistant studio manager at Ford's of Bristol, when the studio manager was Dennis Lewis (q.v.). Became Savages President in 1966, when his old art master Frank Mole (q.v.) was Honorary Secretary. After exhibiting regularly at Savages annual exhibitions from 1948 until the early 1970s, his work took him to London and he moved to Newbury. Was made an honorary member in 1996. The Wigwam has 20 of his evening sketches.

COWELL, Harold FRSA

Born in 1915, he came to Bristol in the late 1930s to practise as an architectural designer, establishing a reputation for black and white floors for cinemas and dance halls. Was a 'Desert Rat', and after being wounded, was transferred to the Special Operations Executive under Sir Fitzroy MacLean. After the war he lived and worked in London and then Cornwall, but returned to Bristol as Head of Art at St Thomas More School, and was elected FRSA. Later became Deputy Head of Kingsweston School. Helped form Bristol Youth Orchestra, played trombone in the Bristol Brass Band and was an accomplished pianist (though rarely heard at the Wigwam). He was a skilled calligrapher and designer, but painting remained his first love, as demonstrated in the retrospective held at the time of the 1998 annual exhibition. He joined the Savages in 1987, becoming President in 1991. He died in 1996.

CRADDY, Eric Haysom ARWA

Born in 1913, he won a choral scholarship to Bristol Cathedral School, then moving to the Bristol Municipal School of Art under Reginald Bush (q.v.). Later apprenticed as a designer with Mardon, Son & Hall, where he worked on original sketches for cigarette cards, the last, on the outset of war, being a series of 50 on the story of navigation. Became an artist member of the Savages in 1937. After war service, rejoined Mardon's, retiring in 1973. In the meantime he had been Savages President three times, the last in 1967. He was a regular RWA exhibitor, and was elected ARWA in 1947. His speciality was marine subjects, in watercolour and oils; appropriately, he was keenly interested in dinghy racing and was Commodore of the Bristol Corinthian Yacht Club. His wife's illness limited his scope, but he continued to exhibit at the Savages annual exhibitions.

CULPAN, Terry
Became a Savage shortly after moving to Bristol in 1993. Specialises in marine subjects, and spent time at sea with the Royal Navy as a guest artist during North Sea exercises. Work in Saudi Arabia in the 1980s saw him broaden his interests to include landscape and architectural subjects. On taking early retirement in 2001, he began running art classes as well as teaching. He shows regularly at Royal Society of Marine Artists exhibitions, and is represented by two galleries in the USA.

CUTTER, George Frederick
Born in Bristol in 1940, his vocational training was as an electrical technician. Taught craftsmanship by Terry Cleeve, he became an artist specialising in pastels. One-man venues have included Rooksmoor Gallery, Bath, Street Galleries, Wells City Museum and Bristol Guild. Enjoys impressionism and modern expressionism.

DAVIES, Brian L
Was elected an artist member in 1927 and active in the studio from 1928 to 1932; he had a picture in the Savages annual show in 1934, before moving to London. The Wigwam holds five of his sketches.

DENING, Charles Frederick William RWA, FRIBA
Born in Chard in 1876, he was a noted architect, influenced by Lutyens. His Bristol work included St Alban's church in Westbury Park, which has been described as 'one of the best pieces of Arts and Crafts Gothic in England'. A fine watercolourist, he joined the Savages in 1919, and almost immediately designed the current Wigwam, supervising its construction from 1919 to 1921. A noted architectural historian, he wrote the magisterial *The Eighteenth Century Architecture of Bristol* and the more modest *The Old Inns of Bristol,* which he illustrated with elegant pen-and-ink drawings. Was President of the Bristol Society of Architects and of the Bristol & West of England Photographic Society. He served as Savages President in 1928, and was later made a life member. Was also an active member of the RWA, serving as honorary secretary and artists' chairman for many years. The destruction of much of old Bristol in the Second World War affected him psychologically, but he steeled himself to undertake many watercolour drawings of blitzed buildings; Bristol Art Gallery holds several examples. There was an exhibition of his war-time work at the David Cross

Gallery c.1980. He died in Stoke Bishop in 1952, a broken man.

DOBSON, Sir Frank RA, ARBS
Born in London in 1888, the noted sculptor was only briefly a Savage. In the inter-war years, with Epstein he was called a 'keeper of tradition', bridging classical and modern sculpture. With war imminent, he evacuated from London to Bristol in 1939, setting up a studio in Clifton Hill and immediately joining the Savages. While in Bristol, he was selected to represent sculpture at the Internat-ional Exhibition in Venice in 1940, and was appointed an Official War Artist. The Wigwam holds two of his sketches and a caricature of him by Donald Hughes (q.v.). His work is held in many public collections, including Tate Britain. He died in London in 1963.

DUFFIELD, FRANK
Born in Warwick in 1901, moved to Bristol in the 1920s to join the Mardon, Son & Hall studio, producing designs for cigarette cards. Elected to the Savages in 1946, he was a popular and assiduous member. A good pianist, he would play popular tunes, always with pipe in mouth, after the Wednesday evening entertainments. His painting of Brigadier Manley Angell-James is in the Imperial War Museum. Awarded life membership in 1973, he died in 1982.

DURMAN, Alan
Elected an artist member in 1946, like many Savages of his generation he was employed by Mardon, Son & Hall. Worked as a mural artist, with commissions from the Berkeley Café, Clifton and Saltford Community Hall. He was also a successful poster designer, one of whose nude studies for British Rail caused a furore in Ramsgate. He was elected Savages President in 1952; a caricature of him hangs in the Wigwam. He died at Saltford in 1963.

EDWARDS, Michael B
Born in 1939, and a successful businessman and management consultant, he became a full-time artist in 1990, supplemented by part-time consultancy work. Joined Bristol Savages in 1990. He has published three books, including *Impressions of Bristol,* along with greetings cards. He holds an annual exhibition at his home in Bisley, Gloucestershire, where he also runs residential summer courses in painting. He works in oils, acrylic and watercolour. Has exhibited with RSMA and RBA.

EHLERS, Ernest RWA
Born in Newfoundland in 1858, but moved to Bristol as a child with his widowed mother, living in Cotham Grove. Studied art in Germany and on his return made painting his profession, living for a time in Edinburgh. Known for his landscapes, notably woodland scenes. In 1896 elected to RWA, making many friends among local artists assembling at his glazed lean-to studio in Kingsdown. This, and other meeting places in friends' houses and a rented studio in Corn Street, led to the setting up of Bristol Savages in 1904. Ehlers was elected the first President. He became a well known figure around Bristol, wearing a Norfolk jacket and knickerbockers and carrying large amounts of paraphernalia. Lived in Clyde Road, Redland and latterly in Vyvyan Terrace, Clifton, where he died in 1943.

FABIAN, Ernest F RWA
Elected an honorary member in 1908, and although an artist, is chiefly remembered as a sculptor craftsman. For 37 years he was modelling master at the Municipal School of Art, retiring in 1929 through ill health. Was a regular exhibitor at the RWA. He was commissioned by Halifax, Nova Scotia to make a bronze model of Ernest Board's painting of the Cabots setting out for America, and his work is to be seen in Bristol Cathedral, which houses a number of models and busts by him. For the Savages, he crafted the silver President's chain of office, the impressive golf trophy, a classically designed plaque for the Bongie Portfolio and a plaster model of a rugby player. A caricature by Charles Thomas (q.v.) shows Fabian as tall and handsome with moustache and thick crop of hair. Lived in Downs Park East and died in 1931.

FARE, Arthur C FRIBA RWA
Born in Bath in 1878, he was a practising architect. His characteristic work, popular with local collectors, was detailed watercolour drawings of Bristol buildings and street scenes. The Wigwam has a good example, of Corn Street, painted as a two-hour sketch. He was regularly seen at Savage gatherings, and contributed many well executed drawings for the club magazine *Grouse.* He is remembered as short, serious-faced, quiet and retiring. He was an accomplished cellist. Exhibited regularly at RWA. His plaque in a sculpture by Ernest Pascoe to their friend Jack Stancombe is in St Nicholas Church. Died at his home in Upper Belgrave Road in 1958.

FISHER, Martin

After serving as a submarine commander in the Second World War, attended the RWA's school of architecture under Gordon Hake. Became an architect with Bath Corporation, working with Sir Hugh Casson on new proposals for the city, before setting up on his own. An excellent draughtsman, in 1969 he produced a folio of prints of Bath. Became an artist member in 1965 and President four years later. Exhibited a range of work at Savage exhibitions from 1965 until 1974; resigned in 1975.

FRINGES, Balthazar

French, he joined the Savages in 1904, attended erratically and resigned twice, finally in 1906. He first suggested the popular annual Artists' Summer Outing, and may have prompted the introduction of Blue Feather membership, after giving a memorable cello and flute duet with his son. An etcher and landscape and figure painter, he exhibited 24 works at Savages exhibitions in the short time he was a member, mostly figure subjects and river scenes. He was long thought to be unrepresented in the Wigwam's collection, but his design for the 1905 House Dinner menu was rediscovered early in 2004.

GALLANNAUGH, Roger
Dip.Arch(RWA), ARIBA,
Dip.Arch.Cons.(Bristol)

Born in London in 1940, qualified at the RWA School of Architecture, where Tom Burrough (q.v.) was lecturing on the History of Architecture. After partnering his father for 36 years, set up his own practice. Worked primarily on local authority housing, Courage's Brewery and the Spectrum building in Bristol. Past-President of Bristol Society of Architects and RIBA Wessex Region. Began sketching and painting in the mid-1980s, his subjects rural and urban scenes. The Savages have a copy of his book of Regil, recording every building in the village in pencil, pen and watercolour. Enjoys painting and walking holidays in Spain, Greece, Gozo, Italy. Exhibited at Savages annual exhibitions and the Bristol Cancer Help Centre in 2000-03. Was Savages President in 1998.

GARDINER, Robert

A restaurateur, he was elected an artist member in 1977. Painting mainly in watercolour, he has exhibited at the Savages annual exhibitions from 1977 to the present day. The Savages hold nine of his sketches.

GAY, Arthur Wilson

For 30 years an artist at E S & A Robinson, he was elected to the Savages in 1928. Known for his large watercolours, he exhibited at many Savage exhibitions. Retiring from Robinson's in 1949, he concentrated on portraits, and was acclaimed in 1955 for his image of fellow Savage Harry Crook in mayoral chains. Painted two Wesley shrines in Cornwall. The Wigwam holds two examples of his work. A quiet, shy man who disliked crowds, he had a nervous breakdown in 1956 and committed suicide in Redland two years later.

GODDING, Ernest

Born 1894. Reginald Bush's son-in-law, he was elected a member in 1927. A member of the Mardon, Son & Hall studio, he specialised in etching and pencil drawing. One of his prints was purchased by Bristol Art Gallery, and he had work in a Chicago Society of Etchers exhibition. He died in 1931, aged only 37.

GUYATT, Henry Coulton

Born in 1857, he lived in Long Ashton. A landscape painter in oils and watercolour, he was elected to the Savages in 1907 and showed more than 150 works from then until 1938, mostly landscapes of the West Country, North Wales and Berkshire. He exhibited 19 paintings at the RWA between the wars. The Wigwam has 20 of his sketches. He died in 1939.

HAKE, Gordon D FRIBA, RWA

Born in 1887, became well known as an architectural artist in watercolour, crayon and pencil. After Christ's Hospital, studied at Ecole des Beaux Arts in Geneva and at the Architectural Association School, London. Moved to Bristol in 1922 to head the newly opened RWA School of Architecture, which he ran with distinction for 30 years. Was elected a Savages artist member, also exhibiting at the RA, RWA and other galleries. He served as secretary of the Bristol Society of Architects and President of the Bristol branch of the Design in Industry Association. He was commissioned by Bristol University to modernise the Victoria Rooms. Served as Savages President in 1930, 1938 and 1939 and for a long time was editor of *Grouse*. On retiring in the early 1950s he was made a life member, moving to Yarcombe to indulge his passion for fly fishing. He died in 1964. The Wigwam has 35 of his evening sketches, and a set of crayon sketches of bomb damage in Bristol was bought by the City Art Gallery.

HALE, William Matthew RWS, RWA

Born in 1837 the son of a clergyman at Claverham, Bath, he was 69 when invited to join the Savages in 1906. His activity in the studio was limited, but he contributed a beautiful watercolour to the Bongie Portfolio. He exhibited at the RWS and RWA and at least once, in 1912, at the Royal Academy. Two of his paintings in Savages exhibitions were purchased for Bristol Art Gallery. He painted some notable Bristol scenes, and the RWA Permanent Collection holds his atmospheric *Bristol Harbour* (illustrated in *Public View: A Profile of The Royal West of England Academy*). Notably, he recognised the talent of the armless painter, Bartram Hiles (qv), coaching and encouraging him to persevere. Died in 1929 in Stoke Bishop, aged 92.

HANNEY, Clifford ARWA

Born in Pensford in 1890, his art training began at the Municipal School of Art under Reginald Bush (q.v.) from 1913-14. After the war, he studied art at the West Marlands School of Art in Southampton until 1923. In that year he was elected an ARWA. In 1930 he became a lecturer at Cheshire County Training College for 20 years, but in 1933 was a founder member of the New Bristol Art Club. In 1951 became an artist member of Bristol Savages, serving as President in 1963. Exhibited at the Savages annual exhibitions from 1951 until 1977, by when he was 87. His work was shown at the RA, RWA, RBA and ROI. He travelled, his painting subjects ranging from St Ives to Hadrian's Wall and Venice and the Italian Lakes. His work was acquired by Manchester and Oldham Art Galleries. He died a few days after his 100th birthday.

HARDIE, Alexander Merrie RWA

Born in Aberdeen in 1910. An engineer, he was a self-taught artist, a colourist in the Scottish tradition, painting mainly landscapes, but still lifes and portraits in later life. Worked in watercolour, pastel, oil and gouache. In 1963, he was appointed Principal of the College of Technology in Bristol, becoming a Savage in the following year. In 1966, he became Pro-Vice Chancellor of the University of Bath. He painted a portrait of the first Vice Chancellor, Dr George Moore. He became Professor of Physics at Bath in 1975, returning to Scotland in 1978 to live at Cromarty, where he died in 1989. He exhibited at Savages exhibitions from 1964 to 1976. Elected to RWA in 1970. He showed with Aberdeen Artists' Society and RSA, with one-man shows at the

Rooksmoor Gallery and Holburne Museum in Bath and the Logie Gallery at Tain in Ross-shire. RWA, Gloucester Education Authority and University of Bath hold his work.

HARRISON, Peter William MSIAD

Born in Bristol in 1935 into an artistic family. His father, Celic Harrison, worked in the Mardon, Son & Hall studio, while his grandfather, a fine illustrator, toured the country to illustrate a wild-west show starring Buffalo Bill. Peter studied at the West of England College of Art, prize winning in 1951-52. In 1953 he became apprenticed to R B Hooper-Jones (q.v.) at the studio of E S & A Robinson, where, national service intervening, he worked until 1968. He moved to Ford's Advertising before going freelance in 1976. Taught illustration and figure drawing part-time at Brunel Technical College. Elected an artist member of the Savages in 1972, exhibiting annually until his premature death in 1989. He was President in 1977, 1984 and 1986. Played clarinet with the Severn Jazzmen, often performing at the Wigwam and the summer soirée. One-man show at Frost & Reed's Bristol gallery in the mid-1970s.

HAWKINS, Bernard William

Born in Tooting in 1940, he studied art in London. He worked at Ford's Advertising in London before moving with them to Bristol. The studio had five Savage artists, including the studio manager, Dennis Lewis (q.v.). Elected a Savage in 1974, exhibiting annually from 1975 to 1995. Always an innovative artist, he was also a skilled craftsman, restoring clocks and making guitars and other musical instruments. In 1998 moved to Poole, where he began a business restoring and renovating old fountain pens for the antiques trade and designing and making pens for this exclusive collectors' market.

HEANEY, Alexander J

Born in 1876, came to Bristol with HM Customs and Excise. Elected an artist member in 1915, and was active in the studio for 20 years. In 1922 he was a highly successful, if self-effacing, President. He contributed to *Grouse* and left the Wigwam two excellent self-portraits. Shy and with a permanently sad expression, he was tall, lean with a thick crop of black hair. When ill health forced his retirement in the 1930s, he concentrated on art, becoming a fine painter and etcher. Although a student at the RWA School, he never exhibited there, but did so at the RA occasionally and once in Chicago. Bristol Art Gallery has a good selection of

his print work (see *City Impressions: Bristol Etchers 1910-1935*). He died in 1936.

HELPS, Herbert P A

Born in 1893, he was elected an artist member in 1911, when living in Westbury Park. As a commercial artist, he was the first of a new breed of Savage. He was a freelance, for many years illustrating the *Bristol Times & Mirror,* and apart from Savages annual exhibitions, there is no record of his ever exhibiting. He had an encyclopaedic knowledge of historical events and costumes, and portrayed old sailing ships with immense accuracy. After a spell with E S & A Robinson, he worked at Mardon, Son & Hall, becoming a specialist in cigarette cards, some of which were considered masterpieces of the genre. A contributor to *Grouse,* he was President in 1933 and in 1955, in which year he died after a sudden illness. The Wigwam has 70 of his sketches and a caricature by Charles Thomas (q.v.).

HERNIMAN, Barry

Born in Middlesex in 1950, he moved to Gloucester in 1959. Working first as a draughtsman, land surveyor and graphic designer, he now has his own graphic design business. After living in South Africa and travelling extensively in South and North America, he returned to the UK in 1980, becoming a mature student at Gloucester College of Art, where he gained a Higher Diploma in Information Design. He is a Member of the Chartered Society of Designers. Held his first solo exhibition of watercolours in Ross-on-Wye in 1991, and has since shown elsewhere in England, Ireland and Canada. Has been a full-time artist since 1998, and was the SAA Artist of the Year in 2001. A regular contributor to *The Artist* magazine, and published his first book, *Painting Mood and Atmosphere in Water Colour* (Search Press) in 2004. The Savages have one evening sketch.

HILES, Frederick, John (Bartram) RWA

His is the most remarkable of all Savage stories. As a young boy of eight in 1880, he suffered a dreadful tram accident in Hotwells, Bristol, necessitating the amputation of both arms at the shoulder. While recovering, he resolved to realise an early dream of becoming an artist, and experimented with a pencil held in his mouth. After diligent practice, he produced a passable sketch. Back at school, he gained a certificate for freehand drawing, moving on to the Merchant Venturers Technical College, where he was

successful in examinations and won prizes. William Matthew Hale (q.v.) encouraged him to take up watercolour painting, and to adopt the name 'Bartram'. At 16, he was exhibiting at the Bristol Academy (later RWA), and the sale of that picture was an immense fillip to his confidence. At 18, he anonymously entered an open competition, winning one hundred guineas and two years' training at the South Kensington Schools, where he won one silver and two bronze medals. After further study in Paris, he returned to Bristol, selling 27 of 30 paintings exhibited at the Frost & Reed Gallery. He moved to London to design postcards for Raphael Tuck, and sell impressionist paintings of London street scenes. In 1906, at the age of 34, he brought his wife and baby daughter to Bristol, living at 21 Constitution Hill, Clifton and becoming a familiar figure in his long Inverness cloak. At Matthew Hale's instigation, he joined the Savages, and was a regular attender for 12 years. In 1908 and 1909 he exhibited at the Royal Academy. His health began to fail in 1920, and the state of his teeth and gangrenous gums, added to the post-war economic depression, made work difficult; this condition was alleviated somewhat by treatment recommended by dentist and fellow Savage C J Kelsey (q.v.). The Savages and the Artists' Benevolent Fund helped him financially, but he deteriorated, dying in 1927 at the age of 55. The Wigwam possesses four photographs of this remarkable man and 20 examples of his work.

HOLDEN, Harold, H ARWS, ARCA, RBSA

Born in Settle, Yorkshire in 1885. Studied at Skipton School of Art, Leeds College of Art and finally Royal College of Art, London. Devoted his life to teaching art, and after an appointment as art department head at Leeds Modern School in 1910, he went on to be principal of art colleges in Cheltenham, Leeds and Birmingham. Exhibited at the RA, RBSA, Royal Watercolour Society and abroad. Later settled in Westbury-on-Trym and died in 1977, having been made an honorary Savage in 1960.

HOLDEN, John H

Artist and administrator who worked as John Holden. Born Leeds, 1913, son of Harold. Studied Birmingham College of Art, then Royal College of Art. Became Principal, Wolverhampton College of Art, Manchester College of Art and Design, and then Deputy Director of Manchester Polytechnic, from which he retired in 1978. Exhibited Royal Academy between 1935 and 1955, but mostly in the 1930s. Lived in Wilmslow, Cheshire. Sometimes incorrectly named as John Hamilton-Holden in gallery lists. Elected to Savages in 1965. Died 1980.

HOLLOWAY, George H

Born in 1882, he was elected a Blue Feather Savage in 1923. Served in the First World War as a staff captain in the Royal Artillery, and was in business with the family printing firm, Holloway & Sons, at one stage chairman of the Bristol Master Printers Association. An elocutionist who specialised in monologues, he made more than 1,000 BBC broadcasts, was a member of Bristol Playgoers Society and a life member of the British Empire Shakespeare Society. Elected an artist member in 1961 at the age 79, he was a talented watercolourist and on Wednesday evenings showed himself to be a fine figurative artist, especially skilled at depicting horses; in contrast, at Savages annual exhibitions from 1962 to 1977 he concentrated on landscapes. He produced some fine black and white illustrations for the *Bristol Illustrated News*. He was made a life member in 1976, and died the following year.

HOOPER-JONES, R B

Elected an artist member in 1934, when living in Clyde Road, Redland, he exhibited for many years. Employed at E S & A Robinson. During the war was in the Savages Observer Squad and designed a poster for the Air Raid Precautions Committee. He worked in watercolours, pastels and oils. The Wigwam has one of his framed works and about 20 evening sketches. He died in 1959.

HOPES, Rex Frederick ARWA

Born in Bristol in 1890, when he was delivered by the cricketer Dr W G Grace. He worked as a window dresser for Austin Reed, transferring to their Oxford Street store in London. While there, he studied art in the evenings at several schools, including the Slade. Returning to Bristol, with his wife he opened a private school for girls at Redland, then Langford and finally Winterbourne. He was a member of the Fabian Society. A good poet, he contributed to local magazines, some of which he illustrated with black and white drawings. Elected an artist member in 1933, he was President in 1946, 1957 and 1967. He painted mainly in watercolours, specialising in flora and still lifes, and exhibited regularly at Savages annual exhibitions and at the RWA. He also depicted theatrical subjects, helped in productions and was a very good character

actor. Multi-talented, he was also a craftsman-designer in fabrics and pottery. Died at Worcester Court in 1982.

HUGHES, Donald James FAI, ARWA

Born in 1881 and educated at Clifton Hill House, Hughes was one of the most famous Savages. Handsome, clean shaven and with grey hair, he carried lightly his fund of knowledge, love of art and command of the English language. Teetotal and non-smoking, he was a keen cricketer and hockey player in his youth. When first elected to the Savages as a literary member in 1914, he was an auctioneer and estate agent with offices in Unity Street. He retired early to devote himself to art, in 1924 holding a one-man show at the Clifton Arts Club, where he was chairman at one stage. He was a student of Iain McNab's at Heatherley's School of Fine Art in London. *Grouse*, of which he became editor in 1930, was a natural outlet for his literary talents. He was a celebrated Wigwam entertainer, reciting poems with solemn face and hands clasped before him, and maintained the Savages' tradition of interrupting the minutes with a witty remark. As an artist he worked primarily in watercolour and crayon, and could work at great speed; during a three-week holiday in Europe he painted 60 pictures. He became an artist member, and the Wigwam has more than 40 of his evening sketches. In 1938 he wrote the text for Kit Gunton's book of lino-cuts of birds, *Birdsworth*. He bought the Blaise Hamlet cottages, and when his offer was refused by Bristol Corporation, he donated them to the National Trust. He put a plaque on his Berkeley Square house to commemorate John Loudon MacAdam, the road-making pioneering who had lived there. Hughes was Savages President in 1934, 1944, 1954 and 1963, and a portrait of him hangs in the Wigwam, as well as a Charles Thomas (q.v.) caricature. He died in 1970, bequeathing £1 to the Imperial Tobacco Company, which he felt he owed them as a lifelong non-smoker.

JOYNSON, Derek

Born in Bristol in 1936, he studied at the West of England College of Art, then serving an apprenticeship at the studio of E S & A Robinson under Ernest Andrews (q.v.). He moved to the Keynsham studio of Fry's, the chocolate makers, and when this was transferred to Bournville he joined Mardon, Son & Hall. He was elected an artist member of the Savages in 1977, and painting mainly in gouache and oils, he exhibited with them until 1984. He was a figure and portrait

painter, but also painted landscapes with figures. The Wigwam has a landscape of his, and a conversation piece depicting artists at work in the Savages studio, where it now appropriately hangs.

KEENAN, John RWA

Moved to Bristol in 1920 and became a Savage in 1946. With his friendly disposition and dry sense of humour, he was a popular President in 1956 and 1965. He worked in the Mardon, Son & Hall studio for many years, and was elected to the RWA. The Wigwam has 22 of his evening sketches, and three of his works hang on the walls, along with a caricature by Harold Packer (q.v.). He died in Redland in 1970.

KELSEY, C J ARWA

Born in 1870, he practised as a dentist in Knowle. Elected a Savage in 1906, he was an enthusiastic member in the studio and in committee, remembered for his friendly mien and impressive appearance, with carefully trimmed imperial beard and moustache. Specialised in landscapes in watercolours and oils, one of them being hung in the 1912 RA Summer Show. Exhibited at the RWA. He was an expert enameller, writing a descriptive article on the subject in *Grouse*. He made the President's jewel worn by the Savages President when attending outside functions, and was instrumental in addressing the serious dental condition of Bartram Hiles (q.v.). Kelsey was elected President in 1926 and remained active in the Wigwam until the Second World War, when he retired to Tickenham to raise exotic plants until his death at 96.

KINGSTON, Thomas ARWA

A bachelor living in Kingston Road Studio with his brother W P Kingston, he was a founder member of the Savages in 1904. Although a very popular and staunch member, his shyness prevented his ever becoming President. He was an associate member of the RWA. A lover of the English countryside and old gardens, he painted in watercolours and oils, the Wigwam holding 25 of his evening sketches. He never recovered from severe influenza in 1928 and died the following year following an operation for appendicitis. He is buried at Long Ashton.

LAIRD, William ARCM, LMusTCL

Born in Northumberland in 1920, he attended Trinity College of Music, London. Worked as a draughtsman at the Ministry of

Works, taught music in Hertfordshire and Bristol and produced music programmes for the BBC from Bristol. Served with the Royal Engineers in the war, and was subsequently a member of the RE band. He was a self-taught artist, working mainly in watercolour and pastel. Was first a Blue Feather pianist and member of the Savages Quintet, but became a Red Feather in 1970, serving as President in 1975 and 1978. Retired to Throwleigh on Dartmoor in 1978, and exhibited paintings, mainly of Dartmoor and its surroundings, at galleries in Chagford and Okehampton. Conducted his own composition, *Overture: Hadrian's Wall,* based on Northumbrian folk tunes, and played the solo piano part in Cesar Franck's *Symphonic Variations* by invitation of Southmead Orchestral Society. Died in 2000.

LANCASTER, Brian C GRA, RSMA, FRSA

Born in 1931 in Atherton, near Manchester, an industrial environment which influenced his later choice of subject matter. Attended Bolton Art College for three years, with a further three years at Southport College of Art; he later specialised in lithography and graphic design at Manchester College of Art. His first exhibitions were at the Atkinson Art Gallery and Southport's annual exhibition. After working as a package designer in England and Canada for 20 years, he moved to Bristol to join the Mardon, Son & Hall studio. Harold Packer (q.v.), the studio manager, introduced him to the Savages, and he was elected an artist member in 1969. He left Mardon's for Ford's as an illustrator and general artist, later working with Barney's Advertising. He has shown at the RWA and regularly at the Savages' annual exhibitions. Had a one-man show at Bristol University drama department in 1988. In 1990 he became a member of the Guild of Railway Artists and in 1998 was elected a member of the Royal Society of Marine Artists.

LEWIN, Frederick George RWA

Born in Bristol in 1861. Started work as a reporter on the *Western Daily Press,* but his real talents were as an illustrator and cartoonist. A self-taught artist, he contributed to *Punch, Zig Zag, Magpie* and other magazines. He illustrated Bristol newspapers for over 50 years, notably cartoons for the *Evening Times* and a series on inns for the *Evening Post.* He designed comic postcards for several publishers, including, E W Savory (a fellow Savage). Between 1903 and 1916 he showed 60-plus works at the RWA, mostly watercolours and

pen-and-ink cartoons, but also a few oils. Joined the Savages in 1906, the year he was elected to the RWA. He illustrated a number of books, including, in 1922, *Bristol, a pictorial record.* No examples of his work are in the archives, but he contributed to the Ehlers Folio of 1907. Died in 1933.

LEWIS, Dennis RWA, FCSD

Born in Bristol in 1928, he left school at 14 and was encouraged to work in lithographic printing. He soon realised that art was his true vocation. After evening classes at art college and army service, he returned to John Lee & Son, by then incorporated into Bennett Brothers, a major firm of master printers in Bristol. He was admitted to the Society of Lithographic Artists on a special shortened apprenticeship in 1948. In 1955 he joined Décor Advertising, specialising in silk screen printing and exhibition display, later moving to Ford's Advertising, where he spent 34 years, rising to chairman of what was by now an international design group. Retired in 1990 to paint most days in his Portishead studio. Has exhibited in every Savages exhibition since 1963; was President in 1972, 1979 and 1987. He was elected an associate academician of the RWA in 1966, becoming a full member in 1970, serving the academy in various capacities. He has shown at the RA, had 10 one-man exhibitions and worked on numerous commissions.

LEWIS, Lowry RWA

A founder member, he was 54 in 1904, already a well known artist then living in Waverley Road, Redland, and an RWA academician. He was born in Falmouth, and founder of the Bristol and District Cornishmen. He spent much time in the West Country painting coastal scenes, mainly in watercolours. He was a keen churchman, serving as a warden of St Agnes Church, St Paul's, and organised charity appeals for children and the poor. He presented several paintings to the Wigwam, including *Come Pick a Bone* to mark the first annual dinner. After his death in 1913, Bristol Art Gallery bought two of his paintings, *Bay of Sorrento from Naples* and *Sennen Cove, Cornwall.*

LINGFORD, George

Born and educated in Bristol, he left for Liverpool, probably in the late 1860s, returning to the city in 1903. He was now apparently a successful artist who could tell fellow artists that he never started a new picture until he had sold the last. He worked in a borrowed studio in West Park, but without apparent success, before leasing

rooms at 39 Corn Street, above Gibbs' gunshop, which the Savages used as temporary headquarters. He was a driving force in the Savages in the early days. Lingford did not attend meetings regularly, although he presented a framed work to the Tribe, and left Bristol for London. There, ill, he fell on hard times, and was helped financially by the Savages. His health appears to have improved, for he emigrated to Canada aged 72, dying in British Columbia in 1933.

LINTON, W Evans RWA

Born in Portishead in 1878, he was the youngest of the founder members of the Savages. His house in Oakfield Road, Clifton, was an early meeting place. Studied art at Calderon's School of Animal Painting and the Academie Julian in Paris, becoming a well known painter of landscapes and animals who exhibited at the RA, the Royal Institute of Oil Painters, the Royal Cambrian Academy and the Paris Salon. Elected to the RWA in 1910, he was on their hanging committee for many years. His book *The Drawing and Construction of Animals and Animal Painting* became a recognised authority. Tall, clean-shaven and bespectacled, pipe-smoking and with 'a somewhat stentorian voice', he was assistant art master at Clifton College and played rugby for Clifton. The Bristol and Huddersfield Art Galleries each have a painting. Died in 1941.

LLOYD, Stanley

A keen and active founder member, who was assistant secretary in 1908. After serving in the First World War, he left Bristol to live in Wiltshire and then Devon and although retaining his Savages membership, never attended again. He was a noted illustrator, particularly of children's books. The Wigwam has three of his framed pictures and about 20 evening sketches, along with a caricature of him by Charles Thomas (q.v.).

LONG, Michael Richard ACSD

Born in Bristol in 1940, he attended the West of England College of Art and was apprenticed at E S & A Robinson in 1957 as a designer and reproduction artist. Taught at Brunel Technical College, latterly Senior Tutor in Graphic Design, and freelance book designer and illustrator. Is an associate member of the Chartered Society of Designers. *The Evolution of Mammals,* copiously illustrated by him, was published by the Natural History Museum in 1986 and sold worldwide, being translated into Japanese and Spanish. In 1996, a one-man exhibition of illustrations from the book was held at

Bristol Art Gallery. Paints mainly in oils and acrylics, his work primarily landscapes, much executed in Somerset and the Cotswolds, and seascapes. Has exhibited in a number of West Country galleries, including RWA. With Michael Edwards (q.v.), founded Dobunni Painters, exhibiting in galleries across the Cotswolds. He has paintings in the John Hill Marine Collection. Played bass for the Blue Notes jazz band from 1958 to 1962. Savages President in their centenary year, having served as such twice before.

MAGGS, John K ARIBA, FSIA

A busy architect, he was elected as a Red Feather in 1959 but spent only limited time in the studio. The Wigwam holds six of his evening sketches. Died in 2000.

MARSHALL, J Miller

Moved to Bristol in 1904 from Norwich, where he had been a member of the Norwich Art Circle since its inception in 1885, working prolifically in Norfolk. Exhibited at the RA, RBA and RI. Founder member of the Savages, he lived in Pembroke Road and was active in the Wigwam to 1915, when he left Bristol, having served as President in 1910. He contributed to the Bongie Portfolio, and the Wigwam holds six of his evening sketches. Died in Minehead in 1935.

MATTHEWS, Les MA(RCA), ATD

Born in Bristol in 1946, attended Gloucester College of Art, 1964-67 and Royal College of Art, 1968-70. Head of art in schools, including Churchill Comprehensive, from 1984. Exhibited RA, RWA, Bath Society of Artists, Bristol Guild and, in 1990 and 1991, Savages annual exhibitions, having been elected in 1990. Has since resigned. Has illustrated for OUP and Transworld Corgi. He works in oil, gouache, egg tempera and watercolour, his wide subject range including the female nude, Egyptology and mythology, chivalry and science fiction.

MAYES, Robert RWS

He was 70 and a member of the Royal Society of Painters in Water-Colours, specialising in landscapes, when elected to the Savages in 1907, probably introduced by Brooke Branwhite. The Wigwam holds two examples of his work, and he contributed to the Bongie Portfolio. He lived in Downend at a house named Ovenhurst, notoriously decorated to his design throughout. In 1918 he died at a painting session at Wilde Parsons' house in Hampton Park. Wilde Parsons subsequently sent the painting to the Wigwam and it now hangs in the studio.

MILNE, Arthur Edward (Hamish) RWA

Born in Edinburgh in 1888, he was a landscape, portrait and flower painter in oil, watercolour and pastel. Moved to the West Country in the 1930s. Was a regular exhibitor at Savages exhibitions from 1931 to 1966, showing 141 works. He carved the figure of St George over the Wigwam door, and renovated and installed the Canynges fireplace and the totem pole outside the studio. Savages President in 1931, 1940 and 1951, he was made a life member in 1961. After retirement he worked at the RWA, restoring paintings. Lived in Weston-super-Mare and then Clifton, where he died in 1981. The Wigwam has a caricature of him, and a nude portrait donated by the sitter.

MILNER, Donald Ewart OBE, MA, ARCA, RWA

Born in Huddersfield in 1898, son of artist James H Milner, he studied at the Camberwell School of Arts and Crafts and the RCA. After teaching in art schools in Birmingham and Gloucester, moved to Bristol in 1937 as Principal of the West of England College of Art. His teaching commitments precluded regular attendance but he maintained a keen interest in Savages affairs, exhibiting at several annual exhibitions. He resigned in 1947. Exhibited RA, RWA, the New English Art Club, Cooling Galleries and Arts Council. His work is in public collections including the V & A. He was a painter, stained glass designer and typographer, producing designs for the Bibliographical Society and publishers Sidgwick & Jackson. Examples of his stained glass can be seen at Bristol Courts of Justice and Bristol University. He served with distinction as the RWA's Artists' Chairman (1967-73) and President (1974-79); there was a retrospective exhibition in 1995, and his work is in the RWA's Permanent Collection. Died at Wotton-under-Edge in 1993.

MOLE, Frank

Born in 1892, he moved to Bristol from Bedfordshire in 1923 to take up an art teaching post. Was elected an artist member in 1933 and served as secretary for 25 years. He was a quiet man who painted watercolours, notably landscapes, especially of Cornish subjects. Also worked in pastels and pen-and-ink, and some of his drawings (e.g. the Oak Room porch and fireplace) are superbly accurate in detail. Adept in making jewellery and a great admirer of Fabian's (q.v.) work, he designed a chain for the President's Lady. A keen

music lover, he was for many years a member of the Bristol Philharmonic Society. On retiring, he moved to the Red Lodge, surrounded by the treasures he loved. He contributed regularly to *Grouse*, and the Wigwam has 36 of his evening sketches. A portrait by John Codner (q.v.) hangs behind the President's Chair. Moved to Worcester Court in 1970, dying in 1976.

MOLYNEUX, Geoffrey BA, MA, ATD, PGCE

Born in Nantwich, Cheshire in 1947, attended Stoke on Trent and Manchester colleges of art. After spells in the police force and the theatre, moved to Bristol, and later the Royal College of Art, to complete his art education. Taught art until 1997, working at the City of Bristol College. Elected an artist member in 2000, he has paintings and prints in many private collections in Britain and abroad.

MOORES, Alfred Nixon

Born in 1914, after showing an early interest in his father's draughtsman's engineering drawings, he won a scholarship to the Bristol Municipal Art School. He then took an apprenticeship at Mardon, Son & Hall, becoming a general designer working in advertising and packaging. Used his draughtsman's skills creating perspective views for the RAF to help destroy enemy U-Boats from the air. His painting Winter Landscape was hung at the Royal Scottish Academy in 1942, while a series of dramatic panels of aircraft in action was exhibited at the National Gallery in 1944. Back in Bristol, he became a Savage in 1946, his depictions of life in war-time Burma helping secure his election, and he served as President in 1960 and 1970. Taught art at Twyford House, Shirehampton, where his classes were oversubscribed, and ran sessions on advanced photography at Filton Technical College. His work has been hung in the National Portrait Gallery, Arts Council of Great Britain, Bristol Art Gallery and RWA. He died in 2000.

NEAVE, Vincent F G

Born in London in 1948. A self-taught artist, he took up art as a profession after a serious back injury in the construction industry. Moved to Bristol in 1969 and gave up painting temporarily in 1983 to convert, with his wife Kate, the *Glevum,* a 150-ton grain barge, into a floating studio and art gallery in Bristol's floating harbour. After selling it in the early 1990s, he now devotes his life to nautical research and painting. Best known for his marine paintings, he is equally passionate about the British landscape. Elected an artist member in 1996, he served as President in 2000. The Wigwam has two of his evening sketches along with his pastel *Sun, Sand and Seaweed*.

ORCHARD, Stanley

As a young artist he showed great promise, and after a short probationary period he was elected an artist member in 1926. In the following year he was tragically killed in a motorcycling accident during a painting excursion to Cornwall.

PACE, Anthony

Born in Australia in 1939, moved to Britain in 1947 to live with his grandmother. Studied at Newport and Cardiff colleges of art. Worked at the National Museum of Wales, Cardiff as designer for the schools service, and on conservation of fine art at Reading University. In 1964 joined TWW television in Cardiff, and for 21 years worked on major films for Britain and America. With the advent of computer graphics, he decided to concentrate on painting. He first exhibited at the Savages in 1985 and from the following year at the Royal Institute, RBA and RSMA, with a one-man exhibition in Bath in 1990. This later toured Devon and Cornwall. Private collectors with his work include Prince Philip and Princess Anne.

PACKER, Harold George

Born in Cotham, 1908 and trained at the Municipal School of Art under Reginald Bush (q.v.). Joined Mardon, Son & Hall as a commercial artist, retiring as studio manager in 1973. Became a Savage in 1936, showing 79 works at annual exhibitions from 1938 to 1978, the subjects including caricatures of fellow members, landscapes and street scenes. A great admirer of Dickens, he produced many illustrations of his characters. The Wigwam has 30 of his figure studies and 20 evening sketches. Died 1999.

PAIGE, E Willis RWA

Born in 1890, he moved to Bristol as Assistant Master to Reginald Bush (q.v.) at the Bristol Municipal School of Art, first living in Cotham and then Trelawney Road. Elected to the Savages in 1926, becoming a great asset. A fine painter, draughtsman and etcher. Of commanding appearance, with goatee beard and charming manner, he was an excellent and witty speaker. Savages President in 1935, 1942 and 1943, and a regular contributor to *Grouse*. Was a member of RWA, exhibiting extensively,

including a noted etchers' exhibition in Chicago. Five etchings shown at the Royal Academy in the 1930s, and Bristol Art Gallery has seven. Portrayed many of Bristol's fine old buildings, including Merchants Hall, destroyed in the Second World War. The Wigwam has two of his framed works and 30-plus evening sketches. Died in 1960.

PALMER, John Frederick RWA

Born in Bristol in 1939, he studied at the West of England College of Art, with a five-year apprenticeship with Mardon, Son & Hall; was an artist and designer there for 34 years. At same time worked privately as a painter, becoming a member of the RWA, and in 1985 receiving the Cornelissen Prize for Fine Art. Artist member since 1972, twice President. Retired early from Mardon's in 1989 to pursue full-time career in fine art, and was elected RWA two years later. Exhibits regularly in South and West, with regular one-man shows in Bristol, Bath and Cheltenham, and in exhibitions at Islington Fine Arts and the Mall Gallery, London. His work is in several public collections, including British Aerospace, banks, building societies and insurance companies. Has illustrated books and magazines. In 2002, the RWA commissioned him to paint the Academy building when scaffolded for restoration work (illustrated in *Public View: A Profile of the Royal West of England Academy*). He teaches informally at art clubs and other venues. Principal other interests include photography, railways and his growing library of books.

PANTER, Kenneth ARIBA, ARWA, FRSA

Born in Cardiff in 1920, he was an architect and member of the Welsh Board of Advanced Technology. Moved to Bristol in 1949 to head the Architecture Department at the Technical College. Elected an artist member in 1956, exhibited regularly at annual exhibitions as well as the RWA. Savages President in 1964. He was appointed Professor of Architecture and Building Technology at Bath University in 1964. He retired in 1977, moving to Chideock, Dorset. Died 1988.

PARSONS, Arthur Wilde RWA

Born 1854, was already a celebrated painter in oils and watercolour of marine and coastal subjects when he helped found Bristol Savages in 1904. He lived in Hampton Park, sharing a studio with his brother Featherstonehaugh, a portrait painter. The

self-taught Wilde Parsons had independent means, and devoted his life to painting. His work was first accepted by the Royal Academy in 1909 and Bristol Art Gallery has 15 paintings, including *The Opening of the Royal Edward Dock*. The Wigwam also has several, including *Waves breaking over Cornish Cliffs*, *The Fight of the Angel Gabriel* and a large watercolour painting of *HMS Formidable*. Queen Mary admired his work, and he contributed to the miniature paintings commissioned for the Royal Dolls' House at Windsor. Quiet and reserved, he sported a beard and pipe and Charles Thomas (q.v.) wrote: 'His kindly and genial personality endeared him to his brothers of the brush'. A photograph of him hangs in the studio. Died 1931.

PEAKE, Wilfred E

Born in 1880 and elected to the Savages in 1908, he was a specialist in medieval scripts. An active member and a talented pianist, he was instrumental in forming the Blue (entertainer) Feather membership. He lived in Royal York Villas, Clifton and was manager of a bank when he joined, leaving in 1914 when transferred to Burton-upon-Trent. All artists contributed to the Portfolio presented to him on his leaving. The Wigwam has his superbly crafted illuminated address in the Bongie Portfolio, along with his sadly incomplete missal of script copied from early monks, for which he designed the ornate capitals. If completed, it had been intended for Bristol Cathedral. Died 1940.

PEARCEY, T Murray

Elected in 1923, but has left no evidence of any studio activity. His payments lapsed, and after settling his dues, he resigned in 1930.

PEARSON, H G ARWA

Elected an artist member in 1908 and a painter in oil and watercolour, although little is known about him. The Wigwam has one evening sketch, and he contributed to the Bongie and Wilfred Peake Portfolios, which indicates that he was a member at least until 1921.

PENNY, Edwin

Born in Bristol in 1930, he studied at the Bath and the West of England Schools of Art and is a wildlife watercolourist. At the age of 21 he was apprenticed as an artist to E S & A Robinson. During National Service with the Royal Tank Regiment he won a painting prize from the Hong Kong government and received tuition in Chinese painting by a local artist. This made him able to blend the principles of Eastern composition with Western ideas. On returning to Bristol, he became studio manager for a printing firm. He joined the Savages in 1956, becoming a freelance artist 10 years later. In 1973 he served as President. Since 1974 he has been represented by Frost & Reed and shows at their London gallery. Noted for his ornithological studies – he admires the paintings of Thorburn and Audubon – his work was included in an international exhibition, 'Birds in Art', which toured America for many months.

PIGOTT, Ronald Wellesley

Born in Ireland in 1932, he was a surgeon specialising in plastic surgery as well as a fine hockey player, representing the Combined Services and Ireland. An artist in pen-and-ink, watercolour and oils, he was elected an artist member in 1969. Resigned in 1979.

PITT, Arthur Edward

Born in Bristol in 1900, he joined the Savages as a Green Feather in 1953, when he owned a shoe shop in Cotham. A talented, self-taught artist, he applied to become a full artist member and was elected in 1959, the first Green to become Red. He moved to Burrington Combe in 1962, painting landscapes and showing at the annual exhibition from 1960 to 1986. He died in 1987.

POPE, Richard J BEd

Richard, usually known as Dick, was born in Bristol in 1946 and is married with four children. He left school at sixteen to undertake a five-year apprenticeship in lithographic printing at Mardon, Son and Hall. He completed this in 1968 but two years later left printing to retrain as an art teacher at Redland College. He has taught art in Bristol schools for 29 years and has been head of department at his alma mater, St Mary Redcliffe and Temple School, for ten. Before his appointment at Redcliffe School he regularly painted and took part in group exhibitions at the Association of Illustrators' Gallery, London, Hamilton's Gallery, Mayfair and the Eye Gallery, Bristol. He collects (very modestly) contemporary art, artists' books and Ravilious ware. His interests include painting and design, gardening, visiting galleries, reading widely, writing Haiku and listening to classical music and modern jazz. He joined the Savages in 2003.

RANSON, Ron

Born in Chesterfield in 1925, he began his career as a technical illustrator with Rolls-Royce, illustrating cars and aero engines. He then worked for many years as a designer at London advertising agencies, and was for 12 years publicity and public relations officer with a major company before taking up painting as a career. A self-taught watercolourist, he has developed a loose impressionist style which has an oriental simplicity. He has shown almost worldwide, and his work is seen regularly at the Royal Institute of Painters in Water Colours. He ran a residential watercolour school at his home at St Briavels in the Wye Valley until moving away in 2003, when he also resigned his Savages membership.

REED, David N

Born in Lancashire in 1939, he moved to the West Country in 1961. Trained as a graphic designer, he was an illustrator in advertising and printing before pursuing his passion for painting. Walking in Cumbria, with the ever changing light, provides inspiration. His work reflects his interest in conservation and the countryside, as well as military history of, particularly, the Napoleonic era. Has had a number of solo exhibitions and in 1997 was invited to join the Savages. President in 2002.

RICHARDSON, Frederick Stuart RA, RI, RWA, ROI, RBC

Born in Clifton in 1855, he studied art in Paris under Carolus Duran. Elected in 1919, he was considered by many to be the Savages' finest artist. Well known as a painter in oils and watercolour of landscape and everyday scenes. He exhibited widely and was a member of several prestigious academies and artist bodies. Shy, retiring and good-humoured, he wore tweeds, smoked a pipe and enjoyed fishing and golf. He contributed regularly to *Grouse* and was President in 1923. He died in 1934.

ROBINSON, Arnold W RWA

An authority on stained glass and first-class artist in the medium, he had his studio above his firm's premises in Park Street. He was a well known figure around Clifton, striding with haversack strapped to his back from his home in Stoke Hill to his studio. He was elected an artist member in 1921, becoming President in 1944. He was a member of the Royal West of England Academy. He worked mainly in watercolour and crayon, usually in dark colours. Contributed occasionally to *Grouse*. His stained glass can be seen in the Berkeley Chapel at Bristol Cathedral and St

Edyth's Church, Sea Mills. He was responsible for the restoration of the Cathedral windows following war damage, and for reinstating glass removed for safety. Never robust, he ceased attending the Wigwam in 1944 and died after a long illness in 1955. The Wigwam has more than 20 of his sketches and a caricature by Charles Thomas (q.v.).

RUMMINGS, Michael MSAI

Born in 1932. An early ambition to be an architect unrealised, he was apprenticed to be a graphic designer, and studied this, along with illustration and life drawing, at the West of England College of Art. Then worked with Robinson's and Mardon's before going freelance, specialising in graphics, architectural design and designs for novelty metal box printing, his clients including many internationally known corporations. Elected a Savage in 1980, he has exhibited several times at the RWA and held the occasional one-man show.

SHELDON, W A

Born in Bristol in 1868, he taught locally, having obtained the Queen's Prize for Architecture and an art master's certificate. Elected an artist member in 1907, he was a regular attender for the next 49 years. He escorted school parties around Bristol Art Gallery, lecturing them on art appreciation. He was a frequent contributor to *Grouse*, and exhibited periodically at the annual exhibition. He contributed to the Bongie Portfolio, and the Wigwam has about 50 of his evening sketches. Gave up attending at the age of 88, was made a life member and died four years later in 1960.

SHIPLEY, John ARCA, NDD

Born in 1932, studied at Harrogate School of Art and as an Associate of the Royal College of Art, London in graphic design. He designed and illustrated for British Rail, BBC Television, Courage Western, John Smiths and Harvey's of Bristol, and was West of England art critic for the *Guardian*. He retired as Senior Lecturer and Hon. Research Fellow at Bristol Polytechnic. Elected in 1991, he was the Savages President in 1997.

SHIPSIDES, Frank MA(Hon) Bristol

Born in Mansfield in 1908, he received a classical grounding in art at Nottingham College of Art. His first job was designing decorations for boxes and trays, including a depiction of Clifton Suspension Bridge for a cigarette tin. Turned down for military service on health grounds, he moved with his wife Phyl to Bristol in 1941. Eventually settled with Mardon, Son & Hall, much of his work being for Imperial Tobacco. Retired in 1968 to devote his life to painting, mainly marine subjects. Held 10 one-man exhibitions of oils and watercolours at Alexander Gallery. In 1977 was invited to collaborate on *Bristol Impressions,* to which he contributed the pen-and-ink drawings and which sold out in weeks. Five books were published by Redcliffe Press, and another, with Sir Robert Wall, celebrated his commission by Bristol City Council to paint the seven HMS *Bristols* for permanent display in the Council House foyer. Another commission was to commemorate the Queen's visit to Bristol to open the Maritime Heritage Museum. In 1989, Bristol University bestowed on him an honorary degree. For many years he designed, constructed and painted stage scenery for local theatrical groups. For this work, he received a Vatican award in a ceremony at Clifton Cathedral. His scale ships' models have won four medals. He has continued painting into advanced old age, working from sketch books. An immensely popular member and probably the best known Savage of recent times, he was President in 1974 and 1980.

SKEENS, Walter Morgan ATD
Born in 1887, elected an artist member in 1927, he taught art in Bristol schools. A good draughtsman and artist in oil, watercolours, pastel and pencil, he was an active and very popular member. Despite a serious cycling accident in the early 1940s, he painted with the Savages for 40 years. He loved old Bristol, sketching its notable buildings and street scenes. The Wigwam has 13 of his evening sketches. President in 1953, he was made a Life Member when he moved to Weston-super-Mare in 1969, the year in which he died.

SKELTON, Joseph Ratcliffe RWA
Born in Newcastle-upon-Tyne, he was a founder member in 1904. He worked in watercolours and oils, specialising in figure painting, and also achieved some success as a black-and-white illustrator. He exhibited widely, including the RA, RWA, Royal Institute of Painters in Water Colours ands the Royal Institute of Oil Painters. In Bristol, he did not achieve the success expected of him; somewhat depressed, he tried his luck in London some time before 1908 but was no more successful there, despite commissions to illustrate books for

Arrowsmith's. He retained his Savages membership, sending five paintings to the 1912 annual exhibition. Today there is no trace of *Sabot Market, Concarneau,* the one example of his work recorded as purchased by the Wigwam. He died in straitened circumstances in 1927.

SKINNER, Cyril L ARWA
Born in Luton, he moved to Bristol around 1930, and was elected an artist member. He was active in the studio for some years, and exhibited annually until 1939, when he returned to Luton to head the Arts and Crafts School there. He retained his membership until 1965, dying suddenly on a visit to Bristol in 1970. He contributed to *Grouse,* and the Wigwam has three framed works and five evening sketches.

SPEIGHT, Joseph
Joseph Speight, usually known as Joe, was born in 1945. He spent his formative years abroad, particularly in the Far East, which had a significant influence on his style and colour rendition. He favours oil on canvas because of a tendency towards intricate detail in seascapes and still-life pictures. Marine subjects are top of his list, particularly ships, followed by action themes such as the American Civil War.

Watercolours are an occasional departure for landscapes, and are well suited to the Cotswolds, where he lives. Although he has painted all his life, he has never been serious about it until recently, holding only occasional exhibitions to sell pictures to make room for new ones. He joined the Savages in 2003.

STACY, Henry Edward
Born in 1838, he was a well known artist when invited to the inaugural Savages meeting in 1904, having regularly exhibited at Newcombe's Gallery in Park Street. Already 66 and sporting a beard, he soon became known as Daddy. In the 1870s he lived in Weston-super-Mare, where he founded the local art school. In 1880 he moved to Bristol, living in West Park in a house he put at the disposal of the Savages in their formative days. In 1908 he moved to the country at Bitton, and rarely visited the Wigwam again. A perfectionist, he left no evening sketches, but presented the Wigwam with what he considered his best painting, a watercolour landscape of Kelston Hill from his Bitton studio. He disliked parting with his work. He died in 1915 and is buried at St Anne's Church, Oldland.

STANILAND, Lancelot Norman RWA
Elected an artist member in 1927 and active for three years, until he moved to Newton Abbot. He continued to exhibit at the annual exhibition and in 1954, on moving to Clevedon, he resumed work in the Savages studio. He specialised in watercolour landscapes, some of which he contributed to *Grouse.* The Wigwam has two framed works and seven evening sketches. He died in 1970.

STODDARD, Robert W
Has the distinction of holding the shortest term of membership. An architect, he was elected in December 1920 and within the year had resigned when he moved to London for business reasons. There is one evening sketch in the Wigwam.

STOKES, Adrian
Born London in 1902, he studied at the Euston Road School under William Coldstream in the late 1930s. Married the artist Margaret Mellis in 1938. Moved to Carbis Bay, St Ives just before the Second World War, where he was a central figure in the Modernist circle of Ben Nicholson and Barbara Hepworth. An influential critic, he was more significant as a writer on art than as an artist; his paintings, 'hazy and subdued, glow with a gentle light and colour, the forms often deliquescent', according to the critic Frances Spalding. Had a one-man show at the Leger Galleries in 1951, and there were retrospectives at the Serpentine and Tate Galleries after his death. The Arts Council and the Tate hold examples of his still lifes and landscapes. His books included *Cezanne* (1947) and *Reflections on the Nude* (1967). Was elected an Honorary Savage c1950. Died in 1972.

STONELAKE, Francis Anthony RWA
Born in Bristol, he lived in Redland where his father ran a bakery and confectionery business. In search of an art scholarship, he submitted a set of horse studies to Briton Riviere, the celebrated animal painter, who urged him to persevere. He developed into a fine exponent of the genre. He was a founder member, serving as President in 1909 and 1924. An excellent raconteur, he was famous, with Charles Thomas, for leg-pulling. He helped establish *Grouse,* to which he contributed regularly. He was a member of the RWA, often serving on its hanging committee. The Wigwam has 10 of his framed works and about 25 evening sketches. Died in 1929.

SWAISH, Frederick George RWA

Born in 1879, he was an early member who lived at Willsbridge, near Bristol, the son of Alderman John (later Sir John) Swaish. Showing early promise, he had attended John Fisher's art school, then joining the Municipal School of Art, coming under the influence of Reginald Bush (q.v.), who encouraged him to apply for a studentship at the Royal Academy. After five years at Burlington House, he spent a year travelling to study Old Masters on the Continent. He then spent three winters in the studio of E A Abbey at Fairford, meeting up with his old friend Ernest Board (q.v.). The evening sketches held by the Wigwam show he was active in the 1920s. Quiet and friendly, he was noted for his wit and eloquence. In 1912 he exhibited at the RA, but was never admitted a member. Bristol Art Gallery hold four of his paintings, and the City Council commissioned *The Building of the Keep at Bristol Castle*. He was a member of the RWA, serving on the hanging committee, and is represented in the Academy's Permanent Collection. In later life he turned to portraiture, probably his best work, including the much loved portrait of Bongie in the Wigwam. He died in 1931.

THOMAS, Charles William RWA

Born in Portishead in 1884. His early aim to become an architect was thwarted when his employer went bankrupt. He was only 20 when elected a Savage for his talent as a cartoonist and storyteller in dialect. Served in the First World War as a camouflage officer. After the war he managed Benson's cigar shop in Bristol and later joined the *Evening Post* as a columnist and cartoonist. He was Secretary of the Royal Empire Society, meeting some famous people, introducing Scott of the Antarctic and the *Punch* cartoonist George Belcher to the Wigwam. He was notorious for his humorous interruptions of the Secretary reading the minutes. A devout Christian, he preached in Bristol Cathedral. In later years, many considered him abrasive and high-handed, leading to resignations. However, he had many friends and admirers, who presented him with a small house at Portbury on his retirement. He was summed up as 'an artist of some ability, chiefly with soft watercolours, and a cartoonist of genius'. The Wigwam has 80 or so of his evening sketches, plus many caricatures. Died 1958.

THOMAS, Stuart J G

Lived in Bristol before moving to St Ives to live on a houseboat. A painter, etcher and sculptor, he exhibited five works at the RWA from 1922 to 1928, mostly landscapes plus a sculpture. He showed 29 works with the Savages from 1928 to 1938, including marine paintings and Cornish and Dutch landscapes.

TITCOMB, John Henry

Born in London in 1863, he studied art at the Slade under Brown and Tonks. He exhibited at the RA and the Royal Institute of Painters in Water Colours, and was an established artist when he moved to Bristol in 1916. He was a younger brother of William Titcomb (q.v.), who moved to Bristol and joined the Savages seven years earlier. After only two years, he joined the artist community in St Ives, dying there in 1952. The Wigwam has two of his evening sketches.

TITCOMB, William Holt Yates RBA, NEAC, RI, RWA, RBCA

Born in Cambridge in 1858, an older brother of John Titcomb (q.v.). After winning a prize for pencil drawing at Westminster School, he studied at the Royal College of Art, at Antwerp under Verlat, Paris under Boulanger and Lefevre and at Bushey under Herkomer. He exhibited at the RA from 1896 onwards and won medals at the Paris Salon (1891) and at the Chicago International Exhibition. In 1892 he married the painter Jessie Ada Morison. Moved to Bristol, joining the Savages in 1909, setting up a studio over the arch in Boyce's Avenue, Clifton. He painted many local street scenes but his pictures were often of a religious nature; a major painting showed the Red Maids singing in church, another was a 1918 reconstruction of *John Wesley preaching in St Mark's before the Mayor and Corporation in 1788*. Bristol Art Gallery has examples of his work, and he is represented in Doncaster and Dudley Art Galleries and elsewhere. The Wigwam has seven of his evening sketches. He died in 1930 and is buried in Brompton Cemetery, London.

TOOPE, Arthur E

Joined the Savages in 1906, while living in Knowle. As a painter, he had a partiality for soft colours, but was also skilled in black and white and silhouette work. He was a constant contributor to *Grouse,* and in 1931 was elected President. He moved to Hallatrow, Somerset, in 1932, but retained his membership and regularly sent pictures to the annual exhibition until 1952. The Wigwam has more than 30 of his evening sketches. Universally known as 'Curly' he died in 1954.

TRUMAN, Herbert ARWA

Born in Devon in 1883, he studied art at the South Kensington Schools and St Martin's School of Art. He first exhibited at the RA in 1912, and for many years showed at leading provincial galleries. Versatile in oils and watercolours, he used strongly contrasting light and colour. For some time he worked for the Egyptian government in Cairo, assisting the secret service in the war against drugs trafficking; in 1914 he became head of the political section of Cairo CID. T E Lawrence (of Arabia) was a great friend. Truman started an art school in Cairo. He moved to Bristol in 1946, living in Upper Belgrave Road. On becoming a Savage he was immediately active in the studio. He painted *The Wigwam,* which also has two of his evening sketches. In 1949 he was elected an associate of the RWA. His *Queen Elizabeth II entering the Council Chamber* was painted in 1957 and is considered his masterpiece. It hangs in the Royal Empire Society's premises. His work is also to be seen in the Lord Mayor's Chapel, the Crypt of St Nicholas Church and in Bristol Cathedral. He also painted Bristol buildings and streets, Avon Docks, Blagdon Lake and the caves at Cheddar. He designed and illustrated the jacket for Thor Heyerdal's book of the Kon-Tiki expedition. Quiet and reserved, his harsh features belied a gentle disposition.

WARD, The Rev Louis Arthur RWA, FCSD

Born in Bristol in 1913, he won a scholarship to the Municipal School of Art. While he was there, the Principal, Reginald Bush (q.v.) introduced him to the Savages, and he immediately became an artist member at the age of 21. Joined Mardon's studio, but continued evening classes at the art school, eventually teaching there. After Second World War service, he returned to Mardon's, but soon went freelance, concentrating on book illustrations, including *The History of the World, Treasure Island* and educational works, magazines including *Woman's Weekly* and scenes for the British Tourist Board. Contributed a series to the *Bristol Evening Post,* entitled 'Ward's World', commenting on current events with line drawings. For some time was vice-chairman of the Bristol branch of the Save the Children Fund. In 1973 he entered Ripon College, Oxford to train for holy orders, and was ordained in Bristol Cathedral. He served as curate at Corsham and vicar of Bitton before retiring to return to painting. When he returned to the Wigwam, he found that every member was wearing a clerical collar.

He has exhibited at the RI, at the RWA and Bristol Art Gallery, the latter an exhibition of famous actors including John Gielgud and Prince Charles in a dustbin in a burlesque of Becket's *Endgame*. His portrait of the Duke of Beaufort, a former Savages patron, hangs in the Wigwam. His paintings hang in the Lady Chapel of Bristol Cathedral, in the SS Great Britain Museum and in Ripon Hall, Oxford. His Derby Day was exhibited at the Festival of Twentieth-Century British Artists in 1992, while the Wigwam has six framed pictures and 45 evening sketches.

WATSON, Alfred John ARCA, ARWA
Born in London in 1858, he studied at the South Kensington Schools and was later elected an associate of the Royal College of Art. He moved to Bristol in 1886 to become Second Master of the Bristol Municipal School of Art, a post he held for 37 years. He was too busy to be active in the Wigwam, but contributed to the Peake Portfolio. Retired to Portishead in 1923 and left the Savages three years later. He died in 1927.

WEAVER, Brian NDD ATC
Born in London in 1937, he was evacuated to Devon and Dorset during the Second World War. After Southall Grammar School he attended Ealing Art School for seven years and gained a National Diploma in Design, Illustration and Printing. Further training at the Hornsey College of Art brought a London University Art Teacher's Certificate. After teaching at a school in Harrow from1960, in 1966 he moved to Bristol as Head of Art at Rodway School in Mangotsfield., and in 1981 he moved to the equivalent post at the Grange School in Warmley. He retired in 1992, since when he has helped run an art club in Winterbourne. He has also built a studio in his garden where he has installed a kiln for firing pottery, which he makes on a wheel constructed from parts of a washing machine, a printing press, and bearings from a Ford Taunus car and a bicycle. Married with three sons, Paul was the first member of his family to become an Artist Member, and since then has introduced his father to the Savages. An odd highspot of his career came when he was sponsored by his school on the children's TV programme Blue Peter to make pots on a wheel, blindfolded, for twenty-four hours. He made 1,225, raising £1,760 for the Year of the Disabled and winning him a still cherished Blue Peter badge. He joined the Savages in 2003.

WEAVER, Paul
Born in 1965. Studied graphic design and illustration at Brunel Technical College, and has worked for several design consultancies and publishing houses. As an artist, specialises in watercolour, his preferred subject being landscape and coastal scenes, along with townscapes and people. As well as being a Savage since 1999, he is a member of SAS (The Society for All Artists), demonstrating and running workshops for local art groups in his spare time. His long-time aim is to paint and teach full-time. The Wigwam has four of his evening sketches.

WHATLEY, Henry Howard
He was elected a member in 1904, leaving Bristol and resigning the following year.

WILLIAMS, Terrick RA, ROI, VPRI
Born in Liverpool in 1860, he studied art in Antwerp under Verlat and in Paris at the Academie Julian. He exhibited at the RA from 1890, and in the early twentieth century won medals at the Paris Salon and at the Barcelona Exhibition in 1911. A landscape and marine painter in oils, watercolour and pastel, he was especially interested in light and its effects on buildings. He painted much in Venice and in France. Lived in London, and for some time in St Ives. He was elected an Honorary Savage c1930. Died in 1936.

WILSON, A J
Born in Yorkshire, he moved to Bristol as a commercial designer with Mardon, Son & Hall in 1935. He designed an Air Raid Precautions poster at the outset of the Second World War. Active in the studio until he moved to Putney in 1948, setting up as a freelance artist specialising in landscapes and architectural subjects. He retained his membership and was still exhibiting with the Savages in 1952, as well as contributing to *Grouse*. He resigned in 1963. The Wigwam has about 10 of his sketches and one framed picture.

WOORE, Edward
He was elected a Savage in 1948, while living in Bristol, but returned to London in 1954. Known also as a portrait painter, he was primarily a designer of stained glass windows, with examples in St Bride's, Hyndland, London (1920), Fenham, Newcastle on Tyne (1934), Salisbury Cathedral (1935) and Westminster Abbey (1952). Exhibited at the RA 14 times. He appears in Savages exhibition catalogues until 1956.

WRENCH, Roy Leslie
Born in Bristol in 1917, he established himself as a self-employed exhibition and interior designer. Self-taught as an artist, he specialises in marine subjects around the coastal waters of Plymouth. He was President in 1992, shortly afterwards moving to Plymouth but continuing to submit work to the annual exhibition. The Wigwam has two of his evening sketches.

Presidents 1904-2004

1904-05 –
1905-06 –
1906-07 EH Ehlers
1907-08 EH Ehlers
1908-09 A Wilde Parsons
1909-10 FA Stonelake
1910-11 A Miller Marshall
1911-12 C Brooke Branwhite
1912-13 C Brooke Branwhite
1913-14 C Brooke Branwhite
1914-15 C Brooke Branwhite
1915-16 C Brooke Branwhite
1916-17 FG Swaish
1917-18 WHY Titcomb
1918-19 E Board
1919-20 GE Butler
1920-21 CW Thomas
1921-22 FG Swaish
1922-23 AJ Heaney
1923-24 FS Richardson
1924-25 FA Stonelake
1925-26 AW Robinson
1926-27 CJ Kelsey
1927-28 AC Fare
1928-29 CFW Dening

1929-30 REJ Bush
1930-31 GD Hake
1931-32 AE Toope
1932-33 CW Thomas
1933-34 HP Helps
1934-35 DJ Hughes
1935-36 E Willis Paige
1936-37 AE Milne
1937-38 F Mole
1938-39 GD Hake
1939-40 GD Hake
1940-41 AE Milne
1941-42 CW Thomas
1942-43 E Willis Paige
1943-44 E Willis Paige
1944-45 DJ Hughes
1945-46 THB Burrough
1946-47 RF Hopes
1947-48 EH Craddy
1948-49 RH Brentnall
1949-50 LA Ward
1950-51 EGH Andrews
1951-52 AE Milne
1952-53 A Durman
1953-54 WM Skeens

1954-55 DJ Hughes
1955-56 HP Helps
1956-57 J Keenan
1957-58 RF Hopes
1958-59 EH Craddy
1959-60 LA Ward
1960-61 AN Moores
1961-62 K Panter
1962-63 DJ Hughes
1963-64 C Hanney
1964-65 RH Brentnall
1965-66 J Keenan
1966-67 KA Cooke
1967-68 RF Hopes
1968-69 EH Craddy
1969-70 M Fisher
1970-71 EGH Andrews
1971-72 AN Moores
1972-73 DR Lewis
1973-74 EG Penny
1974-75 FW Shipsides
1975-76 W Laird
1976-77 MR Long
1977-78 P Harrison
1978-79 PJ Andrews

1979-80 DR Lewis
1980-81 RJ Batterbury
1981-82 PG Collins
1982-83 JF Palmer
1983-84 FW Shipsides
1984-85 P Harrison
1985-86 M Rummings
1986-87 P Harrison
1987-88 MR Long
1988-89 AVT Pace
1989-90 DR Lewis
1990-91 H Cowell
1991-92 JF Palmer
1992-93 MR Blackmore
1993-94 RL Wrench
1994-95 MB Edwards
1995-96 AVT Pace
1996-97 JJ Shipley
1997-98 RS Barber
1998-99 R Gallannaugh
1999-00 AN Carder
2000-01 VFG Neave
2001-02 MR Blackmore
2002-03 DN Reed
2003-04 MR Long

Honorary Officers

Secretaries 1904-2004

1904-05 to 1913-14 WH Quick
1914-15 to 1945-46 HE Roslyn
1946-47 to 1969-70 F Mole
1970-71 to 1974-75 T Cutter
1975-76 to 1984-85 JFC Bedford
1985-86 to 1987-88 ES Franklin
1988-89 to 1995-96 T Cleeve
1996-97 to 1999-00 NR Parker
2000-present JR Cleverdon

Treasurers 1904-2004

1904-05 to 1920-21 FAS Locke
1921-22 to 1926-27 A Bruce Bedells
1927-28 to 1940-41 WJ Sherwood
1941-42 to 1947-48 AK Deane
1948-49 to 1952-53 J McLeod/ HE Hicks
Sutton
1953-54 to 1957-58 HE Hicks Sutton
1958-59 to 1965-66 F Clee
1966-67 F Clee/ T Cutter
1967-68 to 1969-70 T Cutter

1970-71 to 1975-76 HGL Stafford
1976-77 to 1985-86 GE Jones
1986-87 to 1992-93 R Egarr
1993-94 to 1997-98 GE Jones
1998-99 to 2002-03 R Bennett
2003-04 J Oakhill

Entertainment Members 1904-2004

1957	ADAMS	Donald (Hon)	Bass Baritone
1964	ADAMS	Samuel John	Poet
1915	ALEXANDER	Maurice	Violinist
1972	ALEXANDER	Arthur Charles	Cellist & Saw
1980	ALEXANDER	George	Pianist
1988	ALFORD	Michael B.	Conjurer
1990	ANSTICE	Raymond W.	Tenor (ex G/F)
1934	ARGENT	Arthur Stanley	Baritone
1995	ARNOLD	Ian	Baritone
1910	AUBREY	Dr. H. Windsor	Musician, Poet
1908	BABER	Frank H.	Baritone
1934	BABER	Donald	Conjurer
1908	BAKER	Arthur John	Tenor, Organist
1919	BAKER	Arthur Charles	Literary Member
1926	BAKER	A.J.	Pianist, Organist
1950	BAKER	George (Hon)	Baritone
1960	BARBIROLLI	Sir John (Hon)	Conductor
1943	BARNS	Cecil Ernest	Tenor
1929	BEAUFORT	10th Duke of	Hunting Horn
1912	BEDELLS	Bruce	Pianist
1966	BEGBIE	Alexander J.S.	Light Baritone
1909	BIBBING	H. Ernest	Literary Member
1907	BIVEN	Frederick	Singer, Actor
1927	BEILBY	Bernard John	Violincello, Cello
1912	BIRD	J. Osmond	Baritone
1998	BOWIE	Stuart	Conjurer
2002	BOYD	Robert	Pianist, Musical Saw
1947	BRADFORD	E.W.	Conjurer
2001	BREDDY	Roy D.	Conjurer
2001	BRISTOW	Daniel	Violin
1934	BROOKMAN	George	Bass-Baritone
1910	BROWN	W.S.A.	Literary Member
1976	BRYANT	Martyn Douglas	Cornet
1937	BUDD	Stanley H.	Tenor
1952	BURCHALL	Sidney (Hon)	Baritone
1960	BURT	M.B.	No Details
1935	BUSSELL	Reginald F.	Bass-Baritone
1937	BUSSELL	Hooper	Baritone
1966	BUSSELL	Brian A.	Pianist, Organist
1979	BUTTERFIELD	Michael	Pianist
1968	BUTTRESS	Frank	Conjurer
1970	CALDERLEY	Denis	Pianist, Organist
2003	CALVIN	Wyn (Hon)	Actor, Comedian
1948	CANN	Arthur	Alto
1916	CARTER	Desmond	Rhymester
1904	CASTLE	Richard	
1960	CHALLENGER	Harry Raymond	Conjurer
1921	CHAPMAN	J.H.	Ex Gr. Feather
1960	CHIVERS	Gordon	Baritone
1956	CLAREMONT	Dr. Louis E.	Pianist, Organist
1947	CLEAVE	Bernard	Baritone
1924	CLEE	Frank	Baritone
1955	CLEE	John	Poet
1963	CLINCH	James	Oboist

1967	COLLAR	Arthur Roderick	Elocutionist
1958	COLLIER	Reginald J.	Tenor
1908	COOPER	A. Morley	Singer
1951	COOPER	Joseph (Hon)	Concert Pianist
1931	COOKSLEY	George	Violinist
1941	CORNISH	E.J.	Pianist
1980	CRABBE	Anthony R.	Conjurer
1935	DANIEL	Mervyn	Tenor
1921	DAVIES	E.A.	Bass
1926	DAVIES	W.E.	Tenor
1957	DAVIES	A. Vaughan	Pianist
1986	DAVIES	J. Nigel	Pianist, Organist
1961	DAW	David P.	Guitarist
1981	DAWSON	Hylton	Poet, Author
2003	DAY	Tony C.	Trumpet
1938	DEANE	Alan K.	Ex Gr. Feather
1952	DIXON	Ralph	Conjurer
1964	DODD	Nigel	Pianist
1911	DORE	Lionel	Bass
1952	DRABBLE	P.C.	Ex Gr. Feather
1966	DYER	Charles J.	Bass-Baritone
1937	EASTMAN	Glyn	Bass-Baritone
1917	EBERLE	George F.	Ex Gr. Feather
1921	EDRIDGE	Dr. Ray	Elocutionist
2002	EDWARDS	Stuart	Wind Instruments
1957	EMERY	Lewis G.	Bass
1922	EVANS	John Eaton	Tenor
1982	EVANS, Q.C.	Mark	Tenor
1937	EVERETT	Leslie	Literary Member
1908	FARQUHAR	Clifford J.	Singer
1979	FARROW	Clive	Singer, Raconteur
1931	FORWARD	Richard	Pianist
1983	FOULKES	Stephen C.	Bass-Baritone
1920	FOWERAKER	Richard W.	Singer, Elocutionist
1958	FOWERAKER	David Bruce	Elocutionist
1968	FRY	Reginald Henry	Tenor
1932	GALPIN	Howard	Violinist, Pianist
1943	GARCIA	Louis	Violinist
1912	GARDINER	F.	Musical Member
1999	GARDINER	Andrew	Tenor
1919	GASS	W. Irving	Bass-Baritone
1924	GASS	T.A.	Rhymster, Raconteur
1914	GAY	Wilfred	Counter-Tenor
1951	GAY	Rev. Percy	Raconteur
1935	GEDYE	F. Stanley	Ex-Green Feather
1914	GEORGE	Ernest	Pianist
1978	GIBBS	David	Viola
1988	GIBBS	Keith B.	Pianist, Organist
1933	GILMER	Charles T.	Violinist
2002	GITTINGS	Philip	Oboe
1955	GODFREY	Isadore (Hon)	Pianist, Conductor
1985	GOLDING	Norman A.W.	Trumpeter
1910	GOODFELLOW	Wilson D.	Rhymester
1966	GOWER	James J.	Bassoon

1957	GRIFFITHS	Neville (Hon)	Tenor
2002	GRIFFITH	Tony	Conjurer
1952	GROVE	Maurice Edgar	Raconteur
1912	HALL	A. Bingham	Baritone
1923	HAMBLIN	Monty L.	Baritone
1961	HAMEL	Gerard van	Bass
1972	HANKS	Peter Edward	Tenor
1989	HARDINGHAM	John W.	Poet, Raconteur
1980	HARKCOM	M.G.	Baritone
1910	HARRIS	Colin	No Details
1908	HARRISON	W.G.	Elocutionist
1906	HEMING	George Thomas	Bass-Baritone
1907	HEMING	Percy (Hon)	Baritone
1946	HEMING	John F.	Baritone, Photo'gr
1909	HEMMENS	Tom	Literary Member
1985	HENDERSON	Tony	Pianist
1910	HICKS	H.C.	Elocutionist
1948	HIGGINS	Geoffrey Joseph	Pianist
1931	HOBBS	Sidney	Ex-Green Feather
1926	HODGE	Stanley	Bass-Baritone
1912	HODGSON	Percival	No Details
1907	HOLDSWORTH	G.	No Details
1926	HOLLOWAY	J. George	Elocutionist
1927	HOLLOWAY	John F.	Baritone, Actor
1924	HOOK	Montague C.	Baritone
1966	HOOKER	Alan	Singer, Guitar, Pianist
1916	HORSELL	J.	Alto
1992	HOSKIN	Niall P.	Baritone
1961	HOWELL	Kenneth	Baritone
1988	HOWSE	John	Accordian
1942	HUGHES	Ellard	Elocutionist, Poet
1908	JAY	Thomas	Literary Member
1971	JENNINGS	Christopher	Baritone
1951	JONES	F. Norman	Comedian
1962	JONES	Stuart Walter	Bass
1928	KILLIP	Kingsley	Pianist, Organist
1946	KNIGHT-ADKIN	J.	Poet
1937	LEWIS	Harold Essex	Elocutionist
1919	LLEWELLYN	David	Pianist, Tenor
1998	LOADMAN	Ray	Cello
1904	**LOCKE**	**F.A.S.**	**Poet, Rhymester**
1941	LOCKIER	Charles	Ex Green Feather
1938	LOUIS	Kenneth	Singer, Char'tr Actor
1908	LOVE	Frederick T.	Ex Green Feather
1955	LOVELL	Kenneth Barclay	Conjurer
1912	LUCAS	Merrick	Ex- Green Feather
1968	LUCENA	Geoffrey	Baritone, Guitar
1927	LUTON	Eric	Cellist
1931	MACINNES	Charles	Ex- Green Feather
1940	McLEOD	John	Ex- Green Feather
1988	MANKELOW	Christopher	Bass
1933	MASON	F.H.	Tenor
1969	MATTHEWS	Kenneth E.	Music Hall Singer
1966	MEARNS	James	Tenor
1944	MEIGHAN	John	Ex- Green Feather
1924	MENDHAM	Geoffrey	Pianist
1948	McGREGOR	R.J.	Literary Author
1964	MICHAELS	Mark	Flute, Piccolo, Guitar
1948	MICHAELS	Mitchell Q.	Violinist
1948	MICKLEBURGH	Edwin Roy	Ex- Green Feather
1947	MORGAN	William	Baritone
1948	MORRIS	Cyril	Baritone
1924	NEALE	A.F.M. Pearcy	Bass
1958	NEWBY	Bert (Hon)	Tenor
1954	NICHOLAS	Allen Robert	Tenor
1931	NORGROVE	J.W.	Poet
1982	NORTHAM	Christopher	Concert Pianist
1941	O'DONNELL	Elliot	No Details
1961	OGDON	John (Hon)	Concert Pianist
1964	OGILVIE	Vivian	Author, Raconteur
1965	O'KILL	John L.	Pianist
1956	OSBORNE	Leonard (Hon)	Tenor
1924	PARDOE	C.B.	Tenor
1909	PARKMAN	Alfred	Bass
1981	PARR	Ken	Tenor
1958	PAYNE	Robert Samuel	Bass-Baritone
1910	PATCHETT	John Dixon	Elocutionist
1910	PEDDIE	David	No Details
1999	PEGLER	Geoffrey	Accordian, Violin
1948	PELMEAR	W.G.	Pianist
1925	PENNY	Thomas	Singer
1908	PEZZACK	R. Henry	Literary Member
1911	PICKERING	A.C.	Violinist
1906	POLLARD	Sidney	Musical Member
1954	POPE	Thomas F.	Tenor
1933	PORTER	E. John	Bass
2003	POTTER	Stuart	Pianist
1994	PRAEGER	Paul	Conjurer
1958	PRATT	Peter (Hon)	Actor, Singer
1999	PRICE	Jonathan D.R.	Organist, Pianist
1968	PYMAN	Martin	Guitarist, Singer
1904	QUICK	Richard	Literary Member
1904	**QUICK**	**William Henry**	**Literary Member**
1932	RIDER	Graham S.	Pianist, Organist
1933	ROBERTS	Cyril E.	Poet, Rhymester
1953	ROBERTS	Henry Thomas	Tenor
1910	ROBINSON	W.J.	Ex- Green Feather
1972	ROBINSON	E.J.	Conjurer
1905	ROSLYN	H.E.	Literary Member
1960	ROYALL	Cyril H.	Tenor
1914	ROYCE	J.G.	Singer
1907	SALISBURY	W.H.	Ex- Green Feather
1953	SALTER	Maurice Herbert	Pianist
1906	SAUNDERS	Lionel G.	Pianist, Banjo
1935	SAUNDERS	Mervyn	Singer
1987	SCHILLER	Allan	Concert Pianist
1958	SCOTT	Basil	Alto
1976	SCOTT	Hamilton	Baritone
1985	SEACOME	Michael	Conjurer
1994	SHELLARD	S. Alan S.	Composer, Pianist
1922	SHERWOOD	W. James	Tenor
1948	SMITH	James	Tenor
1964	SMITH	Ronald Stanley	Tenor, Raconteur
1989	SMITH	Graham R.	Violin
1916	SPILLER	H.V.	Bass-Baritone
1966	SPRAY	Grahame H.J.	Raconteur
1921	STAMPER	Christopher G.P.	Poet
1926	STARR	Paul	Ex- Green Feather

1922	STANCOMB	Rev. John M.D.	Baritone
1909	STEAR	Charles W.	Tenor
1979	STEVENSON	Timothy P.	Clarinet
1912	STEWART-SMITH		No Details
1975	STOKES	Philip	Baritone
1978	STONE	David	Concert Violinist
1932	STRATTON	Rev. A.C.	Poet, Rhymester
1954	STYLER	Alan (Hon)	Tenor
1946	SURPLICE	Alwyn	Pianist, Organist
1920	SUTTON	H.E. Hicks	Ex-Green Feather
1928	TANNER	L.E.	Poet, Rhymester
1937	TAPPENDEN	Reginald E.	Baritone
1930	TAYLOR	Richard V.H.	Ex- Green Feather
1966	TEWSON	Brian A.F.	Pianist
1983	THAIN	Peter	Elocutionist
1909	THOMAS	Herbert J.	Literary Member
1926	THOMAS	C. Harold G.	Pianist
1914	THOMPSON	Gordon	Baritone
1948	THOMPSON	T.A.	Bass
1949	THONGER	Thomas	Tenor
1987	TORPY	Christopher J.	Raconteur, Actor
1938	TORRENT	Marcel	Violinist
1966	TURNER	A.D. Clive	Illusionist in E.S.P.
1909	VALENTINE	J.E. (Hon)	Ex- Green Feather
1932	VALLENCE	Frederick	Conjurer
1909	VENN	Lionel	Tenor
1931	WAITE	Colston Delauney	Baritone
1947	WAITE	Vincent	Author, Pianist
1957	WALSH	George Frederick	Bass
1991	WATKINS	Jeremy M.	Baritone
1980	WATSON	M.D.	Classical Guitar
1981	WATTS	Clive	Tenor
1925	WEATHERLEY, K.C.	Frederick E.	Poet, Versifier
1919	WENSLEY	Francis H.	Tenor
1925	WETHERED	Judge E.H.C	Conjurer
1943	WHITWILL	T. Norman	Ex- Green Feather
1959	WILKINSON	John Desmond	Pianist
1906	WILLIAMS	A.F.	No Details
1926	WILLIAMS	A.H.	Violinist
1946	WILLIAMS	Peter	Tenor
1919	WILSHIRE	F.A.	Musical Member
1949	WINSTONE	F. Reece	Photographer
1933	WOODLAND	Philip G.	Alto
1930	WOODRUFF	Arthur	Alto
1974	WOODRUFF	Geoffrey Tom	Dialects Raconteur
1985	WOOLFORD	Ernest J.	Pianist
1962	YOUNG	Roderick Stephen	Tenor, Actor
1957	YOUNGHUSBAND	Derek	Films, Lecturer

Bold Type: Founder Members

Bristol Savages 2003-2004 Session

Life Members

LG Adams Kenneth J 54
LG Anstee John W 88
LG Bennett Reg E 88
LG Cleeve Terry 67
LR Craddy Eric H 37
LB Dodd F Nigel 64
LG Eberle John L 46
LG Franklin Eric S 66
LG Garcia Moss 53
LG Jones Gordon E 73
LR Lewis Dennis R 63
LG Morgan Norman G 53
LG Parker Norman R 71
LB Payne Robert S 58
LR Shipsides Frank 69
LB Spray Grahame HJ 66
LR Ward Louis A 34
LG Wilson Michael G 77
LG Yandell T Jeffrey 84

Honoured Savage Members

HG Broadbelt John 85
HG Brown David 82
HR Cooke Kenneth 47
HB Garcia Louis 43
HG Long Richard C 77
HB Mearns Jim T 66
HB Royall Cyril 60
HG Thomas Nicholas 80
HG Thomas Richard CN 57
HB Wilkinson John 59

Honorary Savage Members

Calvin Wyn 03
Heighton Martyn 89
Kingman Sir John 97
Miller Martin A 94
Stockton Earl of 96
Wilson Arnold 78

Red Feathers

Barber Roy S 83
Batterbury Reginald J 59
Blackmore Mark R 82
Carder Anthony N 95
Codner John W 37
Collins John F 85
Collins Patrick G 69
Culpan J Terry 93

Cutter George F 95
Edwards Michael B 90
Gallannaugh Roger 94
Gardiner Robert J 77
Herniman Barry 03
Lancaster Brian C 69
Long Michael R 72
Molyneux Geoff 02
Neave Vincent FG 97
Pace Anthony VT 84
Palmer John F 72
Penny Edwin G 56
Pope Richard 03
Reed David N 98
Rummings Michael H 81
Shipley John J 91
Speight Joe 03
Weaver Brian 03
Weaver Paul 99
Wrench Roy L 88

Blue Feathers

Alford Michael B 88
Anstice Ray W 90
Bowie Stuart 98
Boyd Robert 02
Breddy Roy D 02
Bristow Daniel 01
Bryant Martyn D 76
Crabbe Anthony P 80
Davies J Nigel 86
Dawson Hylton 79
Day AC (Tony) 03
Edwards Stuart 02
Evans Mark 82
Farrow Clive E 79
Foulkes Stephen 83
Gibbs Keith B 88
Gittings Philip RJ 02
Golding Norman AW 85
Hanks Peter 72
Hardingham John W 89
Hoskin Niall P 92
Jennings Christopher G 71
Loadman Ray 98
Matthews Ken E 69
Pegler Geoffrey 99
Potter Stuart 03
Preager Paul 94
Price Jonathan DR 99
Schiller Allan 87
Shellard S Alan S 94
Smith Ronald S 64

Stevenson Timothy P 79
Torpy Christopher J 87
Watkins Jeremy M 91
Woolford Ernest J 85
Young Rod S 63

Green Feathers

Abraham Peter J 95
Adams Paul R 89
Adams RD (Bob) 01
Allen Gordon W 92
Allen John D 85
Allt John D 93
Andrews David 01
Anning Paul A 91
Ashford Mervyn A 98
Ashman Marcus N 93
Aylett Nigel D 74
Bailey Alan E 84
Baker David 02
Barnfield Mike 92
Bassett Peter 88
Beacham Ivan 01
Beard L Andrew 89
Bedford John D 80
Benson John P 00
Biddle Norman M 84
Bigger Michael R 78
Blackham M Paul L 98
Blake Richard 97
Bleaden Reginald A 93
Bolt Gordon J 92
Boult AR Ben 96
Brake David E 97
Brewer Brian J 97
Brewer Paul JM 02
Bromhead Christopher JH 77
Brooks Michael L 81
Broome Rodney C 80
Brown Frank AL 67
Brown James G 86
Bryant David L 90
Bryant John B 76
Bunker Mel H 82
Burt Jeff M 01
Bush Peter S 98
Chambers Timothy L 97
Clarke Frank R 93
Clarke Gerald F 97
Cleverdon John R 81
Coe Douglas 87
Comer Pat G 84
Cook Douglas W 73

Coombs Bernard G 90
Copp Brian W 79
Counsell Peter O 91
Creed Ron HW 81
Crossley John 86
Cryer David 99
Cutter Geoff M 94
Davey Peter G 97
Davidson Colin M 81
Davidson Timothy J 74
Davies Christopher 94
Davies Geraint E 94
Davies J Ifor 80
Davies Roger C 02
Dawes Robert A 84
Dellar George R 79
Densham Peter RC 96
Di Mambro Nicholas 86
Dowdney Neill F 82
Dunster Brian L 02
Durston John D 99
Dwyer John M 01
Edwards Paul B 99
Ehlers George T 76
Emery Rex 82
Esbester Michael 65
Evans Mervyn E 78
Evans R Eric 77
Faulkner R Ian 00
Floyd Peter J 64
Forbes-Nixon John D 86
Franklin Stephen C 91
Gammon R David 02
Garcia Anthony C 63
Garland John B 86
Gordon AS (Tony) 90
Goss Gerald 96
Greenfield Lee 01
Greenland Jack 82
Grover Dennis R 87
Gutteridge E Alec 74
Guy Derek W 98
Haas Harold W 82
Halford Martin EH 99
Hall David P 85
Hall Stephen I 82
Hamilton Nigel J 76
Harrison Frank R 91
Harrison John D 86
Harrison Peter 77
Haworth D Paul 95
Hayes George H 82
Heaton-Ward W Alan 59
Hedges Robert HJ 86

Heming D Michael 69
Hewlett Maurice R 87
Hill Alfred E 82
Hill Harvey A 84
Hill Malcolm S 90
Hobbs Jeremy J 82
Hobbs Jack M 79
Hodgson Keith J 86
Holdsworth Beverley M 01
Holtham John G 83
Hopkins David W 96
Horton John R 87
Horton Timothy T 80
Hough Peter LM 92
Howard Mark H 01
Howells DA (Bob) 00
Hughes Stephen G 96
Humphrey Derek K 70
Hunt Dennis JI 89
Hunt Tom A 69
Isaacs John A 00
Jancar Joseph 02
Jarman Clive R 85
Jenkins Roydon 99
Jervis Christopher R 01
Jewell David J 72
Jones Donald K 80
Jones AC (Tony) 98
Jury David 87
Kendall John 89
Kennedy Cameron TC 89
Kingdon Bernard W 82
Knifton Hugh G 97
Kubiak George S 92
Lamb Reginald 96
Langford David H 91
Laurie P 90
Levan Ronald A 89
Lewis Dudley 99
Lindsay Ian T 92
Long Charles N 88
Lowe John CD 88
Luckwell John G 63
Lyons Fergus JF 72
MacCaig Alexander S 90
Mackintosh Ian H 76
Maggs RF (Bob) 96
Malpass David W 91
Marmion Vincent J 89
Marsh R Peter 73
Marshall George W 75
Martin AF (Tony) 62
Martin David J 00
Mason Jeffrey G 97

Massey Michael C 01
Matthews Christopher K 79
Matthews Robert H 75
Mays Neville H 02
McArthur AR Dayrell 68
McArthur James JD 76
McClean A Nicholas 82
McLaughlin James HP 88
Miles John P 74
Mills John 97
Mole D 00
Momber Colin 91
Montague Alan P 00
Morgan-Fletcher Eric G 85
Morley Terence 78
Nash Cedric 99
Nelmes Robert J 89
Nelson Kenneth 01
Neville Brian H 02
Newport Peter L 99
Newstead Michael J 77
Noble Dennis L 01
Norris A Steve 01
Oakhill John A 98
O'Keefe Timothy E 95
Organ Edward J 71
Osborn JS Colin 92
Owen John T 88
Park J Alan 95
Parsons John S 95
Payne Frank 89
Payne Laurence JG 89
Pearce Donald L 95
Pearce John E 88
Pearce Kenneth D 81
Pearce Leslie F 76
Phillips L Trevor 69
Phillips William H 96
Phillpott Roger 97
Pike Hugo R 95
Pinder F Geoffrey 01
Pinson Trevor N 92
Pople Christopher J 93
Pople Donald 85
Popperwell Malcolm R 89
Porter Ronald J 94
Potokar John P 92
Potokar S Leo 69
Pottinger Gerald P 95
Ratliff Anthony HC 95
Ray Clive A 74
Rees Gareth JG 01
Reid C Stewart 92
Renshaw Edward H 00

Richardson Paul EC 72
Riley John M 87
Ritchie Rev David JR 02
Roberts D Glyn 95
Roberts Howard B 96
Roberts Leslie J 99
Robertson David S 01
Rose CG Ian 68
Rosling Geoffrey EF 75
Royle David J 00
Ryder Martyn L 85
Screen Jeffrey H 74
Senior-Stern John M 01
Shattock David J 92
Shellard Dudley ES 78
Shipsides Patrick J 81
Shore G John 76
Silvey Stuart J 88
Silvey T Michael 75
Simmonds Bruce N 84
Simmonds Michael N 74
Sisman Martin 84
Skuse E Frank 69
Smith-Marriott Sir Hugh 84
Somers Martyn J 97
Spray Robin PL 75
Squires Dennis HN 77
Stancombe Robert H 77
Stevenson Alan L 65
Stevenson Roger J 62
Still Trevor A 96
Stone Christopher W 95
Sudbury Martin 99
Sutton David G 00
Taggett TO Stewart 91
Tedder D Derek B 98
Thomas Bill G 85
Thomas Neville A 69
Thorne John D 95
Torpy David M 97
Trewin Edmund A 93
Trigg Michael 91
Trott Ronald W 89
Truscott M Tony 95
Turner Stanley 87
Tyler Peter 02
Tyrrell Kenneth R 91
Uncles W John 84
Vaughan Roy D 78
Waite Leslie 78
Walder Howard A 79
Wall Sir Robert W 82
Walmsley John P 93
Walters John EW 02

Watkins John D 90
Wells Phillip H 98
Westbrook Dennis H 87
Wheeler John W 79
Whitaker Paul K 75
Whitehead D Michael 01
Wills Peter 92
Winstone M Freddie 78
Withers Michael C 86
Wood Colin J 98
Wooster Denys EC 84
Wring Anthony M 87
Yeates Trevor R 88

Junior Lay Members

Dyer Ronald 03
Gill John D 03
Jenkins Roger S 03
March David R 03
Niven Peter AR 03
Pitt A Bryan 03
Quick Douglas 03
Rackham Anthony NDC 03
Read Peter A 03
Saunders EJW (Ted) 03
Stoodley Michael J 03
Timms Michael J 03
Walker John R 03
Watts Peter G 03
White Duncan R 03

Identification:
LR, LB, LG: Life Red, Blue and
Green Feather Members. HR,
HB, HG: Honoured Red, Blue
and Green Feather Members.
Number after name denotes
year of entry.

BIBLIOGRAPHY

Bristol Savages' annual reports

Bristol Savages' press cuttings albums

Bristol Savages' Wednesday evening minute books, 1904-2003

Bristol Savages' committee minute books, 1910-2003

The Story of the Bristol Savages, Colston Waite, private publication, 1971

A Guide to the Wigwam, Colston Waite, private publication, 1972

Not So Savage, a history of the London Savage Club, Norgate and Wykes, Jupiter, 1976

Profiles of Bristol Savages Artist Members, W. Cecil Broome, 1976, updated by Roy Barber and Michael Wilson, 2003, unpublished

Notes and Records of Bristol Savages, W. Cecil Broome, unpublished, 1979

Laughter and the Love of Friends: A Centenary History of the *Melbourne Savage Club, 1894-1994,* Joseph Johnson, Melbourne Savage Club, 1994

Tramlines to the Stars: George White of Bristol, George White, Redcliffe Press, 1995

Wally Hammond: The Reasons Why, David Foot, Robson Books, 1996

Public View: A Profile of the Royal West of England Academy, Redcliffe Press, 2002

A Century of Savage Verse, 2003

Index

Subscribers

Bob Adams
Michael Alford
Gordon Allen
David Andrews
Ray Anstice
Mervyn Ashford
Alan Bailey
David Baker
Roy Barber
Peter Bassett
Ivan Beacham
Joan Bedford
John Bedford
Reg Bennett
John Benson
Norman Biddle
Paul Blackham
Mark Blackmore
Richard Blake
Ben Boult
Stuart Bowie
Roy Breddy
Brian Brewer
John Broadbelt
Christopher Bromhead
Michael Brooks
David Brown
Frank Brown
David Bryant
John Bryant
Jeff Burt
Peter Bush

Anthony Carder
Jack Chalker
Frank Clarke
Bernard Cleave
Terry Cleeve
John Cleverdon
John Codner
Mary Collier
John Collins
Patrick Collins
Douglas Cook
Bernard Coombs
Arthur Court
Tony Crabbe
Ron Creed
David Cryer
Terry Culpan
Geoff Cutter
Peter Davey
Christopher Davies
Geraint Davies
Ifor Davies
Nigel Davies
Robert Dawes
Hylton Dawson
Peter Densham
Marjorie Derwent-Scott
Nigel Dodd
Brian Dunster
John Dwyer
Ronald Dyer
John Eberle

A Edwards
Stuart Edwards
George Ehlers
Rex Emery
Michael Esbester
John Evans
Clive Farrow
Ian Faulkner
Stephen Foulkes
Eric Franklin
Stephen Franklin
Roger Gallannaugh
David Gammon
Louis Garcia
Moss Garcia
Keith Gibbs
John Gill
Philip Gittings
Tony Gordon
Lee Greenfield
Jack Greenland
Dennis Grover
Martin Halford
Nigel Hamilton
Peter Hanks
John Hardingham
Ken Harper
Frank Harrison
Peter Harrison
Robert Hedges
Martyn Heighton
Michael Heming
Alfred Hill

Jack Hobbs
Jeremy Hobbs
Keith Hodgson
John Holtham
David Hopkins
Bob Horton
Timothy Horton
Mark Howard
Bob Howells
John Hughes
Derek Humphrey
Tom Hunt
John Isaacs
Christopher Jennings
Christopher Jervis
David Jewell
Donald Jones
Gordon Jones
Tony Jones
David Jury
John Kendall
Bernard Kingdon
Sir John Kingman
Dennis Knight
George Kubiak
Brian Lancaster
David Langford
Dennis Lewis
Dudley Lewis
Ian Lindsay
Michael Long
Richard Long
Fergus Lyons

Alexander MacCaig
Robert MacEwen
Malcolm MacInnes
Ian Mackintosh
Mary Maggs
David March
George Marshall
Tony Martin
Jeffrey Mason
Bob Matthews
Ken Matthews
Dr Alistair McClean
Jim Mearns
Dr Hugh Metcalfe
John Miles
Geoff Molyneux
Alan Montague
Eric Morgan-Fletcher
David Morris
Cedric Nash
Vincent Neave
Kenneth Nelson
Peter Newport
Michael Newstead
Dennis Noble
Steve Norris
John Oakhill
Edward Organ
John Osborn
Anthony Pace
John Palmer
Norman Parker
John Parsons

Laurence Payne
Don Pearce
Ken Pearce
Geoff Pegler
Bill Phillips
Trevor Phillips
Hugo Pike
Geoff Pinder
Sidney Platel
Richard Pope
Donald Pople
Malcolm Popperwell
Ronald Porter
Dr Leo Potokar
Jonathan Price
Bill Proctor
Douglas Quick
Anthony Rackham
Anthony Ratliff
Peter Read
David Reed
Gareth Rees
Edward Renshaw
Paul Richardson
John Riley
Rev David Ritchie
Glyn Roberts
Howard Roberts
Leslie Roberts
David Robertson
Ian Rose
Geoffrey Rosling
John Rosser

Michael Rummings
Martyn Ryder
Ted Saunders
Ron Sawyer
Alan Schiller
Jeffrey Screen
Mary Seacome
David Shattock
Dudley Shellard
John Shore
Stuart Silvey
Bruce Simmonds
Martin Sisman
Sir Hugh Smith-
Marriott
Grahame Spray
Robert Stancombe
Alan Stevenson
Roger Stevenson
Tim Stevenson
Trevor Still
Colin Stone
Michael Stoodley
Derek Tedder
Bill Thomas
Neville Thomas
Michael Timms
Christopher Torpy
David Torpy
Michael Tozer
Andrew Trewin
Michael Trigg
Ronald Trott

Tony Truscott
Stanley Turner
John Uncles
Michael Vaughan
Robert Vaughan
Roy Vaughan
Nancy Waite
John Walker
Brenda Ward
Lorna Warren
Jeremy Watkins
John Watkins
Peter Watts
Brian Weaver
Paul Weaver
Phillip Wells
John Wheeler
Duncan White
Elizabeth White
Michael Whitehead
Arnold Wilson
Michael Wilson
Freddie Winstone
Michael Withers
Colin Wood
Ernest Woolford
Denys Wooster
Roy Wrench
Jeffrey Yandell
Trevor Yeates
Rod Young